A Grand Teton
Sleigh Ride

A Grand Teton Sleigh Ride

Four Generations of
Wyoming Ranchers Celebrate
Love at Christmas

ELIZABETH GODDARD
& LYNETTE SOWELL

BARBOUR
PUBLISHING

Cover Image: Greg Winston / GettyImages

Published by Barbour Books, an imprint of Barbour Publishing, Inc., P.O. Box 719, Uhrichsville, Ohio 44683, www.barbourbooks.com

Our mission is to publish and distribute inspirational products offering exceptional value and biblical encouragement to the masses.

 Member of the
Evangelical Christian
Publishers Association

Printed in the United States of America.

A WEDDING FOR BELLE

by Lynette Sowell

Lord, you have been our dwelling place
throughout all generations.
Before the mountains were born
or you brought forth the whole world,
from everlasting to everlasting you are God.
PSALM 90:1–2 NIV

Chapter 1

Jackson's Hole, Wyoming, October 1888

The autumn downpour chilled Belle Murray to the bone, despite her good coat with Ham's old slicker worn over top of it all. She shivered, although her black wool dress ought to provide adequate warmth under all the layers.

She hadn't planned on getting stuck in the mud on the trail back to the homestead.

"C'mon, Patch. You can do it." She snapped the reins, urging the horse forward. Patch pulled, his chestnut shoulders straining against the harness, to no avail. The small cart's wheels remained fast in the deep mud.

Belle was stuck two miles from home, and twilight came early in the fall in Wyoming.

Her numb yet still aching heart almost made her predicament seem laughable. If she had the inclination to ride home, she could unharness Patch and ride him the rest of the way. However, she carried a cartful of provisions from the good people of Jackson, and if she left it here, someone might surely take the bit of food. She needed the supplies, even with her brother-in-law having the foresight to prepare for the winter ahead.

Belle sighed, and Patch huffed, the gelding's breath making puffs in the cold air. "I know, Patch. We've gone and done it this time." But there would be no one at home to tease her when she told the story.

Melanie Murray Quinn and her husband, Hamilton Quinn, now lay beneath the earth, still soft enough to bury bodies before winter's cold descended with a fury over Wyoming. The freak wagon accident had robbed Belle of any family she cared about.

She should have taken Ham's advice and left Wyoming before the leaves fell, gone back East. But to what prospects?

Belle sat contemplating her decision to stay in Jackson on her fool's errand. Her supposed mission from God to give some propriety to the Wild West.

The squeak and creak of an approaching wagon made her glance over her shoulder. Here came Zebulon Covington, in all his fur wrapped, bearded, know-it-all glory.

She turned back around. Might as well urge Patch once more. "C'mon, Patch. You can do it." Anything, besides Zebulon coming to her aid. She didn't care much to hear any "I told you sos" from him.

What was it about men treating women as though they couldn't think or care for themselves?

"Whoa." Zebulon pulled up his team, the mules tossing their heads. "Afternoon, Miss Murray."

"Good afternoon, Mr. Covington."

"I see you're in a bit of a bind. Do you care for any assistance?"

She could hear the mocking tone in his voice and dared not look him in the eye to find the twinkle. Why did he always seem to be laughing to himself when he saw her?

"Care? Not particularly. I think. . .I think Patch needs a moment to gather himself, and he'll pull the cart from the mud without much effort."

"Nightfall's coming soon. How long do you plan to wait for Patch to gather himself?"

"Not long. I was just about to try again." She gathered her skirt then swung her legs—carefully and genteelly, of course—to the side in order to climb down from the cart. Her boot slid on the mud, and before she could steady herself, her world flipped on its side and she was left staring up at Zebulon's team, puffy clouds rising from their nostrils while a wet, earthy scent met her own.

Zebulon was off the wagon seat in a flash and by her side. "The mud's a bit slick."

A bit slick, indeed. And it had the consistency of sticky dough, much like the time when she'd kneaded the bread too much. Cold seeped through her layers, and she dared not look down. Wearing Ham's old fur coat had been a wise last-minute decision before leaving for the funeral. They could have had the funeral at the homestead, but she didn't take to the idea of two corpses, especially family, lingering in the house with her alone. Selfish of her, maybe?

She glanced at Zebulon. He'd crouched down close enough she could see the first few strands of silver in his beard. "Thank you, but I can get up without assistance." Although it was gentlemanly of the roughened rancher to help her up. No, the man wasn't a complete beast, but she didn't trust his intentions.

"Suit yourself, Miss Murray." He towered above her as she managed to scramble to her feet, not bothering to adjust her skirts. "Let me see if I can get you unstuck here, and we can both be on our ways."

She stood at Patch's head while Zebulon worked to free the wheels of the two-wheeled cart from the nearly foot-deep mud Patch had pulled it into. "I hope it works."

"You and me both."

He joined her beside the horse. "Here." He took hold of the horse's halter. Zebulon tugged, harder than she would have.

Again, Patch strained against the harness. The cart wiggled. Belle bit her lip. *C'mon. . .*

No. It didn't work.

Zebulon's mules balked and pulled away from Patch when Zebulon tried to use them to assist Patch with pulling the cart. The mules threatened to bolt, but Zebulon grabbed the nearest bridle and they stopped.

"Well, I do believe I'll be giving you a ride home this afternoon."

"But Patch—"

"Tied to the back of my wagon." He glanced toward the cart.

"We'll take whatever's in the back of the cart, too."

She ought to refuse and unhitch Patch from the cart and ride him home. But then she had no sidesaddle, and who knew how long it would be before she could come back to this part of the road and gather the provisions in the wagon, if someone hadn't picked them off by then?

"All right. Thank you. Thank you very much, Mr. Covington."

Well, well, well.

Zeb hadn't expected to find himself in this situation on the way back to the cabin. He'd gone to pay his final respects to the Quinns, along with the rest of Jackson. Those who had the time to make it to town, anyway, with one of the final trips of the season for the visiting preacher, until the spring thaw. Until then Zeb and two of the other men in the area would take turns preaching at the weekly Sunday meeting, for whoever showed up in between snowstorms.

He glanced at Belle Murray, who sat ramrod straight beside him on the wagon seat, her gloved hands folded neatly on her lap. The wagon swayed and creaked, but all the while, Belle managed to keep perfect posture. She'd maintained a form of dignity in spite of the mud covering the lower part of her clothing and one sleeve.

This spring, when he'd met the young and proper spinster who'd joined her sister and brother-in-law out West, he and a few of the others almost began a betting pool to see how long she'd last. Almost, that is. Any money he came by he wouldn't squander on a gamble.

Even if he was pretty sure he'd win. First snowfall and she'd be gone, he told them. The others agreed.

After losing Hamilton Quinn, one of his good friends, he'd modified his tone a bit, as he'd promised to watch out for his friend's sister-in-law if anything ever happened to him. At the time, Zeb didn't think he'd ever be called on to keep that promise. He figured Belle would soon be on her way back East and find her proper self a good spouse.

Belle Murray had stayed in Jackson, though. She had some cockamamie notion of opening some kind of school for young women, but it wasn't a traditional book-learning school. No sirree, she'd told them all she was going to help civilize the West by schooling its young women in culture, poise, and gentility.

The idea almost made him snort, even now, but one of the mules beat him to it.

The mules, dubbed James and John, were apt to act like sons of thunder, but today the mud and chill made them want to hurry back to the warm barn. He didn't blame them.

Shadows continued to gather at the end of this gray day. Zeb had come along at the ideal time. He couldn't envision leaving the young woman stranded on the trail home, left to her own devices.

"I–I'm very grateful, Mr. Covington, that you happened along," Belle said. "I can't imagine what I would have done."

"I'm sure you'd have thought of something. B'sides, I couldn't right well leave a lady on the trail. Wouldn't be proper, nor gentlemanly, of me." He couldn't resist a tease.

"It's quite gallant of you, sir." She paused. "I did think of unhitching Patch, gathering which provisions I could, and riding home, to return for the rest of the items and the cart when the trail dries out."

"Good idea. But you never know who might happen along and see those things. Or the cart. Can't be too careful; they might come up missing."

She nodded slowly. "You're right. Do you expect we'll get snow soon?"

"Possibly. Perhaps tonight."

"It's so cold, already."

"Didn't it get cold in Boston?"

"Yes, it did. I'm sure it still does."

"Well said, Miss Murray."

It was her turn to chuckle at him; the soft bells pleased his ears. He wanted to make her laugh again.

"People think I'm going to leave now, but I'm not." She glanced his way, blinking up at him through long dark lashes framing blue eyes. "I know Melanie and Ham would want me to stay. This is the family's land, and I can't let their legacy go."

"Miss Murray, no offense, but you have no idea of what it will take to winter over in Jackson. There's not someone to dash around the corner to call on, should you need help. Winters are long, and lonely. When the snow gets deep, we don't go much of anywhere. There's no fancy mercantile you can pop over to pick up the latest lady's book."

He couldn't help himself. The idea of a woman living on her own in this part of the country, well, it was madness. Especially one green with ignorance of what living out West entailed. She could die, and no one would know.

"I appreciate the fact I'm not in civilized country. Ham, Melanie, and I have. . .had already formed a plan for the winter. We have adequate provisions, and since it's just. . .just me in the home now, I'll have plenty of food. I can make the fuel last, too."

Zeb shook his head. "Miss Murray, please do me a favor. Please, allow me to pay for your safe passage to the nearest rail station. I'll take you there myself, over Teton Pass. But I suggest you seriously consider leaving Jackson before it's too late and there's no chance of you making it out of here until spring."

Belle frowned, and for a second Zeb regretted being the cause of her somber expression. "Thank you, Mr. Covington. Thank you."

"For passage out of here?"

"No sir, not at all." She stuck her chin out, and he noticed the tiny dimple in its center. "You've made me all the more determined to stay."

The mules' pace had slowed to a casual stroll, and Zeb chirruped to the beasts, who responded more readily than Belle had.

Women. Sometimes, there was no sense in trying to talk

logically to them. This one, anyway.

Stubborn though she was, he had to keep an eye on this one, whether she liked it or not. Her life could very well depend on it. And he'd promised Ham. If he had his way, he'd be toting her over the pass to Idaho, first thing.

Women.

Chapter 2

Belle Murray picked up the primer and held it above Rosemary Smythe's head. They stood before the looking glass in Rosemary's bedroom. The luxury items spoke well of Rosemary's family and her determination to care for her appearance, even out here in the wilds of Wyoming.

"Stand straight; don't slouch your shoulders as if you have a sack of flour strapped around your neck." Belle tapped Rosemary's shoulder gently with a finger.

"All right." Rosemary wiggled her shoulders, thrust them back, and stuck out her chin.

"No, I can't set the book on your head with your chin like that. Your head must be level."

Rosemary lowered her chin. "Is that better?"

"Indeed, it is." Belle released her hold on the primer and let it balance on the crown of Rosemary's head. "There, see? Your posture is perfect."

"I do look taller." A faint glow suffused Rosemary's cheeks. "Am I standing as well as a lady back East?"

"Even better, Rosemary, even better." She realized how much she sounded like Miss Elizabeth Monroe, a governess she'd once served beside while employed by the Skinner family. Miss Monroe had studied in Paris, the woman had told her. Miss Monroe had carried herself ever the bit of a lady, and eventually went on to marry a gentleman who'd done quite well for himself.

To marry well was also Rosemary's wish.

"What is it, Miss Murray? You appear deep in thought." Rosemary turned, and the primer slipped from her head.

"I was thinking of my own inspiration, a Miss Elizabeth Monroe, a refined and genteel woman who found herself in difficult circumstances. I first knew her when I was about your age. I learned from her etiquette, style of dress, manners, and how to conduct oneself in every situation."

"Whatever happened to her?"

"She found a most suitable gentleman, married well, and went on to manage a well-run household. After she wed, I didn't see her anymore." Belle didn't add that Elizabeth Monroe had left the industrial magnate's grand home and never looked back. As soon as Belle could manage it, she did the same.

Instead of finding a most suitable gentleman, however, she'd found herself here, in the West, longing to teach young women such as Rosemary social refinements.

"I'd like to find a most suitable gentleman. I'm nearly eighteen."

"So you are."

"After all, before I know it, I'll be nearly as old as you."

Belle tried not to wince at the reference to her own unmarried state. No, nearly twenty-two wasn't ancient, by any means, but she'd surely envisioned herself married by now. Except, she hadn't found anyone to match her list. Anyone who'd take notice of a self-educated woman whose unmarried parents had arrived in Boston with suitcases and dreams, that is.

"Time does fly, Rosemary. Now, what do you consider most suitable in a husband?"

The young woman sank onto her mattress and pursed her lips. "Handsome, strong. Hardworking."

"Those are good places to start. However, handsome is as handsome does." A brief flicker of memory struck her. She'd nearly surrendered her heart to handsome, once, but God in His mercy had allowed her to see his true colors. "A man should have other qualities. Considerate, respectful. Kind to the weak, especially animals and young children. Submitted with his heart and life to the Almighty."

"Yes, I see." Rosemary looked thoughtful, and placed her finger on her lips. Then she locked her gaze with Belle's and sat up as straight as any debutante before Belle could remark about the slouch. "I know who."

"Who?"

"All those qualities sound like Mr. Covington."

"You mean, Zebulon Covington?" Her voice almost squeaked, but she cleared her throat to mask the sound.

"Oh, yes. I don't know why I'd never thought of him as a possibility before. He's definitely unmarried."

"But he's so. . .so. . ."

"Hairy." Rosemary nodded. "But even trappers-turned-ranchers need to shave, eventually. He has beautiful eyes, so blue. And a kind face under all that beard."

"And he's. . .quite. . ."

"Old?" Rosemary shook her head. "He's not so old. Almost twenty-six, I heard him tell Pa one time. They were talking, not long after Zeb—Mr. Covington—started building his house this past spring. Pa said the man was planning to settle down."

"I see." Zebulon Covington seen as a possible catch? Belle couldn't wrap her mind around the idea. The man was kind enough to have rescued her the other day on her way home, but she didn't see him as possible marriage material.

Evidently, Rosemary knew more about the man than Belle did. Rosemary's face glowed. Perhaps something could come of this and Rosemary could be one of Belle's first success stories.

"Rosemary," she announced, gliding over to the mattress and settling gracefully onto the bed, "if you believe Mr. Covington is a suitable match for you, then we shall see what happens."

"He's. . .he's coming to supper tonight. Ma takes pity on him, says someone needs to feed the bachelors, and Pa said he ought to come while the weather holds, before another snow comes in."

"Well, you should practice tonight on your conversation and manners."

"Oh, my heart flutters at the idea. But what if he's not interested? What if he doesn't want a wife?"

Belle took Rosemary's hand and squeezed. "Dear Rosemary, a man gets to a point in his life and he will see the need he has for a good wife. And when Zebulon Covington does, you'll be right there."

"Please, please, Belle, stay for supper. Ma won't mind. And I'll feel so much better to know you're here. I'm so afraid I'll say the wrong thing or look like an imbecile. And my little brother will only vex me, by teasing me unmercifully. He'll accuse me of putting on airs if I try to show my manners."

Belle pondered that for a moment. "I suppose I can. But I can't stay too late; I'll need to see to the animals in the evening, and I don't like the idea of caring for them in the dark."

"I won't keep you one moment longer than you may stay. Perhaps Pa can send one of his men to your place to feed them."

"I wouldn't want to put them through the trouble. Mr. Tolliver will be coming to work tomorrow."

"No trouble. You'll be helping me, too."

"All right, then. Supper it is."

"Belle, thank you, thank you. I'm ever so grateful. Ma, she doesn't. . .she doesn't understand. It's been hard sometimes, living here. We were in Missouri when Pa got the idea to move to Jackson. Sometimes I miss knowing the latest news, seeing the latest fashions."

"Ah, I see. How long have you lived here?"

"Two years. I miss living back East, but my mother won't agree to send me."

Belle nodded. "I understand. But here, it's so. . .unspoiled. It's beautiful." Beautiful wasn't an adequate word to describe the Teton Range. "I still remember the first time I caught sight of the mountains. I had no words. All I could do was stare."

"Yes, they look like they're so close they could fall on you, don't they?" Rosemary stood then crossed the small room to stand before the mirror again. "So, should I change my dress before supper? Is this day dress good enough?"

"You look just fine. Besides, manners and decorum will make up for any lacking in wardrobe, although a lady should always try to look her very best in any situation." Belle joined Rosemary at the glass. "Perhaps we should do your hair again, with a fresh braid and pins."

"We should." Rosemary pulled the first few pins from her hair. "Because I want Zebulon Covington to notice me, and notice me but good."

Zebulon noticed the Smythes had set an extra place for supper at the table, making six for supper instead of the expected five. The four Smythes and him, plus one more.

"Coffee, Zeb?" Mary Smythe asked from her place at the stove.

"Yes, ma'am." He removed his hat and set it on the nearest empty hook on the wall by the door.

"Mary, I hope the brew's hot and strong tonight," Jake Smythe said as he gave his wife a peck on the cheek.

"Strong and hot, just like you like it, Jake." She took the coffeepot from the stove and poured coffee for all of them. "We have another guest for supper, my love. That sweet, young Belle Murray. She's spent the afternoon tutoring Rosie."

"As long as we have enough to feed her, too."

"Oh, you—" Mary grinned and shot her husband a look, and the two commenced a banter perfected after nearly two decades of marriage.

The sight was both mighty cozy and mighty constricting at the same time. Zebulon knew, sooner or later, he ought to take a wife. No, he didn't need to take a wife. Not really. He could darn and mend passably, he could cook meals he liked, whether or not anyone else did. He didn't keep clutter around the two-room cabin he'd finished adding to in August, giving him some more breathing room than the original single-room building he'd constructed not long after staking his claim. He didn't have time to pay attention to a woman, what with all the cattle needing his attention, and fences, and general everyday chores.

Of course he found the couple's conversation constricting. Wasn't quite sure he cottoned to someone requiring his attention. Made a man itch like a scratchy wool blanket.

Still, though, there was something comforting about it. Jake's warm look at Mary as she basted the chicken she'd had roasting in the oven all afternoon, if judging by the mouthwatering aroma in the kitchen. To have companionship, supper cooked to perfection, and coffee on the stove. Now that was something a man could look forward to. A man could stand to give a lot in a marriage, but oh what he'd receive in return.

The clatter of shoes on the cabin floor announced the entry of Christopher Smythe, a towheaded, much younger version of his father. "Supper ready yet?"

"Nearly," Mary said. She glanced at him, her eyes narrowing. "Did you wash your hands?"

"Yes ma'am." Christopher slid onto the nearest empty chair. "Howdy, Mr. Covington. How are ya?"

"I'm doing well; looking forward to your momma's cooking." At his words, he glanced up to see two young women entering the kitchen area. Miss Murray, and the Smythes' only daughter, whose name he couldn't recall. He studied her face, trying to remember. At his glance, her skin flushed red, as if she'd been outside in the snow on a sunny day.

"Good evening, Mr. Covington," Belle said. "Mr. and Mrs. Smythe, thank you for letting me stay for supper."

"We're glad to have you." Mary carried the pan of chicken to the table. "I couldn't bear the idea of you going home to an empty house, all alone."

"It's—it's not so bad. Quiet, but not so bad."

"You be careful out there. Old Gus Tolliver been helping you?" Jake asked.

"Yes, he has, thank you. I'm going to stay in Jackson, I've

decided, once and for all. I can't let the claim go. Melanie and Ham put almost all their years in. If I stay through the winter and make it until spring, it'll be our family's land forever." She stuck out her chin, just a little.

If Zeb thought she'd been determined and stubborn the other evening after the funeral, well, tonight she was downright resolute, her heels dug in. He had to admire that.

"Nothing like being able to say your land is your land," Zeb said aloud. He'd earned his claim fair and square, had grown his herd, built his first home this year in celebration after receiving his patent from the government.

"But our land isn't really our land, is it, Father? As you said, we're to be caretakers of this land God created." At last, the Smythes' daughter spoke. Her skin had resumed its normal creamy tone. However, at his glance, she colored again to the tips of her ears. Someone had twisted her braid around her head as if it were a golden crown.

"Miss Smythe, we don't really own the land. But I like to know that legally, in this country, no man can take from me what I've earned."

"You're quite right, Zeb." Jake nodded then looked toward the stove, where both Belle and Mary picked up bowls heaped with roasted potatoes and squash for the meal. The aroma of freshly baked bread wafted in their direction.

"Bread?" Belle said as she took the seat beside the Smythes' daughter, who nodded then cut a slice from the loaf. She kept her focus on the bread, but Belle kept her focus on him.

"Let's bow and pray before we eat." Jake reached for his wife's hand.

As they bowed, Zeb couldn't help himself. Still holding Belle's gaze, he winked.

Chapter 3

Belle's neck burned with a hot flush throughout the meal. She didn't need a looking glass to know it existed, and the reason her neck felt hotter than summertime was Zebulon Covington. Thankfully, no one, especially Rosemary, seemed to notice what Zebulon had done. Nervy, bold, brash—none of the qualities in a suitable man that neither Rosemary—nor she—should find appealing.

But part of her did, and she almost wanted to simper as Rosemary had whenever Zebulon looked in her direction.

Belle reminded herself of tonight's purpose for staying for supper, besides a delicious meal she didn't have to cook. Rosemary definitely needed schooling and training. The poor girl's heart would fall prey to the first eligible man who smiled at her the right way. Better it be someone like Zebulon Covington, and not any of the far less savory bachelors in the area.

Tonight was turning out to be nothing short of a disaster, as it soon became apparent that Zebulon didn't even know Rosemary's first name. If Rosemary were to have any chance of making a match with Zebulon, the young woman needed to step forward just a bit more.

In spite of the rowdy wink from the man across the table, Belle knew Zebulon was a good man. She could see it from Rosemary's description and knew it from the way Ham had spoken of him during her months of living in Jackson.

The sunlight in the one window had faded by the time Mary poured another cup of strong coffee. Belle's home lay but a few minutes' ride away, but she ought to leave before the light dwindled altogether.

Melanie had told her of long winters and short days; the cold felt deeper here than back East, too.

"Winter's not here yet," Jake Smythe told her when she remarked about the chill before leaving. She tried not to shiver at his words.

"But Christmas is coming," Mary said. "Don't forget, we're going to have a program on Christmas Eve at the church, for anyone who'd like to come. We'd like you to join us when we practice a few Christmas songs, and perhaps have a bit of a choir."

"I'd like that, very much." She would make the time to meet with the group of ladies and the few men that Jake Smythe had managed to recruit.

"You sure you won't join in, Zeb?" Jake asked while Zebulon was putting on his hat and coat, and Belle was doing the same.

"No, I'm successful at making a joyful noise, but nothing anyone would want to hear."

"Maybe you can say a few words, then. It's not likely that the traveling parson will make it through, and it would be nice to have someone give a message. I believe you're the most qualified out of the lot of us."

"Why's that?" Belle heard herself ask.

"Zebulon here went to seminary, could have ended up a traveling parson himself," Jake replied.

Seminary? She stared at him as she tied her wool bonnet.

He glanced at her as if he'd heard her unspoken one-word question, and shrugged.

Belle said nothing more about Zebulon's singing skills or lack thereof, or the seminary, but bade the Smythes good night, promising to see them on Sunday if the weather was good. She politely refused Jake's offer to send someone to help her saddle Patch; she was used to seeing to her horse herself.

She entered the snug barn, where Patch stood tied not far from Jake's own mount, a dark bay mare.

"Ready, Patch? It's going to be dark soon." She found his saddle and set to putting it on, tying the girth.

A shadow blotted out most of the remaining light coming through the doorway.

Zebulon, of course.

"You ought to carry a weapon with you, Miss Murray. Either that, or confine your outings to daytime hours only," he said as he passed by her to get to his horse.

"It's still daytime." She glanced toward the barn door. Well, it wasn't exactly twilight yet.

"It's unsafe for a woman to travel this time of day, unarmed, alone. I'll see you to your claim."

She didn't want to argue with him again and held her tongue. Never mind he'd made her feel like a child, as if she always needed escorting somewhere.

"You're irritated," he said.

"Not really," she replied, giving Patch a pat on the neck. Truthfully, she was out of her element here. Not for the first time did her nerves make her insides tremble.

"But, do you carry a weapon of any kind with you, Miss Murray?"

"Ah, no, I don't."

He shook his head. "You ought to. What kind of weapon did Ham have?"

"A shotgun and a pistol. I've touched neither of them."

"You need to learn, get comfortable with them. Carry one of them with you at all times. Don't be frightened. Better safe than sorry."

Yes, she'd had a lot of sorry lately, with losing Melanie and Ham.

"Miss Murray, my offer still stands."

"Offer?"

"I'll take you myself across the pass, to the nearest train station. A few more weeks, a month at the most, and you'll likely be stuck here until spring, unless there's an unexpected change in the weather. Which could happen. But, you never know."

"No. I'm staying. Ham and Melanie worked hard for their claim. I'm going to fulfill it then file the patent myself as owner. It's the least I can do, for their legacy."

"And then what? Stay? Do you have any idea on how to run a ranch?"

"I know enough. I've watched Ham, and helped Melanie."

He gave a long sigh. "But you can't do it all yourself."

She paused. "I can try. Zebulon, I can't leave. I have nowhere, no one to go back to." Her voice quavered for a moment, and she swallowed hard. Nobody saw these moments, because she wouldn't allow it. Somehow, in the growing dark, it felt safe to let Zebulon know.

"Then, Miss Murray, I advise you prepare yourself for the hardest winter of your life."

"I'll be ready, Mr. Covington."

"I like it better when you say Zebulon."

Now her cheeks blazed again as they had earlier that evening. "Zebulon, I'm ready to go home." She could follow the trail, the snow lit by the pale moon beginning to rise. The sooner she was home again, the better.

I like it better when you say Zebulon?

Where in the great wide world did that come from? He dropped the thought as soon as it entered his mind. He needed to get home, see to the barn animals then get to bed. Morning would come early, and he had much to do, a few strays to round up, along with picking up some hay from Gates Browning, a few claims over. Then there would be work on the sleigh he'd begun crafting that summer, to use when the trails were impassable by wagon.

They headed out into what was left of the dusk, with the surrounding world glowing white, leaving the trails home darkened.

Belle sat primly on Patch, although she rode astride. The gelding moved on sure steps. "So, Zebulon. Mr. Smythe said you've been to seminary."

"Yes, a long time ago. I was a little younger than you are now, fresh out of preparatory school."

"Preparatory school?" she echoed back.

"Yes, ma'am, I'm completely educated. Six years Latin, four years mathematics, two of economics, four of English, three of French." He let that sink in, wondering how her highfalutin airs took in the revelation.

"Where did you attend seminary?"

"In Chicago. I thought I wanted to be a minister, have a church."

"But you stopped. Why?"

He let Buck's reins go lax; the horse could find his way better on the trail without his own interference. "Looking back, I'm not sure. Pride. Stubbornness. Not sure I wanted to answer to anyone."

"A man can be a minister without standing behind a pulpit."

31

Her gentle words gave him a nudge he hadn't felt in years. The headmistress at the orphanage had told him so. *You don't have to be a preacher to do God's work.*

"I feel the same way."

"Well, a man ought never to be ashamed of having an education." Belle's voice rang out with an air of confidence. "A strong brain is just as impressive as a strong physique."

"I'll keep that in mind, Miss Murray." The turn of conversation almost made him squirm, but there was a kindness in her words.

"So you came here, to Wyoming. That's a big change from Chicago."

"Yup, sure is." He'd come on a whim, almost a dare, really. Trapping had given him a freedom that years of academia hadn't.

"So, you were a trapper and then staked a claim."

"Yup. Finished my cabin addition this spring, new barn, too." Honestly, she was cross-examining him with the skill of an attorney. He almost asked where she was headed with her line of questioning but figured he didn't want to know. Not quite.

"I must say your prospects are excellent."

He chuckled at her tone. "I'm glad you approve."

"But what about your family?"

"Orphaned, as best I know. My mother never married, my father, not sure about him. But I won a scholarship to preparatory school for my grades, and the same followed for seminary."

"How sad about your family."

"I'm thankful for what I have. My family is here, among the locals. Soon as I saw the Teton Range, I felt like I'd come home." Funny, how the low light could loosen his guard.

"Yes, it's lovely here. So free, and wild."

"That it is, Miss Murray."

They fell silent, and as Zeb listened to the soft plunks of hooves on the trail, he shot a prayer of thanks heavenward that the questions were over. For the moment, that is.

Then Miss Murray continued.

"Mr. Covington, have you ever thought of taking a wife?"

He darted a quick glance across the trail at her. "My, my, my, Miss Murray, aren't we being forward?"

"Oh, ah, I don't mean me," she sputtered. "I'm in no position to marry right now."

"Well, who did you mean?" He tried not to laugh.

"Never mind. I'm just curious. There are a number of eligible men in Jackson's Hole, and there comes a point when, I'm sure, a man must know he needs, or wants, a wife. If you are at that point, I'd like to help you find a suitable spouse. Because as you know, there aren't many eligible women in Jackson. A lady will have plenty of choices, but not all would be an, ah, ideal match."

A matchmaker. She was trying to be a matchmaker. The idea made him laugh out loud, and the sound rang against the trees.

"You find my offer humorous?"

"Yes. No. I don't need a wife, Miss Murray. I don't know as I ever will." He looked ahead on the trail, to the edge of a fence with the Quinns' mark on it, the edge of their claim. "It looks like we're here."

"Well, thank you, Zebulon." She reined in her horse and stopped at the gate. "And like I said, never mind about what I said about needing a wife. I have a young lady in mind who I think would be a most suitable wife for the right man. But she can't entertain notions about just anyone."

He didn't wager but guessed the likely candidate was the nervous and giggly Rosemary Smythe he'd sat across from that evening at supper.

"Good evening, Miss Murray. Don't forget what I said about the guns."

"I won't, Mr. Covington. Thank you for seeing me to the gate."

He found himself wishing he could see her smile better in the deep twilight, because he could hear it in her voice.

No, he didn't need a wife. But tonight, he almost found himself wanting one.

Chapter 4

On Friday morning a week later, the snow began to fall, and it continued for the next twenty-four hours. The wind began, howling as it swept down from Grand Teton, the highest peak of the range.

Nobody had warned Belle about the sound it made, a wailing noise that made her want to plug her ears and burrow deeply under the quilts stacked on the mattress.

She cleaned the three rooms of the cabin until they gleamed then whiled away the afternoon watching the white world outside. The snow had stopped, and at last the sun broke out from behind the lead-gray clouds.

Not for the first time did she feel a mixture of grief and joy when bundling into her heavy coat and opening the front door. The snow came up to her knees, and that was in the meager path between the cabin and the snug barn a stone's throw away. Patch was likely more than ready to eat, not to mention Daisy, the cow. Hopefully the small herd of cattle that had hunkered down near the barn had fared well in the storm. Mr. Tolliver was supposed to come to help with chores yesterday, but the weather had obviously kept him away.

The view outside made her stop and stare, even as a burst of cold air swept into the cabin. The mountains rose into the sky, jagged, wild, beautiful. She thought she'd seen mountains in Massachusetts and New York State. But these? Their height and ruggedness made her feel smaller than she'd ever felt in her life. The empty cabin made her feel more alone than she'd ever felt before.

What was she doing here? Helping young women become more refined? Or merely trying to survive and build a life like everyone else?

She needed to stop wondering and get set with the tasks ahead of her today. Last night, she'd found some snowshoes in the corner of Melanie and Ham's old room, a place she'd left untouched since the horrible accident. She still recalled the sight of their broken bodies after their team bolted. She couldn't bear looking at the horses and sold the team, but she'd kept Patch. Somehow, she knew Ham wouldn't mind she'd sold the team, especially if she might need the money for replenishing supplies in the long months to come.

"Here goes nothing." She managed to strap the snowshoes to her boots then grabbed the milk pail before stepping on paddled feet onto the snow. The sun hurt her eyes; the wind stung her cheeks. Melanie had done this for more than four years? Her sister had said the winters were long and cold; Belle said she knew what cold felt like. At the time, Melanie had laughed. If her sister could but see her now.

Belle took a few strides in the direction of the barn. One step at a time. She concentrated on the snow in front of her then stopped when she heard someone calling out.

"Miss Murray!" A figure in the distance came plodding toward her on snowshoes. "Halloo!"

"Hello!" she called out, squinting against the light. Zebulon Covington, of course. She continued along the path to the barn. He could catch up quickly enough if he wanted to speak to her. Why he'd trudged the distance from his next-door claim to hers, she didn't know. But she knew he'd tell her soon enough.

Belle kicked at the snow in front of the doorway, a feeble effort. Then she dug at it with her milk pail until the door would budge open to allow her to slip through.

"You ever seen so much snow?" Zebulon asked, as he grew closer to the barn. The cattle taking refuge lowed as he approached.

"No, never." She dug at the door a little more.

"Here." He pulled on the door, and the snow wedged higher behind it. "You should have kept a path broken during the storm. Doesn't take much time to do. Makes it easier to get your work done when the snow's over."

"I didn't know."

"I thought as much, which is why I came by." He held the door open. "After you, Miss Murray."

She hesitated a moment. She wasn't accustomed to having a man follow her into an empty barn. Yes, the other evening at the Smythes' they'd both gone to the barn, but they were both leaving, and she wasn't exactly alone on the property as she was right now.

Belle glanced at him before entering the snug, warm space filled with the scent of animals.

"Miss Murray, my intentions are completely honorable. You need a hand with the chores, and I think a few suggestions to help you are warranted." His eyes twinkled with amusement. "And you'd much prefer my help instead of any of the other eligible men, I guarantee it."

"Thank you for saying so." The barn felt warm with Patch and the milk cows inside. The horse greeted her, and she went to stroke his nose.

"He's a good horse." Zebulon headed for the pitchfork.

"Yes. Ham helped me pick him out. I bought him as soon as I arrived, from Sven Olsen." She went for the wheelbarrow. "Here, you'll need this. I'll get to milking Daisy."

At Belle's words, the cow thumped on the wall.

"You got the easy job." He grinned, grasping the wheelbarrow handles.

"You chose first." She grinned right back at him. "You grabbed the pitchfork."

"Quite right, quite right."

They set to work in silence, and Belle leaned her head against

Daisy's flank. She'd never milked a cow before coming west, and found she didn't mind the chore once she'd learned. Melanie had a daily war with Daisy at milking time and had gladly relinquished the chore when she saw Daisy preferred Belle.

Maybe it was because Belle talked to Daisy. During those moments in the morning and evening, she would chatter away to the cow.

"Hang on, girl. Almost done. That was quite a storm, wasn't it?"

"Wasn't so bad." Zebulon's voice came from the stall.

"Eighteen inches, at the lowest parts." She kept squeezing and pulling the udders.

"Wait until it's storm after storm, from January on."

"I don't want to think about it." *One storm at a time, thank you very much.*

"Well, you ought to." Zebulon's voice grew louder, and she glanced behind her to see him leaning over the low wall. "Not thinking can cause frostbite, or worse."

Belle tried not to sigh. "I'm well aware of that."

"I don't think you are."

She stared at the milk in the pail and sighed. "Please, give me a little credit. I'm not about to go traipsing off into the wilds without preparing myself."

"I'm sorry. I don't mean to sound harsh."

"I accept your apology." She stood, trying not to knock the milk pail over as she did so. "Thank you for your concern. I know I'm the greenhorn around here."

He nodded. "I'll be glad to put fresh straw down."

"Thank you. I hope there's enough for the winter. Ham was trying to set some supplies back before. . ."

Zebulon nodded. "I know he was. Your brother-in-law was a good man. A good friend. He, ah, he made me promise if anything ever happened, that I'd look out for you."

"Oh, I see." She hadn't known that.

"Which is why I insisted on taking you to the train."

Belle shook her head. "I can't go back. Not snow or smelly barns or the cold will get me out of here. I'm going to file when the claim time is up and then maybe sell. I don't know. I have no other options."

"Surely there's a ladies' finishing school that would appreciate your services back East."

Belle shrugged. "I don't have a pedigree. No prospects. My parents never married. What woman in high society would want *me* teaching her daughter? No matter the quality of my services. But here, I can show young ladies how to be ladies."

"Belle Murray, you are every bit a lady, even in Ham's overcoat and wearing snowshoes and standing in a barn."

Her throat swelled. "Thank you, Zebulon."

She'd said his name again and somehow the space between them had shrunk, with only the stall partition separating them.

He nodded then turned away. "We'll get them fed, and I'll be on my way."

"I do appreciate you coming." Belle toted the pail of milk from the stall. "I haven't seen to the cattle yet."

"I guessed as much, judging from the greeting they gave us. Do you have enough to feed them?"

"For now."

"They might find something to eat on the open range, but it'll take awhile for the snow to clear enough, even with the wind's help." He didn't know what else to say, but Belle was, self-admittedly, as green as they came.

"I understand. Maybe I can buy some hay, somewhere, if supplies get low?"

"Maybe. It'll come at a steep price, the further along we get into winter."

"Oh." She stopped by the door. "I didn't think about that."

He had hay and feed for the winter and assumed Ham had done as much to provide for his small yet growing herd. "You could always sell off some of the herd. You wouldn't get as much if you tried to thin the herd now, but you would have fewer mouths to feed."

"I see."

She stood in the doorway, waiting, while he threw hay out for the cattle. He returned.

"Here, let me help you with your snowshoes." He knelt before her, strapping the shoes onto her booted feet. A hint of petticoat peeked out from under her long dark blue woolen skirt.

"Thank you. I had quite the time trying to get them on before coming out here."

He grinned at the idea. "I imagine you did. First time using snowshoes?"

"Yes, first time ever."

"I see. Well, you'll likely want to learn another skill for getting around here in the wintertime."

"What's that?"

"Skiing."

"Skiing?"

"For short, quick trips, instead of taking the horse."

"Ah, how would I learn such a skill? I have no skis."

"It's fairly simple to fashion some makeshift skis, and poles."

She set down the pail of milk. "You're teasing me."

"No, I'm quite serious." He stood. Now they had no stable wall between them.

Her blue eyes narrowed slightly and a tiny furrow appeared between her eyebrows. "Huh. Well, I'll think about that skill."

"You want to learn, you'll know where to find me."

"Humph." She picked up the milk. "A lady does not go calling on a man."

At that, he tilted back his head and laughed. "Miss Murray, you're painfully proper sometimes."

With that, he left the barn, and she followed him.

"I know we're far from the civilized East, but even so, we must remember our manners."

"Ah, yes, we barbarians here are one step shy of degenerating into wildness."

"Honestly, that's an exaggeration."

"I'm teasing, Miss Murray."

"Of course you are." She paused, blinking at him in the sunlight. "What you said, about other less savory types. . .what did you mean?"

He took the pail of milk from her. "Exactly what I said. You're young, unmarried, inexperienced, and trying to keep a claim. I'm surprised the men haven't been swarming around already."

"Perhaps they're waiting a respectable time during my. . .period of mourning." She bit her lip.

"Miss Murray, some men aren't respectable, and they won't wait." He didn't want to cause her worry or fear, but truth was truth. Not many unmarried women in these parts, although the general population of Jackson had continued to grow steadily.

Someone like Miss Murray could fall prey to the wrong man. It bothered him in more ways than one.

Chapter 5

A lovely Friday morning, and Belle had ridden to the Smythes' for a morning of needlework and chatting with several women from the Jackson's Hole area. The social time did her good, even while memories of sitting with Melanie and working on mending pricked at her heart.

"Belle, how are you getting along, out there on the claim by yourself?" Mary Smythe asked as she worked her knitting needles.

"I'm managing. I'm more tired than I've ever been in my life." Belle set down her own needlework. "Part of me wanted to stay home today, but I needed to get out of the house."

"True, true." Ivana Olsen nodded. "It is just me and the little one while Sven works with the horses; sometimes I must get to town. But this time of year, it gets more difficult."

After the ladies' morning of mending and needlework, they would have a simple lunch. Not high society, by any means, but the warmth of fellowship and sharing. The women's conversation buoyed Belle's mood. She'd struggled to shake the grief over losing Melanie and Ham. Nothing had turned out as she'd expected when moving to Jackson.

This morning she felt flickers of hope, even without her possessing any sense of anticipation for Christmas this year. The sensation of loss felt like a scab that had been freshly ripped open. For the first Christmas ever, Belle would be alone.

The morning's activities involved a few of the women fashioning handcrafted gifts for Christmas.

Scanning the room, she regarded each of her friends. They had families, warm places to be, and hearts to hold dear.

"We ought to discuss our plans for a Christmas program," Mary said. "For some it might be an ordinary day. But for many of us, we still want to celebrate the Savior's birth."

"If we had enough young children, we could do a pageant and costumes," Rosemary said. "I don't mind performing a song, if no one objects."

Belle had to agree Rosemary's idea had merit. "Perhaps some of the adults could read parts from the Christmas story, for an adult pageant. That is, if any of them agree."

"Or we could read from the Bible, and sing songs for Christmas." Ivana paused. "Although, my English is not so good. I don't know all the words. But I could sing in Swedish."

The ladies murmured their agreement.

"Maybe we could find a small tree, and decorate it, with candies?" Belle asked. "I'm not sure what traditions are like here, but I've always missed seeing a lovely tree and gifts in the branches."

"You must have celebrated quite grandly back East." Eunice Woods looked over the top of her mending.

"When I worked for the Skinners, they always hung greenery throughout the main living quarters, the parlor, and the music room. It was lovely and smelled just like a forest." Belle smiled at the happy memory of Christmases in the grand house. The family had bestowed kind gifts to her and the rest of the staff. However, a letter from her sister, on the heels of being lied to by a beau, had driven Belle west. No, her sister's words had beckoned her.

"I'm not sure we'd have trees and greenery as you're accustomed to." Mary looked at her slyly. "I imagine, though, if you send Zebulon Covington out to search for a good Christmas tree, he would look high and low."

"Ah, yes, Mr. Covington would cross the pass to find a Christmas tree if you asked him to." Ivana's expression matched Mary's.

"Whatever do you mean?" Belle tried not to fidget as if she were a child.

"It's quite clear that he's taken a shine to you." Mary nodded.

"He. . .he promised my brother-in-law he'd watch out for me, if anything ever happened to him." She tried not to look in Rosemary's direction but did so anyway.

"But you—but you—" Rosemary sputtered. "I was the one. . ." Her cheeks flamed red.

"I—I— Oh, Rosemary, it's not like that." Belle wanted to

deny her own interest in Zebulon Covington, but doing so would be a lie. Yes, he fascinated her. The morning he'd helped her with the livestock, she'd seen how gentle he was. And he'd never hinted at anything improper. He made her laugh. And more often than not, she found herself wondering what he looked like without the beard.

"You know I like him. And now I hear you've been encouraging his attentions." Rosemary stood, her needlework tumbling from her lap.

"No, not encouraging." Belle took in the other women's expressions. "Rosemary. . ."

"My dear daughter," Mary said, shaking her head.

"Oh, Mother." Rosemary strode from the parlor and entered her room, closing the door behind her.

"I apologize for my daughter." Mary sighed. "I'm not sure what's come over her."

"That might be partly my fault, Mrs. Smythe." Belle frowned. "Yes, I've been tutoring her. But she also asked me to school her in how to carry herself as a lady, to, ah, gain the attention of a suitable man for a husband."

"Well there's certainly a wide selection of men here," Eunice observed, "although I'm not sure how many of them are suitable."

Mary glanced toward the closed door to Rosemary's room. "Her father and I have considered sending her East in the spring. It's been rather difficult for her here. She misses our family and friends. There are more opportunities for her, and yes, more suitable men."

"That's probably true enough."

"Well, we can't worry about it now. We need to weather through the winter, and in the meantime, we have Christmas to look forward to." Mary beamed, but then her smile faded. "Oh, Belle, this year with Christmas coming, it must be especially difficult for you."

Belle nodded. She'd pulled herself along, focusing on learning how to deal with the winter stretching ahead of her, questioning her decision to stay, and missing Melanie with an ache only the bereaved could understand. She glanced down at her black dress.

"I miss them, very much."

"And you have no one else?" Ivana leaned forward, squeezing Belle's hand.

"No. Ham. . .Ham has a brother over the pass. But he's not my family. Melanie and I lost our mother a long time ago." She didn't add more about her lack of family, and the others didn't ask further.

"Humph." Mary frowned. "I've heard of that Abel Quinn. As lazy an incompetent as Hamilton Quinn was industrious and capable."

"He and Ham had some bad blood between them a few years ago. Ham told him never to come back, asking for money again." The man was lazy, given to much drinking and cards, and both Melanie and Ham barely spoke of him during the time Belle had lived with them. Even after his brother had perished, Abel hadn't come to the funeral. What kind of a man would act in such a way, not paying his respects to his own brother?

"That's the kind of man I want Rosemary to stay away from the most." Mary shook her head and tsked.

Rosemary's bedroom door clicked as it opened, and Rosemary reemerged, her shoulders squared and her head held high.

"Belle, Mother, Ivana, and Eunice, I apologize for my outburst a few moments ago." Rosemary settled back onto her vacant chair and picked up her needlework. "I'm not sure what came over me."

"I know you've been lonely for your friends." Mary's knitting needles clicked as she worked them. "Your pa and I have discussed it."

"I do have a friend here, though." Rosemary smiled at Belle. "Thank you, Belle, for being my friend. If Zebulon Covington prefers you, there's not much I can do about that."

"Oh, Rosemary." Belle set down her work and crossed the parlor. "I'm glad you're my friend. Don't worry about Zebulon. I'm not sure that anything will come of it. In fact, he told me he doesn't see the need for a wife." She hugged the young woman, who responded in kind. She dared not mention that Mr. Covington said he would teach her how to ski on Sunday afternoon, if the weather held.

After church meeting on Sunday, Belle ate some leftover stew and bread and tried not to watch the clock until the hands read three o'clock, the agreed-upon time for skiing. Somehow, the subject had come up during the small gathering, and the Olsens said they'd like to join Belle and Zebulon for an afternoon excursion.

"More than likely, they'll enjoy the diversion of seeing me slide around on my hindquarters," Belle murmured to herself as she tied on her bonnet over top a woolen scarf. But ever since the conversation during the ladies' gathering at the Smythe place, she found herself looking forward more and more to skiing with Zebulon. Perhaps Ivana and her husband and small child coming along to ski would be a diversion for her as well. She missed playing with little ones, and the Skinners had had an energetic band of children.

She fastened her coat, topped it with Ham's overcoat, the warmest combination she could think of, then watched until Zebulon, along with the Olsens following by sleigh, arrived at the claim.

Belle went out to meet them. "Oh, a sleigh! How beautiful."

"Yah." Ivana nodded. "Sven finished it in time." She climbed down from the sleigh then pulled her small daughter off the seat.

"Good afternoon." Sven Olsen shook her hand. The tall blond man had few words but radiated love for his small family.

"Are you ready?" Zebulon dismounted from his mule and

unstrapped the skis from the saddle.

"I suppose I am."

"We skied quite often back home." Ivana adjusted Tilde's earmuffs. "This will be Tilde's first time skiing, now that she's old enough. I expect she will fall often."

"It's my first time, too, so I will likely be falling right alongside her." Belle smiled at the petite toddler with blond curls, a round face with a peaches-and-cream complexion.

Sven and Zebulon stood near the Olsens' sleigh, talking and pointing at its rails.

Zebulon crouched lower, examining something on the runners. He straightened to stand upright, his eyes bemused.

"I've been building my own sleigh," he explained. "I'd hoped to have it finished sooner, because it'll make hauling things a lot easier in the winter."

"Not to mention we can all go on sleigh rides on fine Sundays like today," Ivana said. "Here, Tilde. Let us put some skis on you." She continued in Swedish, pointing toward the sleigh. The little child complied, chattering away in her family's language.

The two of them stepped back as Sven drove the sleigh to a shelter beside the barn. He tied their horse to one of the hitching posts nearby.

"Here, I'll help you with your skis first." Zebulon held a pair of straight, narrow slats of wood, with the front ends slightly curved to form makeshift skis.

"Did you make these yourself?" She studied the curious-looking devices. She'd seen skis before but nothing made like these.

"I did. Now, step over here." He gestured a few paces away from where Ivana stood with Tilde.

Belle followed him to a cleared but snowy expanse of the ranch yard. He knelt before her, much as he'd done when helping her with her snowshoes. His large roughened hands strapped the skis, his touch gentle, yet firm, as he tied the straps. Her foot, now firmly buckled into the ski, began to slide as she lifted her other foot.

"Whoa." He grabbed her calf while she simultaneously gripped his shoulder. "Hold on, you can't go anywhere just yet."

Belle had no doubt he'd catch her if she did lose her balance but fought to keep her footing. Surely, she could ski and still keep some sense of dignity. But she'd never had a man grab her leg like that before. Most improper, yet unavoidable. Clearly, it was harder for a lady to stay proper in the West, not out of lack of regard for propriety, but out of necessity. She'd much rather have Zebulon touch her leg than she end up breaking a bone or her dignity by falling.

While the Olsens worked with their little one to cover some distance on the snowy ground, Zebulon worked with Belle.

"Aren't you going to put your skis on also?" she asked.

"Not yet. I want to make sure you get your footing first. All right, you'll need to bend your knees. Slightly; don't squat."

No, she wasn't about to squat. She did bend her knees a little. "Like this?"

"Yes. Now push off with the poles." He'd handed her a pair of poles, crafted from slim yet strong branches, to help her balance and steer. "Don't tighten your knees. Keep them loose."

How he had an inkling that her knees had stiffened underneath all her skirts and long johns, she had no idea.

Belle began to slide, the skis providing support for her. Yes, she could do this. She tried to keep the tips of the skis from touching, but her toes wanted to turn in. She kept going, gliding past the Olsens. Ivana scooped their little one from the ground. She'd slipped and fallen on her first try and sat on the snow, pouting.

Ivana leaned over her daughter, speaking to her in Swedish. Belle understood the caring, encouraging tone well enough.

Belle glanced over her shoulder. Immediately her balance shifted and her foot wobbled. Zebulon's mouth gaped, likely to warn her, but too late. How did one stop with these things?

Her skis tangled together and sent her face-first toward the snow. The cold sucked the breath from her body, and she inhaled sharply as she sat up, brushing the snow from her face and coat.

At this rate, she figured until the spring thaw, she'd remain snowbound or use snowshoes to get to town in the worst of the snowy weather.

"Are you all right, Miss Murray?" Zebulon rushed to help her to her feet.

Their hands lingered as he helped her up, and the cold didn't seem so hostile anymore.

"I'm quite all right." Heat bloomed through her cheeks.

Chapter 6

They made for a soggy and wet group—at least two of them, anyway, as they sat in the snug Quinn kitchen after Belle and Tilde skied and fell, skied and fell. A few times, though, Belle even laughed out loud when Zeb passed her on the trail. After an hour or so, Belle suggested they join her in the house to warm up before they all left for home.

She'd capably added more wood to the stove and had the kettle heating for coffee. If she felt any wounded dignity after the hour of sliding and falling, she didn't let on. Instead, she served up some shortbread cookies as if she were in a grand kitchen, offering the first cookie to little Tilde, who perked up at the mention of sweets by her mother.

"So, you will do the scripture readings on Christmas Eve?" Sven asked Zebulon.

"Yes, I will."

"Good."

"And we ladies will make our traditional Christmas treats, from our home countries, and bring to share on Christmas Eve,"

Ivana said. "Do you know what you will make, Belle?"

Zeb caught a flicker of a frown across her face. Did she not have the means to make anything for Christmas Eve? She'd said she had provisions, but usually provisions didn't include ingredients for a holiday meal.

"I. . .I'm not quite sure. I thought of making a clootie dumpling. I haven't had one in ages. My. . .our mother used to make it for us when we were children, every Christmas." She pulled out some mugs. There were four, one of which had a missing handle and chipped rim.

"I'll skip coffee," Zebulon said.

"Nonsense." Belle shook her head. "You'll have coffee."

"So, what is this clootie dumpling?" Ivana asked. "Is it sweet?"

"A bit. It's like a fruit pudding. But I'm not sure if I'll have the ingredients." Belle poured coffee into the three mugs. "If not, I'm sure I'll figure something else out."

"Whatever it is, I know it will be good." Zebulon did his best to encourage her. He knew she probably didn't feel like celebrating this Christmas.

"Thank you, Zebulon." She handed him a steaming cup then gave cups to the others. She sat down in the chair beside him. "I'm really not much of a cook, so I can't guarantee you how good it will taste."

"Ah, but I know you'll do your best," Ivana said. "I know Sven had to put up with a lot of my burned meals before I learned to cook better."

"I lost ten pounds during our first year after the wedding." Sven gave his wife a warm look. "But now, I must watch I do not overstuff myself with her cooking."

Zebulon found himself envying their interaction. Belle sat beside him, and he wanted to know if she'd felt what he'd been feeling these past days and weeks. Ever since the meal at the Smythes, something had happened.

No, really, it was since losing Hamilton and Melanie. Not as though he'd never lost anyone unexpectedly to an early death before. But maybe it was the promise he'd made to Ham not long after Belle moved to be with her sister and brother-in-law. If anything happened to him, Zeb would be there for Melanie and Belle.

Despite her bravery and determination, he still saw her vulnerability. He admired her persistence and unflinching resolve to stay here. Being in this part of the country, especially at this time of year, demanded it.

To lose the determination and resolve could mean death.

"You've fallen silent, Zebulon."

He snapped out of his reverie to see the three of them looking his way. Little Tilde had fallen asleep in her mother's arms.

"I'm thinking is all."

"Well, be happy, man," Sven said. "Tell me, how much more to finish your sleigh?"

"It's the runners. I need to make sure I have the supplies to attach them."

"If you need some help, I can give you a hand."

"I appreciate that." He shrugged. "I thought I'd have this done sooner, but no. There's been a lot to do on the claim. Or, I should say, the Covington Ranch."

"So, when do you think you're going to settle down?" Ivana asked.

"I think I'm pretty settled right now."

"I mean, take a wife. You need a partner, someone to run the ranch beside you." She flicked a glance at Belle, who suddenly bolted to her feet and went for the jar of cookies. Good. He liked the cookies, shortbread, very much and could probably polish off the entire jar himself.

Belle set the jar on the table. "Here. Help yourselves to more." She lifted the lid.

Of course, a man had to obey. Zebulon picked up another cookie to give himself time to form a response to Ivana's suggestion.

"Well?" she asked, blinking at him.

"Ivana. . ." Sven's tone was low, gently chiding. "When a man's ready, he's ready."

He chewed as they both eyeballed him, and Belle kept herself busy with loading cookies on a plate. She didn't direct her focus in his direction but picked up the cookie jar and put it on the makeshift table by the window.

"Ah, I suppose you're right, Sven."

The couple exchanged glances as Tilde commenced to wail.

"Here." Ivana reached for a cookie. "We should go now, the little one fusses."

"Thank you for coming. I enjoyed your company very much." Belle smiled at Ivana. They were likely not so far apart in age. Zeb didn't miss the wistful look that crept into Belle's eyes when studying little Tilde.

Marriage might mean companionship, but marriage also led to babies. Zeb swallowed hard.

The land was hard enough to work, without supporting a wife, and children. The right woman, however, would be up to the task.

The four of them said good-byes after Belle followed them outside to their respective means of travel. Zebulon let himself linger while Ivana and Belle embraced and the young family headed off toward their claim, with promises to see each other next time the church meeting assembled.

Suddenly, his tongue seemed to have swollen to twice its size, his brain grinding to a halt. He stood by his mount's head and held the bridle.

"Well, thank you for the lesson. I enjoyed it, very much. Except for the falling parts." She laughed at herself, and he also laughed at the memory of seeing her sliding and falling into the snow. She'd picked up the skill by the end of the hour, not expert by any means but enough to start.

"You're very welcome. I enjoyed watching you learn." He let himself take her by the hand. She didn't pull away but looked up at him with her blue eyes bright in her face.

Then he surprised himself by tugging her closer and planting a kiss on her lips. She stepped closer still, and he put his free arm around her.

He caressed her cheek then jumped on his horse and rode away before he said anything foolish.

Belle sat humming to herself as she worked at knitting a muffler from leftover yarn. The finished project would be warm and multicolored, and also serve as a Christmas gift for Zebulon.

She hoped she wasn't being too presumptuous. Although his quick kiss good-bye surprised her the other day, it also pleased her. He'd skittered away like a spooked horse at his own action. She'd stood there, her lips burning, not sure of what to do.

A kiss. It hadn't bothered her, only that she'd had a fitful night's sleep that same evening.

Zebulon was sweet, and his kiss had been sweet, chaste, showing him to be so unlike her beau back East. Their relationship had been disastrous. The man, more a beast than a man, believed women were objects, no matter what their station.

Times like this, she missed her sister desperately, having someone to talk to. Rosemary was a kind enough young woman, but she was naive, and so far the only tragedy in her life had involved leaving her life back East. Not that she minded Rosemary as a friend; truthfully, Belle thanked God every day for the people she called friends now.

But the empty chairs at the table each morning and evening reminded her of her aloneness. The only times she'd allowed herself the luxury of grief was in the moments right before bed, but she was usually so tired after chores and such that sleep came swiftly. Or immediately upon waking in the morning, she'd miss hearing the sounds of someone else in the household.

She still didn't understand losing Melanie and Ham. But then everyone knew the risks of living in the still-untamed territory of Wyoming. Not only that, the accident could have happened somewhere else, even in the city.

Times like this she wanted to tell Melanie about Zebulon. Of course, her sister knew the man better than she, had known him longer. He was Ham's friend, and Ham had a good reputation. Because of Ham, Zebulon had agreed to keep an eye on Belle.

She disliked the idea of anyone "keeping an eye" on her, one of the reasons she persisted in hiring Mr. Tolliver to help with the animals three times a week. She couldn't afford a full-time hand. And she wasn't about to have Zebulon here every couple of days, not when he had his own spread to care for.

She kept knitting the muffler, its length falling past her knees, as she sat by the window.

Maybe giving him the gift of a muffler *was* presumptuous. After all—she wasn't giving gifts to anyone else. But then she could always sneak it to the Christmas Eve meeting and get Ivana to help her deliver the present anonymously. Zebulon had been a good help to her, and for that she was thankful, especially when he would accept no payment.

The sunny afternoon gave the solitary window a soft glow. The days had grown shorter, the closer Christmas came. She ought to haul more wood to the pile to ensure she had enough close on hand before another storm rolled through. Thankfully, Zebulon had chopped a good deal of wood the last time he'd stopped by.

As her hands worked the knitting needles, she looked at her fingertips. The roughened areas had increased. Back East, she'd put lotion on her hands every evening. Ladies took care of their hands.

But her lotion here had dwindled, and she didn't know when she'd be able to purchase more. The local store only carried necessities, and luxuries like lotion had been low on her shopping list. She'd have to special order the product and have it taken over the pass. The cost would be double that back East.

Perhaps next time in town, she'd order a container of lotion to reward herself for making it through her first winter in Wyoming.

Someone approached the house, and she squinted to see the figure, astride a mule. Zebulon. Whatever did he want?

She stood then stashed the muffler on the seat. Whatever he wanted, she wasn't going to risk the hint of impropriety by inviting him into her home, alone, for any period of time. Also, in such an enclosed place, he'd likely hear the thrumming of her heart.

Belle pulled her shawl around her shoulders and opened the front door.

"Mr. Covington," she called out.

He slid off the mule's bare back and tied the reins to the nearest post. "Miss Murray."

He covered the distance to the front door in but a few steps. "I apologize for the late hour of coming by. I know it's going to be dark soon, but I couldn't let this go another day."

"Let what go another day?" She looked up at him, his figure filling the space of her vision. Much too close for her liking at the moment, and she recollected his nearness in a similar stance and the kiss that followed.

"I must give you my apologies for my actions when. . .when I taught you how to ski."

She clasped her hands in front of her. "Why should you apologize? It was unexpected but not unwelcome." Oh, but she was being bold. She'd never spoken such improper words as this, like a flirtatious young woman.

"Perhaps not, but I should have asked permission. I should have—"

Belle stepped forward, stood on her tiptoes, and gave him a peck on the lips. She'd gone beyond presumption and hurtled headlong into sauciness.

"There." She stood there and smiled at him.

Zebulon shook his head. "Miss Murray. I'm. . .I'm not in need of a wife. I don't simply hand out kisses. I'm not sure why I did."

"All right, then." Belle nodded. "Fair enough. Apology accepted. Good day, Mr. Covington."

She stepped backward, nearly tripping as she crossed into the warm, snug home, and closed the door firmly.

Now she knew. If he didn't need a wife, or romantic entanglement, she'd stay away from him but good. And how humiliating, her leaping at him with a kiss. What he must think of her now. Or not. Especially since he didn't need a wife anyway, or so he said.

Belle glared at the jumble of knitted yarn on the chair. She'd give the muffler to Mr. Tolliver. He'd been helpful, reliable, no matter the pittance she could afford to pay him to help.

Chapter 7

Zeb stood staring at the door Belle had just firmly shut. Or slammed, rather. He deserved it.

But it was better this way. He'd avoided much complication, and his head was now clear after being honest with Belle. Despite the fact he'd seen how the Smythes interacted together, as well as the Olsens, he'd been on his own for too long.

Jackson's Hole was developing year after year, and in time to come, the place would be less harsh to outsiders. Maybe then, when it was easier, he'd entertain the idea of settling down.

He strode back to James the mule, and hopped back on. But he didn't want to head back to the ranch just yet. A quick ride into town would do, as quick as he could go on a mule anyway. Unless James had ideas of his own. He would check the post to see if anything had arrived for him. He didn't often receive mail but thought it would be worth a try.

He'd been a cad, pushing her away in no uncertain terms after the kiss. But he was being honest. He shook his head and urged the mule along.

He didn't need anyone.

But what had scared him so badly about a brunette blue-eyed beauty who jumped in headlong into western life?

He didn't know. He'd sooner face a night in the wild, alone, than confront his reaction to her. It wasn't fair to subject her to his uncertainty on how he felt. One moment he wanted her gone. Another moment he wanted to help shelter and protect her.

Despite Belle's getting stuck in the mud and whatnot, she didn't need rescuing. However, that could change. The worst part of the winter wasn't yet upon them. He knew it, but he didn't think Belle understood what could lie ahead.

Half of him wanted to tote her and her belongings over the pass, the other wanted to beg her to stay.

Yet he'd just told her he didn't need a wife, straight out, to her face.

What was wrong with him?

He continued on his way to town, with James ambling along, trusty and true. The critter was unpredictable, but Zeb understood his animal's moods and ways, so the occasional stubborn streak and balking was easily dealt with.

On a fine afternoon like today, it seemed like everyone in Jackson's Hole had descended on the town to do business, catch up on news, and interact with fellow humans until the next patch of weather came through.

"Christmas is coming, the goose is getting fat," someone was singing as Zeb stepped into the general store to pick up his post.

"Gus, we don't have any geese." Zeb nodded to the older man playing checkers by the woodstove. "And if we did, they might be getting a bit skinny by now."

"Oh, you spoilsport." Gus Tolliver glanced across the board at his opponent, Bud Leach, another old-timer come to town, likely for human interaction as well. "Right, Bud?"

"I'm not getting in the middle of a poultry controversy. I'll eat either one, skinny goose or fat." The man stroked his gray handlebar mustache. He reached for a checker and skipped two of Gus's. "Ha. Take that."

"You win." Gus shook his head then stood and stretched. He glanced toward Zeb, who continued on his way to the counter.

Zeb inquired about any post that had come for him, but nothing. He turned and nearly ran smack into Gus.

"Mr. Tolliver."

"Mr. Covington." The older man studied his face. "You look like a man who's highly conflicted."

"I'm not sure, sir. Thought a ride to town and back would help. Better than staying cooped up at home. Not as though there's nothing to do." Zeb shrugged.

"I understand, Zebulon, I understand. Care to step outside and talk about it?"

"I'm not sure it would help much, sir. I've prayed about the matter, yes, but there seems to be no ready answer."

Gus clapped him on the back. "Ah, often the ready answer isn't the easy answer, or the comfortable answer."

Zeb wasn't about to debate that idea with the man. "No, I guess sometimes it's not."

"I wonder if it has anything to do with the young Miss Murray?"

He didn't answer Gus but knew his expression likely gave it away. A rider approached outside on a scrappy-looking dark mount that looked like it could use a good meal and a brushing. The pair halted at the hitching post, and the rider swung off the horse's back.

Zeb had half a mind to offer the man money for the horse, if only to rescue the beast. He pulled his mind back to the matter at hand.

"Well, where Miss Murray is concerned, all I can say is if you're afraid of something, sometimes the best thing to do is charge in and do it anyway. I near about passed out when approaching my missus, before she became Mrs. Tolliver. There she was, refined and pretty as the sunrise. There I was, not having a care in the world with no one to claim my time but myself. Until I saw her."

Zeb could relate to that sentiment. Much as Sven had told him before, sometimes a man didn't need a wife, but he wanted one.

"There's no crime in wanting what the Lord put in our hearts to desire. Companionship, a helpmeet, someone to weather the winters with, enjoy the springs and summers, to gather in the harvest with." Gus's eyes took on a sparkle. "I don't regret it, not one bit."

Chapter 8

A knock sounded at the door some hours after Zebulon had left. The noise made Belle jump and almost drop the scarf.

"Who is it?"

No answer.

Her pulse pounding in her throat, she tiptoed to the window and tried to see whoever had knocked at the door. A horse stood tied to the nearest fence post. She didn't recognize the mount, a dark bay with a scraggly mane.

The shotgun. Belle reached for it where it hung on the rack over the coats. Good thing for her, she'd been practicing like Zeb had suggested. "Who's there?"

"Belle Murray, open the door." A male voice. Not Jake or Sven or Zebulon, or even Mr. Tolliver.

"Tell me who you are, first."

"Abel Quinn."

"I prefer not to have gentleman callers inside my home if I'm alone." As soon as Belle had spoken the words, she realized her error in doing so. But she had a gun. And so far Ham's brother hadn't given her any cause for alarm other than arriving unexpectedly.

"Ma'am, I'm not here on a personal matter. But what I have to tell you, I'd prefer to be inside out of the cold."

She unlocked the door and opened it.

Abel Quinn filled the doorway. A smell came from him of animal fur and stale alcohol. She couldn't catch a whiff of anything fresh. He had a leather pouch slung over one shoulder and a rifle over the other.

"Come in." She debated about heating water for coffee, and although the water in the kettle would likely make a lukewarm cup, she didn't want to encourage him to stay any longer than necessary. However, all she knew about him, she'd heard from Ham. Maybe after all this time he'd changed. But then Abel hadn't come to the funeral, she reminded herself.

"Thank you, ma'am." He removed his hat, and she stepped back to allow him inside. He shut the door behind him, the hinges creaking and wood squeaking.

Belle stood in the center of the room, the table behind her, and kept her hands clasped together. "Please, accept my condolences about your brother."

"You lost your sister, so, likewise." Abel nodded. "I can't imagine what my brother told you about me."

"Only that, ah, you'd had a falling out sometime in the past. He didn't speak of you much. I do know, though, he had hoped to reconcile with you."

Abel guffawed. "I bet he did. Well, actions speak otherwise. Always thought he was better'n me. All I can say is look what I have, and look what he's got."

Belle couldn't find the words to comment on the brothers' relationship. Clearly, Abel still bore ill feelings toward Ham, even as his brother lay in the grave. "So, Mr. Quinn, you said this isn't a personal call. I assume, then, it's a business matter of some kind. Although, I can't imagine what business you and I would have to deal with."

"You're quite right, this is a business matter." He removed the wide pouch from his shoulder and strode past her to the table. He opened the flap and pulled out some papers. "I have here some papers that give me the rights to this claim."

"What?" Belle wasn't sure she'd heard him correctly. "My sister's name is on this claim, not merely your brother's." She knew enough to know if her sister's name was on the claim papers, too, Belle had at least the rights to half the claim.

Until now Abel Quinn had been a figure in her imagination; the relative Ham never saw anymore. She'd figured the man cared nothing for the land and what it meant.

Abel shook his head. "Not in the papers Hamilton filed. The papers say the claim was filed by Hamilton Quinn, not Hamilton and Melanie Quinn. Got copies of 'em right here. Look for yourself."

"There must be a mistake." She reached for the papers he

held. She scanned the first page.

"Go ahead, read them. No mistake. Ham always told me this would be his and his lady's place. But it's figuratively speaking, as they say. Her name was never listed on the paperwork."

Belle shook her head. He'd spoken the truth. No mention of Melanie at all on the paperwork. "No. What does this mean?"

"It means this will all be my property come springtime." He folded his arms across his chest and took a step closer. "Now, I suppose I could be charging you rent, all this time you've been living here since my brother's untimely death."

She tried to keep her knees still. She wished Jackson was modern enough for a telephone, or neighbors were closer. Or she could call on someone to get this man out of her house.

Except the house wasn't hers.

"You. . .you couldn't charge me rent. This place isn't yours. Not yet. It's not mine yet." No, she wasn't backing down easily. "Anyway, I should charge *you* a caretaker's fee. I've cared for the cattle, taken care of the cow and my own horse, kept the house clean, chopped wood, and hired help to assist me. Shall I send *you* a bill for everything I've paid for, as well as my own services rendered?"

At that Abel reared back and let out a roaring laugh. "I like your spirit. And you're a smart woman, too. I tell you what, you can stay here, on one condition."

"What's that?"

"You marry me. Because I'm planning to move into my home

on my claim. And right now, you're in my home. It wouldn't do for people to know we're both living here."

She sucked in a breath. "*Marry* you? I'll do nothing of the sort."

"Well, out you go, then."

"Out?"

"I'm sure a lady of your station," he said, eying her up and down, "wouldn't want her reputation besmirched by living under the same roof as an unmarried man. Now, we get someone here straightaway, we can get hitched. You've got spunk, and you appear to keep a clean house. If you haven't noticed, there's slim pickings of women around here."

"No." She shook her head again. "No, I won't marry you. Not now, or ever."

"I realize I may have put you in a bad position, but I'm not heartless." He grinned at her, his grizzly face swallowing up his pouchy dimples. "You have until Christmas Eve to vacate the premises."

"But...that's in only two days..."

"You're smart enough. You'll figure something out. And it'll give me time to find someone to marry us. I hear the preacher might even make a quick stop right around Christmas Eve, so I imagine he'd marry us proper. If you change your mind."

Her mind flailed around for a solution. "What if I buy the place from you?"

"You can't buy what's not mine yet."

He took the papers from her and set them on the table. "Well, think about it. I'll leave this copy with you. There are two."

She had no more words as he took his leave and strode from the house, after giving her a wink.

Chapter 9

At last Zeb had finished his sleigh, in time for Christmas. In fact, he had half a mind to take it to the Christmas Eve church meeting to show the Olsens and other friends. Sven's input had been invaluable when Zeb was crafting the sled.

Now the runners were bolted securely to the frame, and Zebulon spent time rubbing oil into the wooden sleigh to seal the grain. The smell competed with the rest of the aromas in the snug barn, but the result from using the oil would make a sleigh last for generations. At least, he hoped so. A good sleigh meant good transportation in the winter, and this one looked much finer than the glorified box-looking wagon on flat runners.

One of the first trips he wanted to make in the sleigh was a dash through the valley, with Belle Murray at his side. He stood back, admiring the sleigh once again, and wiped his hands on a clean rag.

He'd overstepped a bit by kissing her the other day, and while the gesture had been brief, it had replayed in his mind over and over since.

He'd ended his book-learning days long ago, but a man

could still learn some things after his formal education was over. He knew he was in love with Belle Murray, and he regretted the times he'd urged her to leave Jackson while she could.

Part of him regretted it, anyway. He cared for her, but he cared for her safety more. Although she'd shown spunk and determination in the time after her sister's death, she wasn't skilled in running a ranch.

His conversation with Gus had helped him see clearly. Despite his nerves and, yes, fear, he had so much to gain with Belle in his life. Despite everything that could go wrong, despite the unknown of life here in Jackson.

Getting this sleigh finished became top priority. When a man set out to woo a woman, he needed to take care that everything was perfect and proper. Belle deserved that much.

The jingle of a harness outside the barn drew him out to see Jake Smythe arriving by makeshift flatbed sleigh, with firewood stacked behind him.

"Good afternoon, Zeb." Jake reined in his horse from his perch atop the wood.

"Afternoon, Jake. What brings you by the Covington Ranch?"

Jake frowned. "I wish it were better news."

"What's happened?"

"Abel Quinn showed up at Belle's place, throwing his weight around. Turns out, Belle has no rights to the claim."

"But she's been there, even before Ham and Melanie died, and Melanie's name was on the paperwork, too, wasn't it?"

"Evidently not. Belle came by the house to talk to Mary and me, beside herself. I don't see any resolution to this, unless there's paperwork somewhere showing Belle could have at least half rights to the claim."

"Nervy of him, showing up like that."

"He's putting her out, Zeb. Tomorrow."

"Christmas Eve? Where she's going?"

"She's leaving Jackson. Gus Tolliver said she's paying him to take her over the pass."

"No. She can't leave."

"Well, she's going to." Jake paused. "I thought you ought to know."

"Thank you. Thank you for telling me." He turned the idea over in his mind. He ought to be glad Belle would be leaving, away from this setting she had no experience living in.

"So, what are you going to do about it?"

"Do?"

"Yes, do about it. Nobody's blind to the fact you've taken a shine to her, and she to you. Poor Rosemary cried for a day when she realized it."

Ah, poor Rosemary. "I'm sorry about your daughter, Jake."

"She'll be all right. I just pray she finds another man like you, Zeb. But you, you need to see about Belle. I admit I had my doubts about her staying. At first."

"I agree with you there. I told her a long time ago she'd be better off leaving."

"But now?"

"Part of me still thinks she'd be better off."

"The first winter is always the hardest, you know."

"I know. But I survived. You did, too." Zeb shook his head. "I don't know."

"Well, you'd better know before tomorrow. Gus and Belle are pulling out at daylight, so she can get to the station in Idaho and get her a ticket east."

Zebulon had been prepared to woo Belle Murray.

At a time like this, his decision had been transformed from wooing to something deeper.

Wooing Belle would have given them the opportunity to ease into what was blossoming between them. Yet to get Belle to stay would likely require something more drastic, and more permanent.

Belle had her trunk packed; it was all she'd brought with her and all she planned to take when she left. She wished she could unpack her memories and leave those as well.

She stood and faced the house her brother-in-law had built, small, snug, looking as large as a gnat when compared with the Teton Range. Their shelter might have been small, but oh, the view of God's handiwork made a better backdrop than the finest home she'd ever worked in back East.

And because of Abel Quinn, she couldn't keep it.

"Hire a lawyer," the Smythes had suggested. But who could

she find? She had no means to do so, and the papers she'd read over and over again told her she had no claim to the property.

She'd said her good-byes to them after selling Patch to Rosemary. Mr. Quinn had no rights to her horse, and judging by the condition of his own mount, she wasn't sure how he'd treat him. She'd allowed herself a good cry after the Smythes had left with Patch. Now she couldn't squeeze out another tear if she tried.

"I can't help but think you're making a terrible mistake," Mr. Tolliver said as he loaded her traveling trunk onto the back of the wagon.

"I don't see what other choice I have." She shook her head. "I appreciate the trouble of you taking me. If I could wait until after Christmas, I would. But. . .it will make things all the more difficult, not to mention the weather is good today."

"What about Zebulon?"

Belle hoisted herself up onto the wagon seat as gracefully as she could. "He told me from the very beginning, ever since losing Melanie and Ham, that I ought to leave. He was right."

Part of her wanted to stay as long as possible, to have more time with the people she'd grown to care for, the Smythes, the Olsens, and Zebulon. Especially Zebulon. But she couldn't ask anyone to put her up. No one had room.

Mr. Tolliver said nothing more but chirruped to the team, who stepped out, pulling them on the snow.

Finally, he spoke. "We'll make good time today. You should

make it in time to the station to buy a ticket to head out on the next train. Any idea where you're going?"

"St. Louis." If she could find her old friend Sadie, or the mission where she worked, perhaps they could put her up for a night or two, or even until she found live-in work.

They glided along in silence, with Belle taking in the sights around her. The sun on snow, the brisk air. The blue sky with the mountains reaching higher than anything around them.

The very idea of being in the city made her throat catch. Stifling, so many people around.

Belle allowed herself a glance back at the tiny house.

Mr. Tolliver caught her glance. "Don't worry. The Smythes will head over straightway for the household items, and sell what they can for you. Quinn might think he has the property, but it doesn't mean everything it contains."

"Thank you." She didn't have any fight left inside her. The very memory of that horrid man and his outrageous marriage proposal made her skin crawl.

"I sure do appreciate you giving an old man some work. I'll tell you this much: I'm not helping Abel Quinn with that land. He'll get no favors from me."

"Mr. Tolliver, you helped me immeasurably, and for that I'll always be thankful." Her throat caught. The wagon jostled as they headed toward the pass, to Idaho, and to the train where she'd leave it all behind.

"We'll miss you, girlie." His beard trembled and his breath

made puffs in the frosty air.

Silence reigned again, until Mr. Tolliver started singing hymns in his gravelly voice.

Dear Lord, there must be some other way.

After a sleepless night filled with tossing and turning, Zebulon hitched the mules to the sleigh. He knew what he had to do; he only prayed he was in time. Gathering clouds to the west told him snow was coming. Not sure when, or how much, but Gus Tolliver had to be crazy to be taking Belle across the pass, no matter what she was paying him.

The mules pulled the sleigh along with their typical resolute plod. One day he wanted to have some fine horses to use for traveling. In the meantime, the mules were cheaper, sturdier—and slower.

No matter how much he chirruped and urged them to speed along, they merely pinned their ears back and continued the same plod-plod-plod along the trail to the pass.

The wind picked up, and Zeb pulled his coat collar more tightly around his neck. He had to reach them, had to.

After an hour of plodding, Zeb thought the sky looked as though it had dropped below the mountaintop, and the snow fell, a dainty white snowfall. But he knew that could change within minutes, and the weather wasn't fit for anyone to be outside, let alone heading over the pass.

He caught sight of a wagon ahead, coming toward him.

Gus Tolliver with a passenger.

The old man pulled his team to a halt as Zeb approached.

"How-do, Mr. Covington."

"I'd be doing better if I was somewhere warmer." He spoke to Gus but kept his focus on Belle, who'd bolted up straight on the seat beside Gus.

"Zebulon." She appeared as though she were ready to leap from the wagon but clutched the seat.

"I found you in time."

"We decided to turn back; a bit of weather's coming in." As Gus spoke, the snowfall intensified.

"Good. Because. . .because I'm here to give Miss Murray a ride back to Jackson. . .to her home."

"I don't have a home in Jackson anymore." She looked down at her lap, her shoulders now drooping.

Zeb hopped down from the sleigh and strode in their direction. He stopped at the side of the wagon.

"Yes. You do. Come, ride with me in my sleigh." He glanced at Gus. "Mr. Tolliver, I'll take things from here."

The cold pulled at Belle with icy fingers as she and Zebulon headed back to Jackson, her traveling trunk strapped to the back of the sleigh.

But she was warm and snug beneath the fur robe he'd covered her with, and her shivering soon stopped. That and she let herself sit closer to Zebulon on the cushioned seat, closer than a lady ought to sit beside a man who wasn't her husband.

Zebulon didn't seem to mind, not one bit. And a warmth suffused through her, down to her toes.

"What do you mean, I still have a home in Jackson?"

"I. . .I was wrong, Belle. Flat out wrong in telling you all those times you should leave while you could." She could feel the rumble from his voice in her side as he spoke above the sound of the wind. "Everyone starts somewhere. You might be green, but you're not stupid."

She wanted to thank him for that observation, but she had a more pressing problem. "But, Zeb, I have nowhere to go. I can't live with the Smythes, I can't afford—"

"Miss Murray, I have a solution, if you're willing. But I must do this right."

Do what right?

"What do you think of my sleigh?"

"It's. . .it's beautiful." She touched the carved front panel, covered with elegant scrollwork. The sleigh wasn't just for hauling things and doing inglorious work. It was meant for joyful times, for a couple riding together on a romantic winter outing. A labor of love.

"Well, I decided awhile back, I wanted the woman I love to be the first to ride in this sleigh with me."

Love? The woman he loved?

"Oh, Zebulon." He loved her. Yes, he'd stolen that kiss. Had anyone else tried such a thing, she'd have probably slapped the man. If he'd tried such a thing months ago, she'd have probably slapped him, too.

However, now she'd had time to see him and know him, and see what high regard people like the Smythes, the Olsens, and Mr. Tolliver thought of Zebulon Covington.

The sleigh had carried them closer, and the trip back to Jackson seemed as though it passed more quickly. Maybe because it was downhill, but the trip also carried her closer to her heart.

Zebulon pulled the team to a halt on a lovely portion of the trail. She could almost glimpse a few of the claims, spread out in the valley.

"Miss Belle Murray, I don't want you to leave. You can't. You won't. I. . .I love you. But if you stay in Jackson, your home must be with me. Always."

With him? She turned on the seat to face him.

He took both her hands in his. "I would get down on one knee. I would ask your father, were he around, before I spoke to you. Miss Belle Murray, would you do me the honor of becoming my wife? Not just for you to stay here in Jackson, but because I want you to stay. I said I didn't need a wife. But I want a wife, and I want her to be you."

She'd thought he was a confirmed bachelor, liking his solitude. Now he was preparing to give it up—for her?

She felt herself nodding. "Yes, yes, Zebulon Covington, I'll marry you. I'll be your wife. But. . .how soon? I have nowhere to stay."

"The Smythes said they will let you bunk with Rosemary until the preacher arrives tomorrow."

"On Christmas Eve? Tomorrow?"

"Yes. The preacher thought he might make it from Flat Creek in time for the service, and with the weather coming in, he's not going to leave the area until after Christmas. So, yes, a Christmas Eve wedding."

But it made perfect sense.

Absolutely perfect sense.

"All right, Mr. Covington." She smiled at him. "We'll get married tomorrow."

Epilogue

One year later

H urry, we're going to be late." Belle tried to pull her coat around her middle, but the toggles had quit meeting up a good month or so ago. She'd already cleaned the cabin, top to bottom, and a wonderful feast would await them upon returning from the church service.

"I know why you're in a hurry. Rosemary's home from college."

"Yes, I haven't seen her in forever, it feels like." Another wallop came from the little life inside her. Or, not so little anymore.

"I'll bring the sleigh around. Can't keep a pregnant lady waiting long, can we, Mrs. Covington?" Zeb winked at her before stepping outside.

She laughed and let the effect of Zeb's wink wash over her.

Oh yes, she loved being Mrs. Zebulon Covington. She loved it even more when he'd bought out Abel Quinn who was desperate for money, and Zeb titled the claim over to Belle in the springtime. She loved it especially when Zeb held her in his arms and all propriety flew from the room. She loved it when she heard his warm, rich voice as they took turns reading to each other on a cold winter's night.

The sound of sleigh bells peppered the air, and she went to the window, new paned glass they'd installed. There stood the team, Zeb's pride and joy, waiting for them. Zeb hopped down from the sleigh and trotted to the house.

Just as he opened the front door, Belle's water broke.

"Oh, Zeb, it's time."

"Time?"

"Get Mary Smythe." At that, a contraction ripped through her.

"I'm not leaving you here alone." With that he swooped her up into his arms and carried her to the sleigh.

A change of plans, in his arms. Where she always wanted to be.

She knew great pain would come, but as long as Zebulon was beside her, she could face it.

As he gently placed her on the sleigh's seat, she grabbed his coat sleeve, making him pause.

"Zebulon Covington, I love you."

"I love you, too, Mrs. Covington."

He gave her a swift kiss before they sped off to welcome their baby into the world.

A MIRAGE ON SNOW

by Lynette Sowell

Chapter 1

Jackson's Hole, Wyoming, November 1919

The whistling wind bit into Emily Covington's cheeks; she squinted against the snow pelting her face at the same time. Her muffler had crept away from her nose and chin, but the urgency of her mission didn't allow her the luxury of stopping.

Mother would be horrified when she saw Emily's chapped skin.

The thought almost made her smile, but childish notions wouldn't help her right now. Focus. She had to keep focused on the trail as she and the others raced back to Jackson.

The fool they'd all headed out to rescue claimed to have been going for a simple hike in the foothills. Simple and hike didn't go together in the Teton Range, which towered above them in the gathering dark.

Her six sled dogs surged ahead, pulling, as their momentum carried her and the sled closer to the ranch. They knew a hot meal awaited them, along with a towel-dry, and pats and kisses from Emily. They'd earned any of the scraps she managed to procure tonight.

Because of them, Billy Adams would live.

Somewhere nearby on the trail, he lay wrapped in a blanket on a flatbed sleigh, a contraption made by Sven Olsen and used for pulling everything from hay to firewood, and now, frostbitten humans who'd been stupid enough to go for a hike.

She'd lived here in Jackson her entire life and couldn't imagine calling anywhere else home.

Billy Adams had left when he was about nine years old, his mother exchanging the shadow of the mountains for the security of the city and family. His sudden absence at their schoolhouse left an empty desk. She'd missed her onetime schoolmate. But the lawyer who'd hung his shingle in Jackson before October's first dusting of snow wasn't the young boy she once knew.

Faint lamplight glowed here and there in the valley as the team drew her closer. When she was but a little girl, the homes were much farther apart and more sparse.

"A man's losing his breathing room," her Pa liked to say. The Covington spread, over six hundred acres now, seemed like the entire world to her, and she didn't understand what he meant by the saying.

Now she knew, as she saw the town growing. Once Jackson got electricity, Pa would likely lose what breathing room he had, save for the acreage. More people all the time got the urge to try their hand at life in the once-wild West.

The grayness descended along with the snow, and the increased cold helped take the edge off Emily's aggravation with going to rescue Billy Adams.

She almost scolded herself for her attitude. Billy was someone's son, someone's family. She'd done her share of foolish things without considering the consequences. Thankfully, she hadn't nearly died or been in as bad a spot as Billy.

No, her mood wasn't because they'd had to leave the supper table and go on a rescue.

The dogs slowed ahead of her. Sven Olsen had reined in his team and glanced over his shoulder at her. She could barely make out the shape of Billy Adams, covered in blankets and lying on the rear of the open flatbed sleigh.

"Emily!" Sven's voice rang out against the trees. "Billy wants to talk to you."

"Whoa, whoa!" Emily stepped from the runners to slow the sled's forward motion, and the dogs skidded to a stop. "We really need to get home, Mr. Olsen. The temperature's dropping every minute."

"Please, Miss Covington," came the voice from the back of the sleigh. "I must apologize."

Trying not to sigh, she left her sled and hiked over to Mr. Olsen's sleigh. "Billy. . ."

"It's Will," he said. "I don't go by Billy anymore. And I'm sorry. I'm sorry for how I treated you just now. You were trying to help, and I was being. . ."

Emily bit her lip. She thought of several adjectives. *Condescending. Pompous. Hurtful.*

Relax. He had no idea who she was at first, and in her trousers and long coat, how could he not assume she was a man, although a bit on the short side?

"Apology accepted, Will. You. . .you didn't know. You were delirious with cold, or something. It's. . ." She glanced at Mr. Olsen, who sat patiently waiting for them. "It's getting late, and you need to get indoors as soon as possible."

Billy rolled onto his side and reached toward her. He caught hold of the sleeve from her fur overcoat. "Miss Covington, I promise you our next encounter will be more pleasant. I am in your debt, and Mr. Olsen's, and everyone else who went out to search for me."

"Thank you. I. . .we really should go. It's almost too dark to see very far down the trail anymore." The dogs knew the way in the dark, but even she was starting to feel the chill through her coat and layers.

"Until next time, Miss Covington."

"Until next time, Mr. Adams." She stepped onto her sled's runners and called out to her team. Mr. Olsen urged his own horse team along, and they continued on their way.

At last she and her team arrived back at the Covington Ranch, where the stately home stood, welcoming her. But first she headed for the barn along with the dogs. It had taken some begging and convincing for Pa to let the dogs have their own area. But she'd paid for everything herself, their pen and shelters.

She wondered how long she ought to wait in the barn, caring

for the dogs. Perhaps her pa, or maybe Sam, would take Billy back to Jackson. If Mother had her way, and often she did, Billy Adams would likely be thawing out by their fireplace in no time, instead of in his room behind his office, in town.

Will Adams fought against the drowsiness threatening to overtake him on the Olsens' makeshift sleigh. He ought to have known better, getting himself into this kind of a pickle. He'd only been a child when he left Jackson, but he still remembered the tales of at least one man who'd gone off on a trek in the foothills and never returned. They hadn't found his body until spring, frozen solid.

He'd stood with the others on the muddy main street of Jackson and watched as the rancher who'd found the man toted his body, laid out on the back of a wagon, all the way through town, to his widow's doorstep. The women's gasps and the men's murmurs echoed in his ears, and Emily Covington whispered into his ear.

"Think we can get a look at the body? I've never seen a frozen person before."

The wagon had rolled past, with a tarp covering the frozen corpse.

He had glanced at Emily, who looked prim and proper as her mother from hat to boots, save for some strands of hair that had escaped her ponytail, and a sparkle in her blue eyes. Her eyes reminded him of the sky above the Teton Range. He'd never seen a blue like that in all his years back East.

Those same blue eyes crackled tonight when she spoke to him.

He should have known better than to remark about the "short blue-eyed musher fellow" who'd nearly plowed over him when pausing under the tree, where Will had taken cover behind a makeshift windbreak. He hadn't intended to sound irritated when the sled nearly ran over him. He should have sounded more grateful.

All these thoughts tumbled through his head while he fought to remain conscious. Or he could succumb to the weariness, the exhaustion borne of being out in the elements for hours. He'd already lost enough face in front of everyone.

Another stray thought jolted him awake.

The election. With him considering a run for city council come spring, what would the locals say about him being so fool-ish? He had a few of the men backing him, hoping his good sense would help steer the town of Jackson into the twenties.

No worries, though. He'd heard a rumor that some of the women were discussing the idea of running for office—he had nothing against women running for office—but the local men might shy away from voting for a woman instead of someone like him.

Their pace slowed, and Will found himself able to roll over on one side to see if they'd arrived in town. No, not town. A ranch, and he couldn't quite make out the signage. It was somewhere warm, and that was all that mattered. He sank back onto the sleigh. Soon he'd have something hot to drink and hopefully sit by a roaring fire.

Oh, Lord, surely You've preserved my life tonight. Thank You...

He listened to the wind, whipping in a gust now, the creak of harness and the whoosh of runners on snow, and Sven Olsen murmuring to his team in Swedish.

At last they pulled up before a home with light spilling onto the snow. Shouts, banging doors.

"You found him, then?" a female voice asked—not Emily's.

The sound of barking and bells nearly drowned out the woman's voice.

"Emily did, just in time. If she'd arrived moments later, he might be dead."

"All right, Mr. Adams. See if you can sit up." Sven stood beside the flatbed sleigh. Will braced himself, trying to put his numb legs over the side.

"I can manage." He glanced from Sven to the older woman, about his mother's age, her dark hair streaked with silver, her blue eyes narrowed. He'd seen that expression before. This had to be Emily's mother.

"Let's get you inside. I've stoked the fire, and we've kept back some supper for you." The woman tugged on his elbow, her shawl slipping off one shoulder. "Can you walk?"

"I can." As soon as he stood, his legs turned to the consistency of breakfast mush, but he fought against gravity. He'd had enough humiliation for one evening.

"Watch your step." Sven nodded while Mrs. Covington stepped aside to let him enter.

"Ah, there goes Emily." She shook her head. "She'll be seeing to those dogs before she even enters the house."

Which suited Will fine, for now. "I'm much obliged, Mrs. Covington, for you and Mr. Covington allowing me to stop."

"You are most welcome, Mr. Adams." She turned her focus outside. "Thank you, Mr. Olsen."

Will realized he hadn't adequately thanked Sven for his help, nor had he thanked Emily or any of the others who'd gone out searching for him that evening.

"What. . .what time is it?" He scanned the walls, one of which sported several mounted elk heads, for a clock.

"Nearly eight," said Mrs. Covington. "Now we'll give you some privacy. I've brought some of my husband's clothes, and I have coffee on the stove. You change, and I'll be back in a few moments with your supper. You're not going anywhere this evening. My husband is in the study and will be out shortly."

A pair of trousers and a flannel shirt were shoved into his hands. "Yes, ma'am."

She turned on her heel with a swish of skirts, and marched from the parlor.

Well, if he was going to jump into Mr. Covington's clothes, he ought to get a move on before someone came waltzing in. No sooner had Will removed his outercoat, along with his hat and muffler, and dumped them on the hearth, than a young man clomped into the parlor. Sam Covington.

"You're the one they went off to search for today." Sam strode over to the nearest wing-backed chair and plopped onto the cushion.

"Yes, that was me." He tried not to shiver, now that he'd dumped off his coat, and picked up the clothes Mrs. Covington had offered him.

"You don't look like an idiot greenhorn to me." Sam crossed one leg over the other and rested his elbow on the armrest, using his hand as a convenient chin prop. "Not a greenhorn, anyway."

"So I look like an idiot?"

"Not my words. That would be my sister's. You're the lawyer from back East." Somewhere in the house, a grandfather clock gonged the hour.

"Yes. My father was William Adams. Died back in '01." After that his mother had sold off quick as anything and bustled him back East.

"So why'd you come back here? I've seen ya at church meetings but never got the chance to ask."

"It's the mountains. I always remembered them. Too much going on in the city. Too much noise. And I want to make sure the good people here are served legally in the way they ought to be, by someone with real credentials."

"You know you're in for a campaign, running against my sister."

"I know. She's always been quite the, ah, character." Another flashback to her impishly saying she'd never seen a frozen body before. What kind of a girl asked questions like that?

But he reminded himself that Emily Covington wasn't a girl anymore. Under all those layers and manly garb, she was most definitely a woman.

Chapter 2

Someone, probably Pa, had left food scraps out for the dogs, who dashed straight for their feeder as soon as Emily removed their harnesses. She sank onto the nearby pile of straw and watched Niki, her lead dog, nudge Felix out of the way. No matter that he outweighed her by a good ten pounds. All the dogs knew Niki ate first, just as she broke the snow first along the trails.

Emily's stomach grumbled, but she didn't move to head for the house. Not quite yet. How long would Billy—or Will—Adams be there? She suspected he'd be fed a hot meal, and if Mother didn't have a bath drawn for the man (which likely wouldn't be entirely proper), she'd at least offer him dry clothing.

Her own ire at Billy's earlier treatment of her waned. She glanced down at her trousers, formerly owned by Sam, who'd shot up in height and had left them behind several inches ago. Mother had long ago become resigned to the fact that Emily wore trousers around the ranch, and even to town on occasion.

The finishing school, once her mother's dream, had dwindled

to a mere trio of young women who visited the ranch two Saturdays each month, where Mother schooled them in diction, manners, and how a respectable young lady ought to carry herself in society, at dinner parties, and other occasions.

Oh yes, Emily knew exactly what to do if she found herself at a formal social event. However, she didn't see the need to fuss quite so much in everyday life.

She couldn't picture herself being able to mush the dogs tonight if she had skirts and such to get in the way.

Niki, finished with her meal, ambled across the sheltered end of the barn and flopped beside Emily on the straw. Her tongue hanging out, her eyes brightened as if she smiled at Emily. Sam liked to tease her, saying dogs couldn't smile.

"But you do smile, don't you, girl?" Emily rubbed her dog's head, and Specks, a black, gray, and white female mutt, moved closer for a few pets as well. "Here's a pet, Specks. You were all very, very *good* dogs tonight."

The animals amazed her, how they worked together and followed directions. Always happy, always ready to go. And for the next months, they'd be her primary way to get into the backcountry. They could take her places a horse and sleigh couldn't go.

Which was why her presence tonight had likely saved Will's life. If she and the dogs hadn't slid into his feeble attempt at a shelter—

She refused to think about it.

Did he remember the man someone had found, frozen in the foothills, when they were but children?

Tonight, rescuing Will had brought the memory back to her. Having the dogs, she'd hoped to save someone. She never imagined it would be Will Adams.

The remaining few dogs, Felix, Branch, and Maggie, finished the last of the food and set to lapping from a pail of melted snow. Emily licked her lips, realizing she, too, thirsted. She glanced at the pail. Not for her. She could melt her own snow, but why pretend she was taking shelter at a remote cabin with her dogs? The main house lay not fifty yards away, with its warmth, Mother's homemade stew and soft pretzels, and possibly even a slice of pie, made from berry preserves they'd canned at the end of the summer season.

Emily's stomach growled again. "All right, I'm going inside." She rolled to her knees then stood, brushing straw from her coat and trousers. She might as well get a move on and stop avoiding the inevitable. However, she could plead fatigue, gobble a quick bowl of stew in the kitchen, then scurry away to her room and avoid Will completely.

She gave the dogs one last longing look, almost wishing for a blanket to bed down on the straw. But a lady didn't sleep in a corner of the barn with the sled dogs, and especially not during a snowstorm when a perfectly adequate home and a soft bed waited for her.

The cold bit into her once more as she closed the barn door

and made for the house, aiming for the rectangles of light glimmering through the falling snow. Emily pulled her coat tightly around her, climbed the porch steps, and entered the house.

Warmth, along with the aroma of Mother's cooking, embraced her as soon as she entered. She headed straight for the bootjack and tugged against it until she removed the boots—another castoff from Sam, another bit of attire Mother tolerated.

"It's me. I was taking care of the dogs," she called out.

"Supper's on the stove. There's plenty," Mother replied from the parlor. "Mr. Adams is at the table, having supper as well."

Ah, so he was. She shouldn't let her nerves get the better of her, nor her own embarrassment of how she'd treated him earlier. Regardless of how he'd treated her.

"Thank you, Mother." She paused in the entryway to the front parlor. She sniffed. In addition to the hearty aroma of stew, another aroma hung in the air.

She sniffed again and lowered her nose to her sleeve. Sure enough, the aroma was coming from her. Emily shrugged out of her coat and kept on the castoff flannel shirt, this one formerly Pa's. She wore it over her shirtwaist. Perhaps Mother couldn't tell the additional smell came from Emily.

"You may wish to bathe this evening, my dear." Mother gazed over the top of her reading glasses at Emily.

"Yes, ma'am. But after supper, though. I'm very hungry after all those hours outdoors."

"There should be coffee on the stove, too."

"Thank you, Mother." Emily nodded at Mother and walked on socked feet to the kitchen. Will Adams sat at the table, taking his time on a bowl of stew.

He glanced up at her when she entered, rising slightly as she did so. "Miss Covington."

She inclined her head toward him slightly. "Mr. Adams."

He took his seat again. "Your mother makes the best stew I've ever eaten. Either that, or exposure to the elements heightened my taste buds."

"It's probably both," she said, stepping toward the shelf and taking down a bowl. Her hunger won out over her wounded pride, and she put a generous dollop of beef stew in the bowl and took the last soft pretzel from the plate.

The remember-whens began halfway through Will's second bowl of beef stew. He'd embarrassed himself by wolfing down the first bowl. He had manners, but after being lost for hours in the driving snow in the hills, his body's need to survive ignored things like chewing slowly and taking time between bites.

Emily sat across from him, her blue eyes sparkling as he finished telling an old story of the time he dared her to sit on the family's unbroken colt and ended up sailing into a patch of manure in the corner of the ranch yard.

"I think the worst thing I hurt that day was my dignity." She wiped her mouth with her napkin, folded it, and set it on the table beside her spoon. "Oh Will, we did used to have some good times as children."

"We did. Those times were the best things I remember about living here." The memory of leaving Jackson, heading over the pass with what seemed like crates of belongings, still stood out in detail in his mind. He'd cried because he didn't get to say good-bye to Emily, or any of his other friends. Mother was in a hurry, raw with grief and wanting to leave.

"You're a big boy. Big boys don't cry."

"So, what do you think of the changes since you left?" She stood, picking up her cup. "More coffee?"

"Yes, please." He raised his cup for her to take, and ignored the sensation of her fingers brushing his. "Thank you."

"You're welcome." Emily stepped over to the stove.

"Some things seem smaller, but there's definitely more houses closer to town now. Your family's home is larger."

"Yes," Emily said, returning to her chair. "Pa built onto the house not long after Sam was born. Then John got married, and he has his own place now but still works the ranch. Pa keeps talking about there not being much elbow room around here, and he's bound and determined to keep the Covington Ranch a working ranch."

He knew about the downturn in cattle ranching, but he also knew the Covingtons had plenty of pluck and determination to keep their legacy alive.

"That's admirable." He took a sip of the strong brew. Finally, a thaw had settled into his bones and he no longer had to fight the urge to keep from shivering.

"And there's the Elk Refuge. That's something new since you've been gone."

Another memory came to him of an especially harsh winter. "I remember that one winter; we'd go out and help feed the elk. So many of them starved."

Emily nodded. "And the one time we found a young calf, tried to talk our parents into letting us bring it back and take care of it."

"We had some good times." And then his mother yanked him away from everything he'd ever known to live in St. Louis. But it had never felt like home, as Jackson had.

They both fell silent, then Emily went to the pie safe and pulled out a pie. "Berry pie?"

"I can't say no. Did you make it?"

"Oh, horrors no. Mother did. She's far more skilled at making piecrust than I. The last time I made piecrust, it had the consistency of mush even after it was baked."

"Not too domesticated, are you?" This didn't surprise him.

"Not as far as cooking goes. Tonight's supper is entirely Mother's doing."

"I think she could do better, if she practiced a little more," Mrs. Covington said as she entered the kitchen. "A man appreciates a woman who can make a good piecrust, doesn't he, Mr. Adams?"

"Ah well, yes, I do appreciate good piecrust." He cleared his throat as Emily darted a glance at her mother. "But there are other attributes that come in handy, such as intelligence, a quick wit, and being able to operate a clothes wringer."

"Ha." Emily snorted.

Mrs. Covington picked up a clean mug and poured coffee. "Bringing coffee to your father. He and John are back from bringing hay to the closest part of the herd." She left the room, and Emily's features relaxed dramatically.

She turned her focus on him. "So, I'm surprised you didn't take up something, ah, more physical, with you coming back here to Jackson. I never would've pegged you for a lawyer. I bet you own half a dozen suits."

At that, he chuckled. "I'm only just starting out. For your information, I only have two suits. My everyday, and my Sunday and meeting suit."

"Good. So you're not completely fancy-fied then." Her eyes took on a familiar gleam, and a dimple in her cheek winked at him.

"Not completely." He wanted to bring up the subject of the spring election, and now was as good a time as any. "So, I understand you're thinking about running for Jackson City Council in the spring."

"Yes. My pa talked me into it." At her words, footsteps echoed in the hallway.

"Talked you into what, Em?" Mr. Covington stood in the

doorway. He held a cup of steaming coffee.

"Running for Jackson City Council."

"Why didn't you run, sir?" Will asked.

"I'm all for making changes in our community, but I think a younger generation will best help do that. And my daughter is one of the best in the younger generation." He nodded at Emily, who beamed. Clearly, as the only daughter in a trio of Covington children, Emily had been the one doted upon.

"I'm sure she is. The reason I mentioned it is I've thought about putting my hat into the ring as well. I know I haven't been here as long as some of you, but I believe I can bring another perspective, no offense intended." And it helped that the name of William Adams, Senior was still held in high regard by the good people of Jackson.

"You're running, too?" Emily shook her head. "Why didn't you say anything?"

"I decided after church service on Sunday. Haven't told anyone else besides Dr. Turner. He said there's going to be a public meeting at the schoolhouse next week to hear the candidates speak."

"Yes, I know. I'm going to be there, along with the other ladies contemplating running for office."

"Well, it should be a most interesting public meeting."

Chapter 3

The Jackson schoolhouse ran out of seating before the town meeting began. The good weather held out, so the powers that be decided to go forward with the evening's program—namely, a discussion of the issues facing the town.

Emily's pulse pounded in her throat, and the pressure fought against the collar of her dress. She kept her feet together beneath her skirt and willed her hands to stop shaking in her lap.

If the other ladies had any nerves about standing before the assembled crowd along with their opponents, which would be announced tonight, none of them showed it.

Somehow, Emily just *knew* she'd be pitted against Will. They were both about the same age, and although she had the advantage of having grown up in the Jackson area, Will's automatic status as a lawyer and his education might make him seem more appealing—particularly to the men.

"Ain't no woman goin' to tell me how to run the city," someone murmured behind Emily. She wanted to turn and see who the speaker was and where he sat, but maybe she didn't really want to know.

Women had the right to vote in Wyoming, and the women in other states of America didn't. Now, with the election coming up, perhaps history would be made if all the women running were elected in the spring.

Tonight's gathering would allow interested individuals in the community three minutes to speak. Community members could voice their concerns to the current council about what they believed needed fixing in Jackson. And who knew what might happen in the spring? Others might decide to run as well.

Pa ought to be the one sitting here, or John. But John had refused, saying he'd rather keep to the business of herding cattle and running the ranch. Pa, too. No matter how much she'd tried to convince them.

But the more she'd thought about things in the community that needed changing, the more she realized she wanted to be one of the people making those changes. She clutched the short speech she'd prepared, written and rewritten several times.

She glanced across the room to where Will sat with a few of the other men. He met her gaze and smiled. She returned the smile then let it fade. No, she wasn't about to be mean in this contest. But it was an election, and she wanted to beat him but good, him smugly grinning at her as if he knew he already had the election in the bag.

Maybe he did have a better chance than her to win. If the

mutterer somewhere behind her shared the same sentiment as others in the room, it shouldn't surprise her.

Emily adjusted her hat with her free hand, the other clutching her few words of address to the townspeople.

After welcoming the assembled group, the mayor called for all interested in possibly running for office to raise his—or her—hand. A smattering of hands rose, some reluctantly.

The apathy of some in the crowd galled Emily. Everyone had complaints, but not everyone wanted to do something about them.

"Your turn soon," Pa whispered in her ear. "You'll do fine. Let the naysayers speak what they will."

She nodded. Someone was standing, speaking about city improvements. Emily tried to listen as best she could, all the while tumbling her own words over inside her mind.

"Miss Emily Covington," someone barked.

She'd never liked giving speeches in school, or standing before the class to spell. This was five thousand times worse. She recalled her mother's coaching on how to stand and cross the room like a lady. She wanted to glance in Mother's direction but thought better of it.

Her boots echoed on the plank floor as she stepped toward the makeshift podium. Once she reached it, she clung to it after setting her paper down in front of her.

The faces in the room blurred, then three came into focus: Pa, Mother—and Will. He gave her a slow nod.

"Good evening, good people of Jackson." She paused. She'd just said *good* twice in the same sentence. No turning back now.

"I'm Emily Covington, and I've lived here my entire life. I've watched Jackson grow from the time I was a little girl. While our town has made some progress and advancements, I do believe there are areas in which we can improve."

Someone snorted—or was that a cough?

Another nod from Will.

"Several things distress me, as I'm sure they distress some of my fellow residents. Chief of which, we need to improve the condition of our city's streets. As you know, with the weather we have, snow, sleet, freeze and thaw, we end up with mud and pools of water. This makes it very difficult—and unhealthy in warmer temperatures—for people to walk along the streets. Standing water can cause illness for man and beast alike."

". . .science class. . ." Someone's whisper drifted across the room.

She straightened her shoulders and stood a little taller. Mother gave an encouraging response with her own posture.

"We also want to go forward with a designated area for dumping refuse and litter, which does not include vacant lots in town. We want Jackson to be an example to cities in the East of how a western town can be run. The elbow room around here is decreasing, as my father, one of the early settlers here in Jackson, likes to say. We have a choice now to improve things, once and for all—if we work together. It won't be easy, but I'm confident we can be successful. I thank you in advance for your vote."

There. Her voice hadn't quavered, and she'd found a voice she didn't know she had. Applause rippled across the room, not from everyone but enough for the sound to buoy her spirits as she stepped back toward her seat.

"And now, from William Adams, Junior."

Emily sank onto the seat she'd vacated moments before. Mother patted her hand. She'd done well. The rest was up to the Lord's will and the votes of Jackson's residents in the spring.

Part of her wanted to vanish down some back trail with her dogs, but she scanned what she could of the room while Will moved to stand at the podium. These were her people, the good and the bad of them, and those in the middle.

Will thought Emily had done a fine enough job speaking, but that didn't mean she'd gain the favor of the voters. Being well spoken always helped, and Emily was far from the simpering female type. In fact, he considered her a formidable young woman.

He appreciated the sight of her, sitting mere footsteps away in the front row. A nicer dress than her usual Sunday-go-to-meeting, this one was a smoky-blue color with an off-white collar and sleeve cuffs, and lace on the bodice to match. Her hair, primly pinned up as elegantly as any eastern woman's hair, was capped by a hat that matched the blue in her dress.

Just by looking at her, he forgot what he'd meant to say. He, who'd won awards for his diction and speaking in college and law school, couldn't find the words.

Now she quirked half a smile at him. He wouldn't fall prey to the distraction of her wiles. He tried to remember the trousers and fur overcoat she'd worn the other evening in the snowstorm, her hair sticking out from under her hat and hanging down in two long braids.

"My. . .my name is William Adams, Junior, and I'm honored to have the opportunity to set out my shingle for business back in the town I remembered so well from my younger years." He went on to outline his education, his experience working in cities back East, and several of the ideas he planned to bring to the city, should he run for council.

Despite the apathy he'd sensed from talking to a few others at the general store earlier that day, he knew, with the right motivation and leadership, the city could clean up its act and progress even more.

He shifted his arm and paper rustled inside his suit-coat pocket, a letter from Mother he'd picked up that afternoon. He'd mull its contents later, but he couldn't help but wonder now.

Someone coughed beside him, the mayor. Will's voice drifted off as he tried to reclaim his distracted thoughts. But all was not lost. The town would have another meeting not long before the election, and he'd have another chance to speak. In the meantime, he'd focus on doing the best job he could at helping the folks with their legal matters.

"So, I thank you for your consideration and your time this evening."

Applause, louder than that given for Emily, rang out in the schoolhouse.

Will grinned as he approached his seat, and he waved to the crowd before sitting down again. More applause. A man could get used to this.

One by one, the present candidates spoke their piece, and then the mayor took his spot behind the podium again.

"Now, the election's a ways off, but if anyone else wants to step up, now would be a good time to do so."

After a few more final words, the mayor dismissed the group for the evening. Emily moved from her place on the front row and stood before Will at the corner bench.

"Well said, Mr. Adams." She extended her gloved hand toward him, which he shook.

"Likewise, Miss Covington."

"Hold it, right there. I'm taking a photograph for the newspaper." Stan Bullock motioned to the two of them. "Shaking hands, as you were. There. That's good. May the best man—or woman—win."

"We'll see, won't we, Mr. Adams?" Emily's eyes sparkled as she spoke, then she smiled for the camera while the two of them shook hands again.

"We shall, Miss Covington." Will paused, removing the envelope from his pocket. The reporter scurried off to another cluster of townspeople.

"Oh, what's that?" She studied the envelope in his hand.

"A letter from my mother. She wants me to leave Jackson. She thinks I've made a mistake in coming here."

"Do you think so?"

"No, I don't. I haven't felt quite at home anywhere else."

"Good. I like having you here again. It. . .it wasn't the same here without you." Her cheeks took on a deep red hue.

He nodded. He didn't dare tell her that his mother said his former fiancée was asking about him—regularly.

Chapter 4

. . . Amelia has been asking about you, wondering when you'll come to your senses and return to St. Louis. I told her I simply did not know. I hope and pray you'll see your place is here, not in that wild and Godless place.

I remain always,
Your loving mother

P.S. There is still time for you to take the train back and be here for Christmas.

Christmas.

Will smiled and folded the letter, shaking his head as he did so. Christmas was the furthest thing from his mind at the moment. Not that he didn't want to celebrate. There wasn't much hubbub here, no displays in shop windows like he'd seen on a visit to New York City while in law school. The Jackson General Store carried a few gift-type items, but the prices on some items made shopping a bit prohibitive at times, as anything and everything had to be literally carted over the pass from Idaho.

He remembered his favorite Christmas present from the old days, as he used to call them. His father had hand carved a prancing horse from a single piece of mountain ash, had buffed and oiled the wood until it glowed. The horse, a handmade woolen scarf from his mother, and a small sack of candy were his gifts that year. The last Christmas with his father.

Mother would be smiling if she knew his thoughts. He wanted the familiar, to look out the window and see the same landscape from his memories. But Jackson had changed, and so had he.

Yes, it was a wild place, the stuff of legend. Godless? No. He knew the scriptures. *Where can I go from Your spirit? Or where can I flee from Your presence? If I ascend into heaven, You are there; if I make my bed in hell, behold, You are there.*

Jackson had its rough-and-tumble reputation, but there were still good people here, and he had a chance to make a difference among them. Amelia had begged him to stay in St. Louis, but when he'd heard her and her father planning out the next half century of his life, he couldn't breathe. The city's buildings, too, closed in around him. Then came the arguments, him not wanting to stay and her refusing to consider the idea of moving west. He'd broken the engagement, given notice at the firm, emptied his account of his savings, and headed west to Jackson.

He'd breathed easier since.

The afternoon shadows had grown longer the closer the days slid toward December. He set the letter on his desk and stepped toward the window of the tiny one-room office. The door behind him led to a makeshift bedroom. He found the space a convenient spot to rent until his practice grew.

He gazed out the window at Jackson's traffic, such as it was. People trying to get business done before sundown. He'd had one client today, someone wanting to prepare a will, Edgar Banks.

The start of the process itself had taken perhaps an hour, but then Edgar had remained, talking for almost an hour more. He'd known Will's father, and Will allowed his own curiosity to be satisfied. In fact, Edgar had been the one to buy the homestead from his mother.

A familiar figure, riding a lanky chestnut astride, came into view. Emily Covington. He wondered what had brought her to town this fine afternoon. Maybe she was just like the rest of the Jackson folk, enjoying a sunny day as an excuse to leave the house.

He smiled as she kept her seat while keeping the horse reined in. A lesser rider would have been thrown. The chestnut gave a kick with its hind legs then surged forward. Emily's lips moved. Her hat slipped from her head and dangled from a cord, slapping against her shoulders.

As if satisfied with himself, the chestnut tossed his head and continued at a trot along the street, mud flinging up from its hooves. Emily glanced in Will's direction then maneuvered the horse to his side of the street and stopped at the hitching rail.

She dismounted then tied the lead to the post. Before leaving the street, she gave the horse a pat on the nose. Then she scaled the steps to the office door where Will had hung a simple hand-painted sign: WILLIAM ADAMS, JR. ATTORNEY AT LAW.

He answered the door after her soft knock.

"Miss Covington. Please, come in." Will took a step back so Emily could enter the office.

"Thank you." She wore trousers, a long overcoat, and a brown hat that dangled down her back. Her dark hair hung in a long braid, several shades darker than her boots.

Will tried not to stare; it wasn't the first time he'd seen a woman in trousers, but after years of city life, he couldn't help but take in the sight of her. Wild, western. Lovely, almost as lovely as she'd appeared the evening of the town forum.

"So, what brings you to town today?"

"Errands at the general store for Mother. And Pa, too. I'm on my way to pick up the mail; Pa asked that I stop in and see if you can come to the house to help him with some paperwork. He didn't say exactly what but wants to know if you can come a week from Friday."

"I can do that. Morning, or afternoon?"

"Afternoon, if possible. Perhaps around two o'clock or so?"

"I can put that on my schedule." He moved to his desk. Not that his schedule was full, by any means, but keeping a calendar would be a good habit as his practice grew.

"Good. Pa will be glad about that."

"I'm glad to help him. I should say that's some young colt

you were riding in on today."

"It's a filly; we call her Cinnamon. She's four, still a bit green. But I wanted to give her a ride out to town. She's sassy, but she's learning fast." Emily went to the window and looked down toward the street.

He joined her at the window. Cinnamon stood at the hitching rail, occasionally stomping one hoof or giving a swish of her tail.

"I've been meaning to ask your father about buying a horse from him, or if he knows anyone with a good mount. I've borrowed and rented a horse, here and there, when I need to go out to ranches. But I'm at the point now when I could use a horse. In the spring, that is."

"He should know someone. I'll mention it to him at supper tonight."

"Thank you." It was a flimsy excuse. He could have asked any number of people about buying a horse, including Edgar or even Sven Olsen, but he trusted Zebulon Covington's judgment. "Well, thank your father for me, also, about the opportunity to do business with him."

"I will." She paused, then opened her mouth to continue, then closed it again as if reconsidering her next words.

"Yes? Were you going to say something else?"

"Ah, I'm sure Mother won't mind if you stay for supper. I'll. . .I'll have some work with the dogs to do, but it would be very nice to see you at supper." Her cheeks bloomed a deep shade of pink.

"Why, I'd like that very much, too." He watched a wagon pass by, the driver reining in the team. Gus Tolliver came over the pass. And sitting next to him, wide-eyed and chattering away, sat Amelia Clark.

What on earth? Surely his eyes deceived him.

"Wonder why they're stopping here." Emily glanced his way. She probably saw his dismay, shock, as Amelia stepped down from the wagon with Gus's assistance. Amelia squinted up at the building. Her face brightened and she waved.

"That's..."

Footsteps sounded on the steps as Amelia made quick work to get to the door.

It opened and she stepped inside, accompanied by a swirl of cold air.

"William, I made it." Amelia shut the door firmly behind her. "Mr. Tolliver is taking my bags to the inn, but I thought I would stop here first."

Emily's gaze bored into him. "William?"

"Ah, Emily Covington, this is Amelia Clark."

"Good afternoon." Amelia's gaze traveled from Emily's braid, her hat askew, until it settled on the hem of her trousers and her boots' toes. "How do you do?"

"Very well, thank you." Emily inclined her head briefly.

"I'm William's fiancée."

"I see. I wasn't aware William had a fiancée." Emily's voice held the slightest edge. Her eyes held a hint of white-blue lightning that only Will could recognize. She nodded at him. "Mr. Adams, we'll see you next Friday at the ranch, if not at church service on Sunday."

She left, allowing a fresh blast of cold air into the office.

Emily knew she shouldn't be angry. Yet she feared the piles of snow might melt as she passed them on the way to the hitching rail. Cinnamon tugged on the lead.

"Hang on, Cinnamon. We'll be out of here, lickety-split." She slung the lead over the saddle horn before gathering the reins and sticking her foot in the stirrup then swinging up onto Cinnamon's back. She ought to have done the errands first, and she'd be on her way back home. But no, she had to ride to the general store yet and get the shopping done.

Fiancée. He'd never mentioned a fiancée to her, not during the months he'd been in Jackson. If he was engaged, surely he'd have mentioned it to someone in Jackson?

She allowed her anger to burn out as she exhaled. Thankfully, Cinnamon's moments of friskiness were over, for now anyway. She nodded to the Olsens, passing by on their sleigh, the one with the cushioned seats. The couple had been her parents' friends since before she was born, yet they still exchanged glances as if they'd been courting for mere weeks.

She hadn't seen glances like that between Will and Amelia, but if he'd found his match, she would wish him well. No matter that since the night of his rescue in the hills, she'd scarcely been able to keep him out of her mind. Well, she'd let the thoughts go.

All this time, all these years, she'd spurned the attentions of eligible men in Jackson. There went one now, tipping his hat to her as he rode by. A woman had to have standards, something her mother always told her. Pa didn't say much about her lack of finding a husband, but as the years ticked along, she imagined Pa had to be a bit concerned. Twenty-eight on her next birthday, and she was a bit "long in the tooth," as the whisper had come from the next aisle in the store one day.

They plodded through the mixture of slush and mud, all the way to the livery, where Emily would keep Cinnamon while she shopped in the store. Mother needed a few things and the weather was good, so Emily could cover the miles back and forth from town without a problem. Today, she'd take the dogs out for a run before supper.

She made quick work at getting Cinnamon settled in a stall then headed for the store. Some salt, other spices, and a sack of flour. Mother intended to begin baking soon, for Thanksgiving next week then Christmas after that.

Emily entered the general store, welcomed by a blast of warmth from the cast-iron stove.

"Howdy." Tom, the shopkeeper, looked up from his place at the counter. "See you made it in on this fine day."

"Yes, sir. Mother needs a few things, so I offered to come to town." She wandered over toward the bolts of cloth and touched a deep burgundy muslin. It would make a lovely skirt to go along with her favorite shirtwaist for Sunday mornings. She could always make something out of denim, a split skirt, which would be ladylike and yet more practical than the pretty muslin in front of her.

"The cloth's new, came on one of the most recent shipments. How much do you want?"

"None today, but thank you. I'd best get my list taken care of, Tom."

"You just say the word, and I'll get it all tallied for you."

"Thanks." Emily pulled the list from her coat pocket and set to work. Daylight was burning and she needed to head home, and to forget about William Adams being engaged.

Less than thirty minutes later, in record time for her, she had her purchases in a burlap sack she'd attached to the rear of the saddle, along with a sack of flour. She headed away from Jackson. She didn't even glance at Will's tiny storefront office as she passed, although she might have heard someone calling out her name.

Home. She needed to be home. Mother would hear her out, as she always did.

But part of her had allowed herself to imagine a life with Will, here in the West. He'd returned—not for her, but for whatever part of his life here he'd missed the most. Perhaps she'd been fooling herself to believe part of the reason was her.

Somebody was hightailing it out of town behind her, the trotting horse's hooves making a squishing sound on the trail.

"Emily Covington, would you slow down for a moment?"

Will.

She reined in Cinnamon, pivoting the horse to face back toward Jackson. "What do you want, Will?"

"I need to explain." His horse halted beside Cinnamon.

"You found a horse awfully fast." She studied the scrappy-looking gray, one of the horses from the livery.

"I borrowed it. I tried to get to the livery before you left."

"Will, it's all right. You don't have to explain. I wish I'd known about Amelia, but I do wish you both the best. When is the wedding? Will it be here, or back East?" She let the words stream out then stopped herself. She sounded like a child and had no reason to be testy.

"Amelia *was* my fiancée. I broke our engagement not long before I moved to Jackson. But she and my mother remain very close."

"Evidently she believes you're still engaged."

"She wants to see how life is here in Jackson, to show me she's up to the challenge. It was one of the things we disagreed about. She didn't want to move to Jackson."

"Where is she now?"

"She's staying at Ma Reed's, where the Crabtrees are renting her a room. I suggested she check with them, as I didn't want her wandering through Jackson, not knowing anyone else."

Emily nodded. "Good idea." She remained silent. He'd given her his explanation. So he wasn't engaged. But then Miss Amelia

Clark intended to stay, presumably to win back Will.

"I don't know how long she's going to stay." Will frowned. "I'm going to persuade her it'll be best for her to head back over the pass, to the train, and out of here. She has no idea what winters are like in this part of the country. She said the snow is beautiful, and what fun it would be to take a sleigh ride through the Elk Sanctuary."

"If she doesn't leave soon, she could be trapped here for the winter." Cinnamon took a few steps sideways, but Emily quieted him. "Unless that's what you want."

Will stared at his mount's mane.

Say something.

But she had no right to demand any answer or explanation. Maybe she'd imagined the possibilities between them. Imagining could be a dangerous thing. She had too much to do to waste time on imagining.

Cinnamon took a few jogging steps, jolting her. "I should go. Cinnamon's carrying more of a load than usual today with this flour, and I have chores to see to."

Before Will could say anything more, she set Cinnamon into a trot and headed toward home.

Chapter 5

S o, what has you looking like a pile of rain-soaked clouds tonight?" Mother's words were gentle, yet probing as only a mother's words could be. "You didn't say much during supper."

Emily sat on a pile of straw in the dogs' corner of the barn. She shook her head. "I'm confused about my feelings."

"Feelings about a particular young lawyer?"

"Yes." Emily petted Niki, who'd lain her head on her lap. "Ever since Will's come back. . .I don't know. We were only children when he left so suddenly, and now I've gotten to know William Adams, the man."

"But?"

"Oh, Mother, he was engaged before he came here. He broke it off, right before he moved to Jackson. They'd disagreed about him moving west, so. . .he left anyway."

Mother sighed then joined Emily on the straw pile, arranging her skirt just so. Mother always succeeded at being just so. Emily didn't know how she did it.

"How did you know he was engaged? When did you find out?"

"Today. When Miss Amelia Clark arrived from over the pass."

"Ah, I see. Is their engagement back on?"

"No. Well, according to Will, it's not. Will said Amelia wants to try life here in Jackson, to show him she can do it."

"Well, I know from firsthand experience how difficult that first winter can be."

Emily nodded. She knew the story. Her mother, alone and grieving the loss of her sister and brother-in-law, and Pa being the one who helped watch over her. Mother, however, was the strongest woman Emily knew. Strong, and elegant.

"I wonder if Will is going to change his mind if Amelia does stay. But then, I really don't know if he cares for me. Like I said, we were children. . ."

"Does he know how you feel?"

"But Mother, it's not my place to tell him. After all, it's not proper." She had to smile at using one of her mother's favorite phrases.

"Funny, my dear. You have to at least give him a strong hint to know you're interested in his attention, and more than the attention of a childhood friend."

"I did let him know that when he meets with Pa next week, I'd like him to stay for supper because we haven't had much of a chance to see each other lately."

"Well then, it should be very clear to him you're interested."

"What should I do? Get a new dress? I don't have time to sew anything. And my hair is so. . ."

"Hard to manage? It's not for nothing I suggested those hundred strokes every night, at which you always balked."

Emily chuckled at the recollection of pleading from Mother and tears from her at the thought of brushing her hair every night. "I was a bit stubborn."

"Be yourself, hair and all." Mother stroked Emily's braid. "And I'll be happy to help you with your hair." She fell silent for a moment.

"What is it?"

"Oh, I'm thinking back to my old friend, Rosemary Smythe."

"Mrs. Rosemary Templeton? Your friend in Boston?"

Mother nodded. "Mrs. Rosemary Smythe Templeton. Had her sights on your father at one time. Before I noticed him. But her heart was back East, and that's where she ended up. Married well, and not to the man of her first choosing. So take heart. If Miss Clark's interest in Will is but a passing fancy, that will become apparent soon enough. A romantic notion doesn't have the lasting strength of true love's commitment."

"Thank you, Mother." She hugged her mother. "I'm sorry I've been so difficult, pants and all. I'm sorry I'm not comfortable dressing up."

"You are still a lady, and you are still my daughter. I wouldn't want to have anyone else to raise, and I'm proud of you." Mother kissed her cheek. "Now, chin up. God will make both yours and Will's paths clear."

Emily's throat swelled with a lump. "I hope and pray so."

"And Christmas is coming. Christmas is always a special time, and we have much to do to prepare." Mother stood, brushing straw from her skirt. "Now, why don't you take a hot bath tonight and have a good soak in the tub?"

"But it's not Saturday."

"Piffle. Go ahead and take one anyway. Sometimes a lady needs some pampering. And I'll let you use a bar of soap from my gift set."

"Thank you, that sounds luxurious." Emily stood, and the dogs all hopped to their feet as well. "No, we're not going anywhere tonight." Maybe tomorrow she'd take them for a good run in the Elk Refuge.

Mother and daughter headed toward the house after Emily petted the dogs and gave them a bit more attention. The wind swept down from the mountains, sending a shiver through Emily. But she didn't mind the crisp, clear sensation.

Mother paused before they entered the house and tugged her shawl around her shoulders. "Anyway, maybe the young Miss Amelia won't be as hardy as your mother, and she'll take the next wagon out of here over the pass. Or perhaps another man will catch her eye, because there's a bit of a shortage of eligible women here. The men are bound to notice her."

"Maybe." They stepped through the doorway and Emily let the home's warmth embrace her as it always did. "Come to think

of it, don't worry about the bath. Sam will complain about helping me take buckets of water to the tub. I think I'll just read for
a while tonight."

"It will be all right, my dear. Give it time."

"I will."

Will met up with Amelia after returning to town and soon
found himself sitting across from her at Ma Reed's hotel, where
the Crabtrees had served up a mouthwatering supper in the dining room.

"The food here is quite good." Amelia popped the last bite
of buttered biscuit into her mouth. "And the fresh air here after
the trip over the pass has given me quite an appetite. But I can't
help it."

Will nodded. "The Crabtrees run the best place in town, in
my opinion, which is why I recommended you come here. You'll
be well taken care of, although it's not quite as grand as what you
might expect back East."

"It's perfectly adequate, and I feel comfortable here in my
room already." Amelia's face glowed; she truly was a lovely
woman. Her small earrings dangled from her ears, the lamplight
catching their sparkle.

"They say we'll have a water-operated electricity plant here
within two years." Will took a bite of his chicken potpie. The
generous portion would stick to his ribs tonight, for sure.

"So it's not quite the wilds here that you made it out to

be, after all." She pushed the vegetables around her plate and frowned. "You made it sound so. . .so. . .remote."

"It was different when I lived here, long ago. Barely a house in the valley. And now there's a town, and it's growing."

"So. . ."

"You do like that word, Amelia." Here they went again. He could feel the discussion coming on. As a lawyer, he'd had practice in appearing before judges, but he didn't practice courtroom law, per se.

"I do." She set her fork down. "William, I want to be frank with you. I miss you. I miss us, as a pair. You don't have to work for my father. You can practice here. I'd prefer living back East, but I want to show you, by staying in Jackson, that I'm open to the possibility of a life with you. Here."

"Oh, Amelia." There was a time when he'd have welcomed those words. Had his opinion changed in but a few months?

"I'm planning to stay the remainder of the winter, to show you I can do it. I can stay here."

"But still, it's difficult." He knew she'd be in for a challenge without a number of conveniences she was accustomed to. But a well-heeled young woman with stars in her eyes over the "Wild West" would be in for a rude awakening.

She tapped the table with her hand, not loud but enough to make her spoon jump. "I'm tired of hearing it's difficult. My family didn't want me to come here. Father nearly threatened to cut me off from my funds. Mother intervened, saying he needed to give me the opportunity, no matter how 'difficult' it would be for me. What is it with you men, anyway?"

He didn't like the turn of conversation. Tonight, he wasn't trying to woo Amelia but wanted to show her how being here, unprepared, could be a disaster for her.

"Amelia, right now it seems fun and novel to you. All the things you've heard of in the dime-store novels, cowboys, ranchers, women fighting the odds. I'm sure it sounds very romantic, but when the days are short, the snow is high, and the pass is closed, you'll have no choice but to stay."

"Here's your pie." An older woman stood beside their elbows. She held two plates of berry pie, each graced with a dollop of ice cream.

"Thank you," Will said, welcoming the diversion.

Amelia nodded. "This looks delicious. I'm beginning to get full, but I do have room for pie."

"I'll top off your coffee as well." The woman glided away, returned with a coffeepot, and refilled their cups to the brims.

Will remained silent as he ate his dessert, and Amelia kept her focus toward the front window of the hotel's dining room. He'd made her mad, but good. And he wasn't about to talk her out of her determination.

"I saw a schoolhouse on the way in. It's quite nice," she said. "Two stories, even."

"Yes. More children here than when I was in school. There's a bank, two general stores, a thriving newspaper."

"I noticed the paper. I saw an old issue. There's a picture of you on the front page. And you never told me."

"We've only now started catching up." He'd seen the article in the paper, from the town forum where they'd discussed the election and state of the community.

"You and that pants-wearing woman, Emily something, I believe, were shaking hands."

"We've discussed running for office. The ladies believe they can help the town."

"Isn't that forward thinking? I knew I'd like it here, as soon as Mr. Tolliver and I reached the top of the pass, and I saw down into the valley." Amelia smiled, but her eyes held a spark of challenge. "Now, tell me about your friend, Emily."

"We were in school together as children." His tie suddenly had the pressure of a noose. "She plans to run for the Jackson City Council in the spring."

"How unique. I'm all for women voting, but really, it seems a bit difficult to try to run for council and tell the men what to do. But she looks enough like a man, wearing trousers and such."

"Emily's a bit unconventional. She can ride as well as any man and I'm sure can shoot as well. She has a sled dog team, too. But I assure you, Emily also carries herself like a lady. I don't appreciate you speaking of her in such a way."

"Oh, sled dogs! How adventurous. I wonder if your friend would take me out on a ride with the dogs?"

Interesting, Amelia ignoring his remarks about Emily and

focusing on the novelty of the dogs. "Maybe she will. She and those dogs saved my life not too long ago."

"Tell me more." She leaned forward, resting her forearms on the table as she did so. Then she straightened her spine.

"I went for a hike on what started as a fine afternoon. I intended only for a short trip into the foothills. Then the clouds covered up the sun, and it started to snow. Somehow I got turned around and couldn't see the trail. Or whatever trail I found wasn't taking me back to town. The snow fell harder. So I hunkered down until almost dark. Emily and her dogs found me. What a sight they were. And Emily. . ."

Amelia remained silent, taking a bite of pie followed by a sip of coffee.

"You and Emily are close, I presume?"

"She was one of my best friends when I left Jackson." He hadn't expected this turn of conversation. He also hadn't liked how he'd explained things to Emily.

Truthfully, until Mother's letter, he hadn't really wondered about Amelia. His thoughts and time had been taken by building a life and practice here in Jackson. He hadn't glanced back.

"Does this mean I have a rival for your affections?"

The lady certainly knew how to pin a man into a corner. He appreciated Amelia's intelligence and her forthrightness. Now he found himself wishing she weren't, because he didn't have an answer she would be happy about. An answer she couldn't ignore, such as his comments about how she'd spoken of Emily moments ago.

"In a word, Amelia? Yes. Yes, you do. Emily Covington means a great deal to me. More than a friend? I can't answer that. Not yet."

"Thank you for your honesty." Amelia reached for her napkin, dabbed it on her mouth, then folded it and placed it on the table. "And thank you very much for supper. I'm sure I'll see you again soon, but I must retire for the evening." She rose from her chair.

Will stood, inclined his head briefly. "Good evening, Amelia." He watched her gather up her dignity and walk from the dining room.

Chapter 6

Emily stared at the list in front of her then gazed at the sky outside the window. A gray day, with flat, dove-gray clouds to the west. That morning when taking the dogs out for their run, she felt a tinge of ice in the air. She wouldn't be surprised if they had another snow in the next day or two. However, on the inside, she basked as if under the sun's glow—Will was coming this afternoon to do business with her father, and staying for supper. Mother sat across from her in the matching chair, working at mending.

Emily dragged her attention back to the list—cookies, fudge, and taffy.

She'd been thinking about anything this afternoon except refreshments for the family's Christmas caroling night. The family would sing carols together, and sometimes the Olsens and their extended family would join them. Some years, other friends from Jackson would take their sleighs to the ranch.

"We've invited William, and his friend, Miss Clark, to the caroling night," Mother said.

"I don't want to sound like a poor hostess, but I must say I'm not overly anxious for Miss Clark to visit." Emily regretted the choice of words. Christmas was the most charitable time of year, and Emily truly bore Amelia Clark no ill will. But that didn't mean she wanted to spend more time with the young woman than she was required to.

"We must include her as well. She's likely homesick, especially now. I know I was. My first Christmas here, I welcomed the chance to celebrate with my new friends. And, your father." Mother looked up from her needlework and stared at the dancing flames in the fireplace.

"They've had supper nearly every night together at the hotel."

"Maybe, maybe not. That bit of information came from Estella Greene, and I don't trust the reliability of her words. I think it's her attempt at stirring the pot." Mother shook her head. "Anyway, don't trouble yourself about Amelia. Better he decide now who he loves, and if there's anything we can do to make it happen sooner than later, all the better for both you and Amelia."

"I don't like feeling this way." Emily set the list and pencil down on the end table. "We spoke at church, and he told me how much he's looking forward to coming today, and having supper, too. He. . .he said he missed me."

"Ah, that's a good sign. Well, I should check on supper. We're having roast with vegetables. And he's going to love the pie you made for dessert." Mother rose from her chair and set her mending on the cushion. Then she tugged on the hem of her shirtwaist. "I'll be back soon."

As Mother stepped from the parlor, the clock gonged two, and at the sound, Emily's heart skipped a beat. She at first resisted the urge to go to the front window and see if Will had ridden into the ranch yard. But no one was there to see her, so she stepped to the window anyway.

The scruffy dark brown horse, ridden by a familiar figure, was in the distance and approaching. Will! He made a good figure on horseback, with his leather satchel bouncing on his hip, his hat slung low over his brow. A gust of wind made both him and the horse duck their heads as they moved forward.

She glanced down at her trousers and everyday shirtwaist that had strands of dog fur on it. Mother hadn't said anything about her appearance earlier, for which Emily was thankful. Of course she wasn't a child who needed prompts regarding her wardrobe. She left the window and scurried up the stairs to her bedroom before Will arrived. Pa would leave John and Sam out feeding the cattle today. In fact, the kitchen door creaked below the moment Emily opened her own door.

"How's my lovely Belle?" her father's voice echoed up the stairwell.

"Doin' just fine, Mr. Covington." Mother's voice held a teasing tone.

Emily smiled as she closed her bedroom door behind her.

Then she marched to her armoire and flung open the door. No, the outfit she'd worn to the town meeting would be too fancy for supper. Trousers weren't an option, either. She pulled out her favorite skirt of gray-blue. Mother said it made her eyes appear bluer. She chose her Sunday-best white shirtwaist to go with the skirt and lost no time changing.

A murmur of voices—Will's voice as he stepped into the house then Pa welcoming him.

She descended the stairs just in time to hear Pa say something about Will and him meeting in the study. Pa's "study." It sounded stuffy, but it contained a simple desk along with floor-to-ceiling bookshelves, reminders of Pa's days studying to be a preacher before he moved west.

Ah well, so she didn't get to see Will before he and Pa went to conduct business. Pa had only said he wanted to file paperwork and needed Will's assistance. Pa hadn't bought any more land in the past few years, that she could remember. So perhaps it wasn't about real estate. Unless he was now enlarging the borders of the ranch because of the general lack of elbow room in his opinion. However, she knew enough about the ranch to know they'd had a hard go of it the past few years but looked ahead to an upswing.

Emily headed for the kitchen, where Mother bustled about. She'd taken the roast from the oven and was slicing a generous chunk off one end.

"Dishing up some supper for the hands. They've worked

hard today, and I figure if we're eating so well, they ought to have a share."

Sam stepped into the kitchen. "Smells good, Ma. Hey, Em, your beau is here."

"I saw him riding up." Her *beau*. She didn't take his teasing bait.

"I guess you did." He studied her outfit. "You look mighty dressed up for a Friday night supper."

"If I want to dress for supper, I can." Really, there were times it seemed as if he were five years old again, tagging after her.

"Here." Ma held a large covered pan in Sam's direction. "Before you take your coat off, run this out to the bunkhouse for Stu and Bud."

"Yes, ma'am." Sam nodded and took the pan from his mother. "Be right back."

"I'll get the door for you," Emily volunteered and headed for the kitchen door. She flung it open and allowed Sam to pass. "Oh, it's snowing."

Lovely white flakes drifted down, peaceful and soft. A breath of wind pelted some of the flakes past her shoulders and into the kitchen.

"What you're proposing is fairly simple, Mr. Covington. However, this isn't part of your will?"

"No. Ownership won't change until after my death, but the land will still belong to the family."

Zeb Covington stood from behind his desk then went to the window. "A man gets to the age when he knows he's looking at fewer days ahead of him than behind."

"Sir, I'd like to think you still have many, many days ahead of you." Will took more notes.

"Thank you, Mr. Adams. Truth be told, none of us on earth knows. But I want more than my soul to be prepared. I want to know they're all well taken care of. I've seen this place grow from barely a house on the landscape to a thriving town. And someday, after I'm gone, I still want there to be a Covington Ranch."

"Well, Lord willing, Mr. Covington, that will happen."

Nodding, Zeb took his seat behind the desk again. "So, young lawyer, I'd like to ask you an important question."

"Yes, sir?"

"What are your intentions toward my daughter? I understand there's another young woman, too, who's come a long way to see you and try out Jackson, to see if it's to her liking." Zeb stroked his beard and stared at Will across the desk.

Will met the full force of Zeb's gaze. "Well, my intentions toward your daughter are entirely honorable. Ever since I've been back in Jackson, she's claimed my attention. Also, she helped save my life. She's a formidable woman."

"I'm sure your intentions are honorable. You're spoken well of in the community, and you're faithful in church and a temperate man. Not given to rage, but a man more given to prayer, I'm told."

Will nodded. "Thank you."

"That said, given you recognize my Emily's attributes, I won't tolerate anyone being double minded about her. She doesn't deserve it. Emily's not like many women. She's got her mother's grace and my backbone."

If this was how Mr. Covington grilled all of Emily's suitors, no wonder she still hadn't landed a husband. Despite the fact there was no woodstove in the room, Will's forehead beaded with sweat.

"I've seen Emily's attributes, like I said. And I would never want to hurt her, or cause her pain."

"But you have this young woman, traipsing around as if she's waiting for you to propose. Again."

"Sir, I had nothing to do with her coming here. I didn't encourage it, not in the least. I've told her, too, that I'm not leaving Jackson, not for her, or anyone."

"Yet still, she stays. Which is why I need to know: if you're not intending to marry my daughter, tell her so. I'd rather her know now, than let more time go by and her end up heartbroken. You proposed marriage at one time to this Miss Clark. That's a very serious thing, indeed."

"Yes, it is. However, I'd always told her I planned to return west one day, and not stay in the East."

Zeb nodded slowly. "Then for Miss Clark's sake, I hope you convince her she's not the one for you."

Will tried not to squirm on his chair. Yes, Zebulon spoke

the truth. Every day that Amelia remained in the West was one day closer to a broken heart, and one day closer to being stuck in Jackson for the remainder of the winter.

He had a sudden recollection of a summer's day, out fishing with his father.

"My father used to have a saying he told me when I was a little boy: fish, or cut bait."

"I'd say that's excellent advice, Mr. Adams."

Chapter 7

The snow continued to fall during supper as they sat, swapping stories and telling jokes while the wind howled something fierce outside.

Emily's heart sang at seeing Will again across the supper table. She had to keep reminding herself that both Pa and Mother, along with Sam, sat at the table with them also. Yet in some ways, it might as well have been a private table in a restaurant, with just the two of them chatting and laughing away.

His eyes, a soft brown in the lamplight, gleamed as he chuckled over one of Sam's jokes.

Another howl of wind drowned out some of the laughter. Mother frowned and stepped to the door, tugging it open. A blast of icy air and a swirl of snow whipped past her.

"I declare, there's more than six inches on top of the snow we already have." She turned to face them.

"Son, I'd suggest you stay here with us tonight," Pa said. "We have the room, and it's not fit to travel in weather like this. Should be all right in the morning, though, as long as the snow's stopped."

"If it's not an imposition, I don't mind." Will glanced at Emily, who dropped her gaze to study her coffee cup.

He'd stayed at the house overnight before, the evening she'd found him lost in the hills. But that night was different. She'd been cranky at him and probably, no definitely, hadn't been the best hostess. Tonight, however, the idea of a few more hours with Will made her heart pound a bit faster.

"Then I'll get extra blankets, and you're welcome to sleep on the sofa, as before." Mother cleared empty plates from the table, and Emily followed suit.

"I'll do the dishes, Mother."

"And I'll help." Will moved to stand.

"No, you don't have to, Will. You're our guest." She felt three other pairs of eyes watching her as she stacked the plates beside the sink.

"I've got some animals I need to see to, if you're volunteering assistance with chores," Sam said.

Pa snorted. "I think you're fine working on your own."

Emily's face flamed, and she was grateful for the lamplight hiding her expression.

"I was joking, Pa. I already saw to the animals." Sam grinned and shrugged. "Well, I'm off to look at some gear in the Sears catalog. Looking for new hiking boots."

"One of these days, we'll have a real hot water heater, instead of using the stove." Mother went to lift the pot of steaming water from the stove, but Pa stopped her.

"Here, I'll do that, and leave the kids to take care of the kitchen for us." Pa winked at Mother as he stepped from the stove to the sink. He filled it with water then set the pot to the side for rinsing.

After her parents retired to the parlor, Emily set to washing the dishes, with Will picking up a towel to dry them.

She decided to inquire about Amelia straightaway, and not put it off. "How is Amelia doing, being here in Jackson?"

"She's doing all right, I believe. She's not fond of the muddy streets, but I expect with tonight's snowstorm, it'll make things prettier to her."

"I can imagine everything must seem so. . .different. . .here, than back East. Especially for someone seeing it for the first time." Emily handed him a dinner plate. "I've seen pictures of back East, the tall buildings standing close together, all the people swarming like flies in the streets."

"What pictures were those?"

"Of New York."

"I've been to New York, twice."

"I'd like to see it, someday, just to say I've been. But Jackson will always be my home."

"Maybe someday we'll see New York together."

His words made her stop rinsing the last of the forks and spoons. She held them above the water. "Maybe."

"Listen, about Amelia. . . I've decided, once and for all, I don't want to renew our engagement. She's not going to be happy here."

"But, do you love her? How do you know she won't be happy here? Has she been here long enough to know?" She handed him the jumble of forks and spoons.

"You almost sound as if you're trying to plead her case."

"No, I'm not. But people can change. My mother was as citified as they come, and she came out here thinking she was going to change the West. Of course, she was very young and wanted to teach young women manners and social graces. The West changed her, but she's still the most well-mannered woman I know. She learned to live here. What's to say that Amelia won't learn to do the same? Would you change your mind about her if she did?" She had to speak the words, to voice the worry inside her. She picked up a clean dishcloth and wiped her hands.

She watched him pause then sit down at the table. He said nothing more, so she continued.

"See? You don't know. If you're not certain, then. . ." Emily shook her head.

"Then what?"

At that moment, Sam entered the kitchen. "I meant to tell you, I didn't feed the dogs tonight." He glanced from Emily to Will.

"That's all right, I've some scraps here I can feed them." Emily picked up the bowl where she'd scraped the plates. "I need to get my coat."

"Sorry, I think I just walked into something right now." He slowly backed from the kitchen.

"Don't be sorry, I need to see to the dogs anyway," Emily said. "Thanks for offering, Sam."

She never knew it could be like this, having feelings for someone and the uncertainty of what lay ahead. Love ought to be easier, oughtn't it?

"I'll come with you," Will offered, heading for his coat hanging on a set of pegs.

She didn't say anything but allowed him to follow her outside, into the wind and snow. The cold nearly sucked the breath from her body, and the wind stung her face almost as much as it had the night they'd searched for Will in the foothills.

He pulled open the barn door for her, the door scraping back the new-fallen snow piling against the barn.

"Thanks," she called out to him then stepped into the barn's warmth. A few greetings from the horses, the bang of a hoof from one of the cows rang against the barn wall.

Will pushed the door shut. "There. Now that we're alone, with no chance of interruption, we need to talk."

The dogs' barking almost masked the sound of his words as Emily headed for the dog pen. "Hello, my beautifuls." She entered the pen then scraped the contents of the bowl into a feeder. Their watering bowls needed filling, but melted snow should work for water supply.

She sank onto the pile of straw in the corner, where the dogs liked to sleep, and the whole passel of them darted between her and the bowl of food. Will stood on the other side of the partition separating the dog pen from the rest of the barn, and smiled at her.

She'd been honest about Amelia and he'd had a slow response. Well, she gave the man credit. She'd seen both of her brothers flummoxed before when posed with a tough question, so Will becoming speechless wasn't quite a surprise to her. What had she expected? Him to proclaim his love for her and describe how he'd carefully spurn Amelia?

Emily cleared her throat. "All right, we can talk."

Will opened the little gate and joined Emily with the dogs, who immediately surrounded him, sniffing and barking. Dogs were often good judges of character, and after the sniffing and barking ended, they went back to the food. But Niki moved to Emily's side and stared at Will with her large dark eyes.

"I wanted to say, about Amelia. I wanted to be sure. I wanted to be. . .to be fair to her." Felix nosed one of Will's hands, and he leaned over to scratch behind the dog's ears. "She came so far. I wanted to know. Because choosing someone to love is a big decision."

Emily stood, realizing then she'd just gotten straw on her best Sunday skirt. "Yes, it's a very big decision."

"But I will tell her, next time I see her." He took a few steps closer to her, the dogs ever watchful.

"When will that be?"

"This weekend; I expect I'll see her at church on Sunday."

"I see."

He was close enough now, she could see the hint of stubble on his chin. Then he lowered his mouth to hers and pulled her into his arms.

Every nerve ending from her scalp to her toes came alive. She couldn't breathe, didn't want to breathe. Her first kiss, from the man she loved. Surely, he must love her, too, kissing her this way. In the circle of his arms, she couldn't hear the sound of the wind outside anymore.

"Are you better now?" he asked.

"Much better." And she smiled at him.

Chapter 8

The Christmas caroling night had perfect weather, a full moon and a crisp winter chill in the air. Inside the Covington's home, Emily hummed as she laid greenery across the mantle. More candles and the effect would be beautiful, peaceful.

Soon the guests would arrive, bringing festive treats as they were able, a musical instrument. Rumor had it Gus Tolliver would even play his fiddle.

First arriving were the parson and his wife, with Amelia Clark. With its swirl of skirts and short train, Amelia's gown would have fit in at a fancy ball in the East. Both women carried baskets.

"Cookies," Amelia said, extending the basket toward Emily.

"Thank you, very much." She couldn't read the woman's expression. Emily carried the cookies to the kitchen table, where Mother had spread a lace tablecloth. Already, half the table was covered with delectable treats.

"Your family has a cozy home." Amelia scanned the room.

"Thank you." She loved every nook and cranny of the sprawling home. Not as fancy as what one might find in the East, but here in Jackson, the place fit in perfectly.

"Well, I suppose you know, so far, you've won."

"Won?"

Emily glanced toward the parlor, where Mother and the parson and his wife chatted. Pa and Sam should be in soon, along with John and his wife.

"Will's affections."

"I wasn't competing, but hoping."

"Oh, but we *were* competing—*are* competing. I knew the moment I stepped into Will's office, my first day here."

Emily squared her shoulders and lifted her chin. "Miss Clark, you've always had the advantage. I only knew Billy Adams, the boy. I've not had long to get to know William Adams, the man. You've known him far longer. You won his heart first."

Amelia smiled. "Yes, I know."

Lord, this woman bears a load of hurt, and I don't blame her. I'd likely feel the same way, were I in the same position. But would I use the same words she has?

She wanted to weigh her words carefully. No, she wasn't backing down from her claim to Will's heart, but she didn't want to ignore Amelia's pain. The young woman had traveled more than a thousand miles to follow her heart, only to learn her love wasn't returned. At least, not in the way she'd hoped.

"I'm sorry you've come all this way, only to be disappointed."

"Not disappointed. You may have won this round, but I still intend to stay and try to change his mind. I thought you ought to know that, too."

Emily nodded, reminding herself she was also a hostess this evening. "I understand. I think your attempts will be futile. This country isn't kind in the winter, so you should think very hard about getting over the pass as soon as possible. In the meantime, may I offer you a cup of tea?"

"That would be lovely." Amelia smiled as someone knocked on the front door.

"I'll have your tea prepared in a moment. Sugar?"

"Of course. And cream, if you have any."

"We do." Emily stepped toward the stove, while Amelia glided from the kitchen.

Her hands shook as she poured the tea. She'd encountered all sorts of wildlife in Wyoming, but nothing like this determined, spurned young woman in a silk dress.

Voices from the front room told her the rest of their guests had arrived. This was how her family loved to celebrate, with a houseful of neighbors and friends.

"A Christmas Eve service isn't quite enough for me," Mother liked to say during this time of year.

"Hello." Will entered the kitchen. He carried a jug. "Pressed cider. It's my offering for tonight's celebration."

"Thank you. I'll get it warming on the stove." She smiled at Will, even as Amelia appeared in the doorway behind him.

"Oh, William," Amelia called out. "I'd love to play the piano for you. Mrs. Covington said I may use theirs. What song would you like for me to begin with?"

He turned to face her. "Why, thank you, Amelia. 'O Little Town of Bethlehem,' if you please."

"I'll join you soon, Will." Emily picked up the teacup for Amelia. "Amelia, I have your tea prepared."

"Why, thank you, Miss Covington. If you could set it on the table, I'll fetch it after I've played the first song." Amelia marched to the parlor.

Will shook his head. "Emily. . ."

Emily shrugged and smiled. "It's all right. I'm going to help set out the food when people arrive."

He stepped closer. "It's good to see you."

"Good to see you as well."

Mother bustled past Will as she entered the kitchen. "Here's another plate. Some Swedish cookies from the Olsens."

"Thank you, Mother."

Will gave her another smile before heading into the parlor. Mother glanced at him as he did so.

After he left, Mother joined Emily at the stove. "You're doing well, my dear. Amelia is fit to be tied, but I'll let her play the piano tonight." The first few notes, the introduction to "O Little Town of Bethlehem," drifted into the kitchen.

"Oh, Mother, it's not easy."

"I know." Mother looked toward the parlor. "Come, join us in the music. Pa and Sam are coming soon. So is Sheriff Daniels."

Mother always seemed to know how to make things feel right again. When Emily entered the parlor, she wanted to stand near Will. However, he stood in the corner near the piano, and others had clustered around him.

Amelia ran her fingers over the keys, coaxing a melody from the piano in ways Emily hadn't ever managed. Her own fumbling piano skills could plunk out songs. Amelia, however, had the graces from far more practice.

She would be a far more fitting woman to marry a lawyer than Emily. However, Amelia wasn't the one Will smiled at across the room.

Will missed home tonight, although Wyoming was home. But listening to the piano music, he recalled times that weren't so wild, or tough, as what he faced now. He smiled as he scanned the Covingtons' parlor. The simple, rustic elegance of the ranch home didn't compare to the refinement he'd seen in certain circles back East. Yet, the Covingtons' home was a far cry from the typical homesteader's place. Zebulon Covington had looked toward the future, to a time like now when Jackson was ever changing.

For now, though, all Will had was two rooms, one to sleep in and one to use as an office. He had nothing but had turned his back on a sure future with Amelia's father's firm.

Tonight, even though he missed the Christmases he'd

always known, this Christmas he was exactly where he was supposed to be.

He could only imagine what Amelia had been saying to Emily, and unfortunately, he hadn't had the opportunity to speak more with Emily and assuage her fears. He knew how Amelia could be, and truthfully, in spite of her fancy frocks, she didn't always treat people in a pretty manner.

He hadn't realized it until lately. And despite his telling her he wouldn't renew their engagement, Amelia stubbornly chose to remain in Jackson. News had it that the pass would soon be impassable. And Amelia wouldn't be able to leave until spring.

The thoughts traveled through his brain one by one during the song, and when the final notes ended, he moved a few steps from the piano and closer toward Emily. The others let him through, the parson and his wife, John and his wife, the Olsens, and then Zebulon and Belle Covington.

Sam shot him a knowing grin when he stopped beside Emily.

Then Sheriff Daniels requested "Hark! The Herald Angels Sing," and Will joined in with the next song.

Emily sang a few phrases, and he didn't cringe. But she couldn't find the melody. The sound was endearing to his ears, and the more he stared at her, the redder her face grew.

The chorus ended, and Mrs. Covington stepped to the piano where Will had stood moments ago.

"We'll take a break now, and there's coffee, tea, and pressed apple cider in the kitchen, along with the delightful treats you've brought and we've prepared."

The group filled the kitchen, and Will kept Emily by his side as long as he could. She only left to help her mother serve coffee and the warm cider, while he couldn't keep his eyes off her. She wore the skirt and shirtwaist she'd worn the evening of the town meeting, and although he still wasn't accustomed to seeing her in a more formal attire, he could get used to it. But he'd never press her.

As they stood, sipping the apple cider and discussing the weather prospects for Christmas week, a pounding sounded on the front door.

"I'll see to that," Zebulon said and left the kitchen. The door creaked open, and a high-pitched voice spoke. Will couldn't make out the words, so he moved to follow Zebulon.

"What's wrong?" Emily whispered to him.

"I'm not sure." He nodded toward the parlor. "Let's find out."

". . . haven't seen or heard from them since they left for town this morning," the man was saying. "Oh, Sheriff, you're here. Good."

He was bundled head to toe, topped with a hat, a scarf around his neck, snowshoes clamped to his boots.

"I haven't seen anyone happen by here today, but then, my boys and I were working." Zebulon glanced at Will and Emily. "We can gather our sleighs and lanterns and help you look."

"Ah, but you're having a Christmas gathering." The man's shoulders sank.

"We'd rather help tonight," Zebulon said.

"Agreed," Sheriff said. "I'll head back toward town and round up a few more people."

"We can help, too," Will added. He glanced at Emily.

"I can get the dogsled ready inside ten minutes." She nodded.

Zebulon put his hand on the man's shoulder. "We'll gather and pray then head out to find them. Come, get something warm to drink, and have a snack before you leave."

Will and Emily followed the pair into the kitchen, where the others exclaimed over the man's arrival.

"It's my brother, his wife, and their baby. They went to town today and never came home."

Bernard and Patience Willoughby, along with baby Edward, had gone to the mercantile to collect mail, shop, and go to the bank in town. They were supposed to return by suppertime, Edgar Willoughby explained, but he had heard nothing from them.

"I want to help," Will told Zebulon. "Other people went looking for me, so I want to do the same for someone else."

"I want to go, too." Amelia set her cup on the counter.

Nobody told her no, although Emily opened her mouth then closed it again.

Will hoped Amelia would be an asset in the search. Then again, maybe this was just the thing to make her realize what living in the West truly meant.

Chapter 9

Emily ended up lending Amelia a pair of her trousers to exchange for the long skirt, and Mother lent Amelia her old outdoor coat, a thick fur coat that, while very old, was still very warm.

"I can't believe I'm going to ride on a dogsled." Amelia didn't complain about her humble clothing but stood in the yard while they all prepared to head out to search for the Willoughbys. Sam and Sven Olsen were already heading down the trail toward town to retrace the missing family's steps. Pa and Will would travel together in the sleigh, but Amelia, for some reason, insisted on riding with Emily.

And I can't believe I'm letting you. Emily said nothing aloud as she fastened harnesses on the dogs, who hopped and bounced.

Even though they'd had a good run through the hills yesterday, tonight they were ready to head out under the full moon.

"We're going to travel where most don't," Emily said. "In case one of them wandered off on foot, for some reason."

It was becoming more difficult to get lost, the more settled

Jackson's Hole became. However, it wasn't impossible. Unless they met with an accident of some kind and were hurt.

"Go no farther than an area you know," Pa said. "Hopefully we'll find them tonight on one of the trails out of town, but if not, we head home and then try again in the morning, with a larger group." The parson and his wife had already set out, along with Sheriff Daniels, toward town to spread the word about the Willoughbys.

Emily had tucked blankets into a large sack and strapped it to the sled, the lantern attached to the sled providing a small circle of light. "Amelia, you can ride on the front here. The sack will cushion your ride somewhat." Amelia complied, and Emily showed her the straps that would help keep her on the sled instead of tumbling off.

She urged the dogs forward but slowed them to stop at the family sleigh. "We're heading out, Pa."

"Do you have your pocket watch?"

"Yes, sir."

"Stay out for no more than an hour, and then turn back." He glanced from Emily to Amelia.

"Yes, sir."

Emily signaled to the dogs to hit the trail, and they were off, racing into the moonlit night. The first surge away from the ranch was always the swiftest.

"Hold on!" she called out to Amelia. "They're getting up to speed."

"All right!" Amelia's voice came back.

"If you see anyone or anything on the trail, or near any trees, let me know."

They raced along. Fence posts made dark spots, punctuating the snow. A home in the distance darkened, its residents likely bedding down for the night.

The Willoughbys, however, lived farther away from town than most. Their spread nestled in the foothills. Emily would go there first; perhaps the family had returned home but then left again, for whatever reason.

"I don't see anything," Amelia said. "It's hard to see clearly beyond the lantern, even with the moonlight."

Emily didn't argue with that, but she found the full moon a convenient and helpful aid in their trek tonight.

After thirty minutes on the trail, they arrived at the Willoughbys' farm, the buildings standing out in stark contrast to the glowing snow. Another trail, the back trail to town, led past the farm. If Emily took the dogs along that trail, she would circle through town then back up the main trail that passed by the Covington Ranch.

"Should we knock on the door?" Amelia asked. "Maybe they came home after all."

"I'll check the barn. You try the door." Emily hurried off to the barn to check for a wagon. All the while, minutes ticked away. If the family was lost in this cold, it could mean life or death.

She found no wagon in the farmyard and met Amelia back at the sled, where the dogs waited patiently.

"No one answered. I knocked loud enough to wake a baby." Amelia shook her head.

"Well, get strapped in and we'll be on our way."

Amelia clambered onto the sled, fastened the straps, and they shot off along the trail.

Emily kept the dogs at a moderate pace. No need to tire them unnecessarily. And by going at a slow enough pace they would see anyone along the trail, or if off the trail, slow enough to see anyone taking shelter.

Another trail led uphill. Not sure where it led, Emily avoided that branch. The cold began to seep through the layers of her clothing. If it bothered her, Amelia had to be suffering.

Indeed, the young woman's teeth were chattering.

"We'll take the route to town." They kept racing along, until Emily paused at a turnoff. What if they'd been going to visit someone? Down this meager roadway lay a few homes, one of which was the doctor's.

What if they'd taken the baby for help, or if one of them were ill?

"We're making a detour," she announced.

"We need to detour home. I can't take much more of this."

Emily shook her head. She should have left Amelia at home. Someone should have insisted she go back to town and her warm hotel room with the parson and his wife.

A few things sprang to mind to say, but none of them would help the current situation. Instead, she turned the team and they headed along the road to the doctor's home.

Not long, and they glided to a stop at the modest home where the doc had lived for years, the son of homesteaders.

They left the dogs in the yard and went to the house, where lamps glowed inside.

Dr. Whitley opened the door immediately. "Yes? Oh, Miss Covington. And a young friend. What do you need assistance with this evening?"

"We're looking for the Willoughbys. Have they stopped by here at all?"

"As a matter of fact, yes. Their young son is very ill. I'm keeping him here overnight, and they're staying as well."

"Mr. Willoughby's brother is very worried about them, and some of us have gone out searching."

After apologies and explanations from the Willoughbys, and politely refusing a cup of tea, Emily turned to face Amelia.

"We'd best get home. My hour is nearly up, and I don't want to worry the family."

Amelia nodded then spun to head toward the sled. "Take me to the hotel, please. We're closer than your home." Amelia's sharp tone gave Emily pause.

"But your clothes."

"I'm done." She waved her hands. "I'm so cold, I can't see straight. My clothes are soaked through. I. . .I can't do this."

"All right." Emily would have explaining to do, once she arrived back at the ranch. "To Ma Reed's, then."

Amelia muttered something as they sped off along the road back to town.

"I'm sorry, I didn't catch what you said."

"I'm sending word to Gus Tolliver in the morning. I'm leaving. You should be happy."

Will and Zebulon covered the route to the west of the ranch and found no one stranded on the road, or any evidence of a wagon.

"I'll see to the team." Zed hopped down from the sleigh. "You go ahead to the house and see to Emily. She's probably back already."

"I don't mind helping."

Zeb shook his head. "Naw, go on in. I'll be but a few moments."

Will left the sleigh then hurried across the ranch yard to the warmth of the house. Now he knew what it felt like to worry about someone out missing in the cold and the dark. Maybe Emily had news.

But one thing made him pause when crossing the yard. No dogs barked from the direction of the barn. He and Zebulon had been gone longer than the agreed-upon hour, and he should have expected to hear dogs when they entered the ranch yard.

What if something had happened to Emily and Amelia?

He shoved the thought aside and opened the front door.

"Ah, hello? Zebulon and I are back," he called out.

"Oh good!" Mrs. Covington called from the kitchen. "Did you find the Willoughbys? Have you seen Emily?"

"No, we didn't find them. And no, we haven't seen Emily either." Will brushed the snow from his shoes then peeled off his gloves.

"Well maybe she was just delayed a few minutes. She might have gone a little slower with having a passenger on the sled, although Miss Clark doesn't look like she weighs more than a gnat." Despite her words, Mrs. Covington frowned. "I've kept the cider warm, and there's coffee on. And we have spiced dough-nuts if you need something to eat."

"Thank you. Just coffee, please."

Mrs. Covington poured him a cup of coffee, which he accepted, enjoying the warmth of the cup on his fingers.

He thanked her then moved to take a seat in the now-vacant living room, where earlier they'd celebrated and sang. How quickly things could change, such as it was in the wilds. In life, really.

A log on the fire crackled then an ember popped. A dog's bark sounded outside, faint at first, then the barking intensified.

Emily!

Will set his cup on the mantel and darted outside to the yard. Snow sprayed up from his boots. Emily was gliding in on her sled, the dogs straining against the harness.

One thing stood out immediately. No Amelia.

He crossed the yard in a few steps and joined her at the sled.

"Where's Amelia? Did you find the Willoughbys?"

Emily nodded. "The Willoughbys brought their baby straight to Doc's home. The baby had a fever and is very ill, so they decided to stay overnight at Doc's until the little one turns the corner."

"And Amelia?"

"She's now safe and warm in her room at Ma Reed's. She couldn't take the cold. I think being out tonight scared her a little, too. Anyway. . ." Emily paused.

"Anyway. . . ?"

"She told me she's contacting Gus Tolliver first thing in the morning and heading back across the pass before it's too late to leave."

"Finally. No matter what I told her, she wouldn't listen."

"I know." Emily shrugged. "You tried. And I don't bear you any ill will for treating her so kindly."

"Well, I suppose I should let you see to the dogs, then."

A strange look passed across her face. "Yes. . . You can join me if you like."

Will caught sight of Zebulon crossing to the house. "I'm going to speak to your father for a moment."

"All right."

Emily unbuckled the dogs from their harnesses and let them run for their water bowls. They'd done well tonight. And she thanked God the Willoughbys were safe. She thanked God even more that Amelia had decided to leave. The young woman's presence had been a burr under the saddle.

But Will, just now, hadn't acted very happy about Amelia leaving. He seemed preoccupied. And it wasn't as warm in the barn as it had been in the house; the barn was where he'd kissed her for the first time. She'd been hoping for a second kiss tonight, except the evening hadn't turned out like any of them had planned.

"Glad you found them, Em." Pa stood on the other side of the partition. "I'll have Sam ride out to the Olsens and let them know in the morning that we won't be needing to search anymore."

"I'm glad, too."

"So Miss Clark is back in town, likely headed out of Jackson soon."

"Yes, sir." She nodded, scratching Felix's ears. The dog licked her hand.

"Interesting development." Pa nodded. "Well, I'm heading in. Don't be too long. I think your young man is inside, waiting for you."

"I'll be in soon." She gave the dogs each a pat and brushed a few of them. Niki had a sore spot on her front paw in spite of the leather booties Emily put on the dogs before heading out, so Emily used a bit of salve she had on hand.

She heard the barn door open then whispers and voices. A horse nickered at someone. A blast of cold air swept into the dogs' area of the barn. Was someone going out again?

A jingling of bells sounded in her ears. Who'd taken out the sleigh bells?

Emily headed for the main part of the barn. "Hello, who's going out now? It's getting a little cold."

"I thought I'd give your Will a hand in hitching up the sleigh for a moonlit ride." Pa stood there, holding the reins, while Will adjusted the bells, which jangled merrily.

"Tonight?" She glanced from Pa to Will.

"Tonight," Will said. "Come. We have a warm fur cover. It's a fine night for a sleigh ride."

She was a bit tired after being out for so long, but the barn had helped her thaw a little. Part of her wished she could change into something better than her trousers and shirtwaist. However, it was dark enough, and they'd be warm enough in the sleigh.

"I'll see you two in a bit." Pa gave Will a nod.

Will took her by the hand and helped her into the sleigh. "We'll take a quick trip, halfway to town and back."

"All right." Emily pulled the fur over her lap, and Will took the seat beside her.

Then he tucked the fur around them securely. "There. Now, here we go."

He whistled to the team, and they headed out easily, plodding along in the nighttime. "I won't push them. It's cold, and they've already been out. This won't take long."

"What won't take long?"

"Ah, Emily, I had a nice conversation with your father. He told me about building this sleigh, how it was special to the family."

"Yes." She tried not to shiver. Will pulled her close to him. It felt a bit scandalous to have his arm around her, but she liked it. And no prying eyes or wagging tongues, and Amelia was likely packing now at Ma Reed's. Either that or thawing out before the fire.

"So, I understand your father proposed to your mother in this very sleigh."

"He did." She loved the story and never tired of hearing it.

"Oh, I do love you so, Miss Emily Covington. I may not say or do the correct thing—like with Amelia. I can argue in court and state my case, but a woman—gets my tongue every time."

"I love you, too, William Adams. Just like you are." Her heart beat a little faster. They slipped onto the road to town. Now the route didn't seem so ominous in the dark, with the moonlight glittering on the snow. The full moon lit William's features, and she stared at his profile.

He pulled the team to a stop and faced her. "Miss Emily Covington, the reason I asked your father to let me take you on a sleigh ride tonight is I wanted to waste no time."

"I see." She smiled.

"I want to ask you tonight, like your father asked your mother, a very important question."

"Ask me what?"

He put both his arms around her and pulled her closer still. "Marry me, Emily Covington."

"Lawyer Adams, that's not a question." She couldn't help but tease him.

"Well then, allow me to rephrase. Will you do me the honor of being my wife, and make this the happiest Christmas ever?"

"Oh yes, Will, I'll marry you." She let him warm her lips with a kiss.

"So, does this mean you'll still run for town council in the spring?"

"I'll not change my mind about that, sir." She grinned. "But you may change your mind, if you so wish."

Will let out a laugh. "Oh, my dear, it will be a most interesting campaign."

Epilogue

June 1920

"Councilwoman Covington, are you ready to become Mrs. William Adams, Junior?" Pa asked as they stood at the doors to the chapel.

Councilwoman Covington. Emily wanted to dance a little jig at the sound of the title, but she was in her wedding gown and a few of the men were still sore about the women of Jackson taking the elections in a landslide.

Their town needed some fixing, and the women, now dubbed the "petticoat government," were glad to lend a hand to make good changes happen.

She'd given Will a walloping in the votes herself, but he assured her he was fine, although his male ego was a tad bruised.

But Mrs. Will Adams? She smiled at the thought. She wouldn't be councilwoman forever, but she'd gladly bear her husband's name the rest of her life.

"I'm ready, Pa. So, so ready." She squeezed his arm, and he clutched her hand; his eyes seemed very bright in the sunshine today. She'd only seen him cry once, when her little brother was born. Today made the second time.

"You know, I'm not quite ready to let you go."

"We're not leaving Jackson, Pa. Not ever."

"Aw, I know that."

They scaled the three steps to the double doors. Miss Etta was plunking out the strains of "The Wedding March."

"Oh, and that legal matter I had your Will help me see to? I'm giving you a few acres of the spread. . .for your future home."

"Pa. . . I don't know what to say."

"I'm not planning to kick the bucket anytime soon, but I want you to choose a spot now, for you and your Will to build a home."

You and your Will.

The music grew louder as the doors were flung open, and she caught sight of her Will standing by the preacher.

My Will, always.

Will stood there, smiling, his eyes gleaming. He tugged at his tie then his cuffs. No doubt, he loved her. She wanted to pick up the hem of her skirt and rush down the aisle to him, but it wouldn't be entirely proper.

Instead, Emily held her head high, let her smile flow unrestrained across her face, and began the walk down the aisle, into her future.

WINTER WONDERLAND

by Elizabeth Goddard

Chapter 1

Jackson's Hole, Wyoming, September 1929

S heriff, I want this man arrested."

Ann Kirkland pressed her correspondence with Mr. Jeremiah Frankston on the sheriff's desk before she lost her nerve. Lose this battle and she might as well return home in defeat.

"What's this?" The stocky Sheriff Daniels wore a warm smile beneath his spectacles. He lifted the papers and tilted his head back, just so.

"I sent Mr. Frankston money to secure his services as a guide. I arrived this afternoon after an arduous trip from New York, I might add, only to be told he's taken up with a different client and won't return for another week. Now what am I supposed to do?"

The train to Victor, Idaho, and then the drive over the Teton Pass had left her drained and devoid of patience.

Though the pristine mountain range had taken her breath, she hadn't realized how isolated this valley was from the rest of the world. She couldn't have dreamed how completely different the natural setting and the culture would be from her life in Manhattan.

Oh, but she had, in fact, dreamed of this.

Dreamed of a complete change of scenery.

Just like so many others who'd come to this valley searching for a taste of the Old West, only in Ann's case, she needed to free herself from the embarrassment of a broken engagement. Daddy would have been furious with her had he thought she'd suffered from anything other than a broken heart—but she couldn't abide with how Tom thought of her. How he planned to treat her once they were married—he cared nothing for her photography or career, but only of Daddy's money.

The sheriff eyed her. "You say you came all the way from New York?"

She nodded.

He gave an understanding nod. "Frankston wrangles cattle and horses but converted to a partial dude ranch about a year ago. We got all manner of writers, artists, and moviemakers coming out here to get their fill of the Wild West, or what's left of it. In fact, a bunch of Hollywood people were here filming a movie. *The Big Trail*, I hear it's called. Lots of wealthy folks from all over come out here, too. So I figured you for a dudine from back East when I first saw you, except you aren't outfitted like some fancy drugstore cowgirl." A grin then. "Not yet."

Ann stiffened.

The sheriff cleared his throat. "About Frankston. Best I figure he took a client out on a long packing trip and got delayed. You staying at the ranch in a cabin? You could wait there for a day or two."

Daddy was very specific when he told her she couldn't stay at a dude ranch. At twenty-three, she was more than old enough to make her own decisions, but since he footed the bill, she had to concur with his wishes. Never mind he didn't want her in Jackson, Wyoming. Technically speaking, she wasn't staying on a dude ranch. "Actually, I made arrangements to stay in Jackson proper for the duration of my business."

Good thing Daddy was on a two-month-long honeymoon in Europe. Her mother had been buried for five years now, and Daddy had found someone new. Ann had taken her own vacation from the magazine to get over her broken heart; at least, that had been her excuse, though it was only partly true. Too bad she couldn't stay long enough to witness the winter wonderland this would become once it snowed, but she couldn't risk getting stuck here—if the stories were true about the pass. She had to be back in New York before Daddy's return.

"I see." He studied her. "And you wanted him to take you riding, hunting, or fishing?"

"I secured his services to escort me safely into and out of the newly established Grand Teton National Park, into the mountains, and perhaps Yellowstone, so that I could take photographs. Places unattainable by automobile, of course. He assured me he could take me places as yet unseen."

"Unseen except by him, you mean." He angled his head and looked as if he might laugh, but he brushed his hand over his chin discreetly enough.

Despite his effort, she was a photographer and had an eye for detail. She wasn't sure if his reaction had to do with Frankston—perhaps he'd told a tall tale—or with her, for believing the man. Or was it something entirely more chauvinistic?

"Sheriff, I know of Wyoming's history. Specifically in this town regarding women. I thank you kindly to take me seriously, too." Women had the right to vote in Wyoming a half century before they had the right to vote across the nation. The town of Jackson was equally progressive with the first all-woman city council. She'd done her homework.

She couldn't abide by a man who wouldn't take her seriously, and that's why she couldn't marry Tom.

"You're right, Miss. . ."—he glanced at her letter and contract—"Kirkland. You're right."

He looked over her shoulder and grinned. "While I can't arrest Mr. Frankston until he comes back—"

"I'm sorry, Sheriff, do you find this amusing?"

"No, miss. But understand I'll question him about his reasons for leaving you high and dry. In the meantime, I suggest you secure another outfitter for your needs. They're aplenty around these parts."

"But I've already paid," she said. "And I'll need that money back before hiring someone else."

At least the deposit, but she needed the deposit back, too, in order to pay the full amount when services were rendered.

"Leave that to me. I know Frankston, personally. He likely hasn't spent your money, but intended a refund and might have placed it with someone else in case you arrived."

"Or sent it back to me in New York. Only I'm not there now, am I?"

Retaining her papers, he opened the door that exited onto the boardwalk. "I have an idea. Would you follow me, please, Miss Kirkland?"

"Where are we going?" Ann walked through the door and stepped onto the wooden sidewalk, or boardwalk—championed by the women's city council, she'd read—so unlike the bluestone side-walks she was accustomed to in the city. The town bustling with people, the businesses were situated to form a perfect town square, the center of which was nothing more than dirt and sagebrush.

What had she been thinking to come here? And against Daddy's wishes? She hoped her flapper younger sister, Edith, kept her mouth shut. Part of Ann wanted to catch the next ride out of town and head back home, where she knew her way around with her eyes closed.

"I'm trying to help, Miss Kirkland, that's all. I'm sure there's a simple misunderstanding. Despite our reputation as being the last of the Old West, we aim to please and want to present our-selves as modernized to the rest of the world, at least where it counts."

She followed the sheriff as he strolled the boardwalk, passing Miller's Bank, Harry Wagner Insurance, Jackson Valley Telephone Company, and even a movie theater. They made their way around the square to the other side where a taxidermy shop and Jackson Meat Market took up the corner. The sheriff stopped in front of J.R. Jones Grocery.

Ann decided she'd best apologize. She certainly didn't need to make enemies here.

"I didn't mean any disrespect," Ann said. "I'm a photojournalist, you see, from *View Magazine*."

Ann wished she'd kept that tidbit to herself until she understood this man better. Photography had gone a long way in developing this area. The town's namesake, William Jackson himself, took the first photographs of the region. Those same photographs aided in persuading the government to create the world's first national park in Yellowstone. Photographs had alerted people about the starving elk due to severe winters and led to the establishment of the US Biological Survey Elk Refuge.

And this year, Grand Teton National Park was created. Ann knew she wasn't the first photographer here, nor would she be the last. But she wanted to make a name for herself, becoming a renowned woman photographer. Daddy loved her, she knew that, but he wasn't any better than Tom, her ex-fiancé. Didn't see her, didn't recognize her talents, even though he was a progressive thinker in his own way as the managing editor and owner of his magazine featuring the lifestyles of the rich and famous.

Ann wanted to earn her way based on her own merits. Daddy could hardly complain that she'd gone to Jackson, Wyoming, against his wishes when he saw her photographs. Of course, there were plenty of photos, what with all the brochures and articles about Jackson's Hole—the valley between the Teton Range and the Gros Ventre Range—but Ann's talent lay in capturing the new and fresh, seeing past the obvious. Once she got her photographs, then he'd have no choice but to publish them in *View Magazine*. In keeping with the tone of the magazine, she'd slip in as many photos of the rich and famous in the valley, all the dudes and dudines, men and women who stayed on the dude ranches and dressed in flamboyant western wear, many of them rich and famous, indeed.

Still, she couldn't exactly show him any if she couldn't hire a guide.

Sam Covington replayed last night's argument in his mind.

Why couldn't his stubborn father see that they could keep the cattle ranch and let the dudes help and accomplish two things at once? The dudes would pay Covington Ranch for the chance. Worst case, Sam could do like Dick Randall had done on the other side of Yellowstone with his homestead—he started the first dude ranch in the country. Sam could start by outfitting and guiding hunters through the Rockies, too.

He almost wished he hadn't already put the word out. He hadn't expected his father's reaction. The man had been anything but happy to hear the news from someone else first.

Thank goodness, his mother had sent him on an errand in town this morning until they had calmed down. Sam hadn't figured calming down would take him all night and through the morning. He wasn't sure what to expect when he got back to the ranch, where he was doomed to live out his days under the rule of his father and older brother, John, if he didn't change something.

Boots clanking against the wood floors in Joe Jones's Grocery, he made his way to the back of the store to the soda vending machine—newly purchased a month ago. Bob, the store clerk, busied himself tallying up a woman's supplies, so Sam didn't bother him with small talk. The soda cost Sam a pretty nickel. He probably paid more than anyone in the rest of the country, because Joe loved the store motto, "It's all got to be brought over the hill."

The Teton Pass was a harsh overlord, closing the road, cutting off the valley residents' ability to get in and out for far too long, at times. But no matter. Didn't look like Sam would go anywhere anytime soon. He opened the bottle and guzzled the soda, a rare treat for him, but he needed the burn down his throat before heading home to face his father.

Problem was, Sam was too progressive a thinker to work under his father, and one day under his brother. Of that, he could be sure. The way they'd laughed at his proposal last night had said it all.

Cattle ranching had been in a slump for years until about three years ago when the price per head started to rise. But it was too late because Sam had already started dreaming about another future. He couldn't let it go. Never mind the price per hundredweight had reached over twelve dollars.

What was wrong with diversifying? He wanted more from life than taking orders from his brother just because he'd had the misfortunate of being born last in the family. Sure, he'd get an inheritance, but he wouldn't get the main ranch—the family business. And that had cost him Rebecca, he was sure. In the middle ages, he would have been sent off to the abbey to become a monk. He could see the future as clear as the stars on a moonless night.

Tourists had already transformed the valley. Wealthy easterners, and even royalty from across the Atlantic, came to experience the West. Sam figured it wouldn't be long before they came by the droves to see the national parks, heading through the town of Jackson if they wanted to see the Tetons and Yellowstone's volcano.

Dude ranches had popped up all over the Rockies and in the valley, and the Covington Ranch was missing that opportunity. Sam took a swig of his drink and glanced to the front of the store where someone came in as the woman exited with her purchases.

He needed to gain the confidence of the well-paying big-game hunters this winter to outfit and guide them and, in the meantime, convince his father to let him try. He might be twenty-eight and could strike out on his own at any time, but having the Covington name behind him made all the difference. And, well, he couldn't just walk away from his family.

Unfortunately, with his competition, he was already behind the game. But Sam figured there would be plenty more coming to the valley looking for a guide.

He would be ready. That is, if he could convince his father before it was too late.

"Bob." The sheriff stepped up to the counter and spoke to the store clerk. "This is Miss Kirkland."

"Hello, miss," Bob said. "What can I help you with?"

From the shadows at the back of the store, Sam watched the introductions. That gave him a chance to take in the small-framed woman in her decidedly fashionable V-necked purplish frock, a matching scarf hanging over one shoulder. A cloche hid her hair, except for the few soft brown curls that clung to her face and the nape of her neck. Her demeanor and fashion told him she wasn't from around here, no doubt there. He knew a little of such things like fashion and culture from listening to his mother back when she tried to teach his sister, Emily, how to act like a lady. That was before Emily got a mind of her own.

"Any news from Frankston? Miss Kirkland paid him in advance to guide her. He's not back yet from his packing trip. May be another week."

Curious, Sam edged closer. Bob was the man's cousin and

might have some news.

He scratched his scruffy jaw. "Don't reckon you're interested in big game, are you, Miss Kirkland? Or are you looking to just ride horses?"

"The purpose doesn't matter," Miss Kirkland spoke up, her tone confident, and yet Sam didn't miss the slight tremor.

Uh-oh, Sheriff Daniels spotted him in the back of the store.

"Sam." He grinned. "Just the man I was looking for."

Sam stood right where he was and nodded. "Sheriff."

The Covingtons and the sheriff went way back, the man a good friend to Sam's father, and to Sam, as well.

"You're looking to guide, aren't you?"

Last night's argument still fresh on his mind, Sam's mind scrambled for a reply. "Depends on who's asking."

Though he knew exactly who, he needed to know *what* she was asking. Sam took the last swig of his soda.

"Miss Kirkland here needs a guide. She's a photographer."

Sam coughed, choking on his soda. He needed his first guiding opportunity to be one that his father would take seriously. Though pretty, he'd give her that, he wasn't sure he should take on guiding Miss Kirkland.

Her brown eyes grew darker, sending poison arrows through him. He needed to build his reputation. This photography frivolity wouldn't do that for him. His selfishness burned, but his future business, though nonexistent at the moment, was at stake here.

Sam tallied up in his head all the chores his father had given him as they prepared to bring in the herd from grazing the free range, so they could ship them to market in early October before the first snow. The head of cattle they'd keep would need an ample supply of hay. The winter shelter needed repairs. Postholes dug. The list went on. No wonder his father had been fit to be tied when Sam mentioned his idea. Even so, he couldn't take her out for at least a week, and Frankston would be back by then.

But Miss Kirkland gave her own mind before Sam could say a thing.

"Never mind, Sheriff. I wouldn't expect this man capable of providing me with the kind of experience I require for my photographs, considering he obviously doesn't understand the important role photography has played in this region."

She lifted her chin and marched from the store.

The sheriff's frustration glanced off Sam. What now, his longtime confidant Sheriff Daniels had to be disappointed in him, too?

"There are other guides that will take this opportunity, Sam. You told me last week you wanted a chance to prove yourself." He shook his head and followed Miss Kirkland out, leaving Sam standing there, holding his empty soda bottle.

Chapter 2

The Covington Ranch encompassed well over six hundred acres and four hundred head of cattle, and meant that ranching was a never-ending job, especially with only five ranch hands. "Boots" Williams helped Sam mend the fence and finally corralled their forty-five horses. During the summer and fall, their cattle grazed in the national forest on a sizeable allotment. But preparing for the winter months meant days on end cutting and stacking hay. As a result, Sam hadn't seen his father or his brother, John, all day, though John had married years ago and had a home of his own for his family on the property—same as Emily—and Sam didn't see him every day.

That was best, until he found a way to bridle his frustration.

He still fumed at himself for rejecting Miss Kirkland outright. If it weren't for the argument he'd had with his father, he would have heard her out, at the very least.

Finished with his chores, he needed to wash up and entered the back of the sturdy log-cabin ranch house built by his father when he decided to settle in the valley several decades ago. They'd since added to the structure and made modern-day improvements over the last few years—electricity from a water-powered plant over at the canyon near Flat Creek. As for the necessary supplies for building and plumbing, they were freighted over the pass.

Even so, the ranch hands still had to use the privy out back since their quarters weren't plumbed yet, if they ever would be. Sam's father had dragged his feet when it came to progress, and Sam hadn't been the only one surprised when the man had agreed to upgrading the plumbing—but Sam's mother had a way with her husband.

Sam doubted he'd ever meet a woman who had the power to sway him like that, but if he did, he wasn't sure that making her his wife would be the best idea. Then again, who better to be his wife than a woman who could persuade him when he needed persuading? Except he'd already tried that, and it hadn't worked.

His mother appeared, pulling Sam from his melancholy. She'd changed into a fresh set of trousers and cotton work shirt, typical ranch-hand clothing. Years ago, his mother had started a finishing school for young ladies. She finally gave it up after Emily fell in love with dogsledding. The last few years, his mother began to prefer trousers over skirts.

Women in these parts worked beside their men, and just as hard. He wouldn't even have thought about it except an image of Miss Kirkland in her fancy dress trotted across his mind. Did she think she would traverse the backcountry of the Tetons like that?

Admittedly, he'd been hard pressed to take her request seriously. So much for his progressive thinking—he should have been more open-minded. She wasn't the first person from back East to arrive in unsuitable clothing. That fact had kept the Jackson Mercantile and Outfitters busy for years, especially during the cattle slump.

"I've been thinking about that woman you met—Miss Kirkland, was it?—all afternoon," his mother said. "Beggars can't be choosers."

Sam grunted.

She squeezed his shoulder. "Sounds like the sheriff was determined enough to see this woman found a guide. Why don't you go in to town in the morning and make an offer."

"All the way into town?" He hated to think of that wagon ride years ago before his father had bought their first Ford truck.

He squeezed her hand. She was the only one on his side these days. He'd shared his hopes and dreams with her, and unlike his father, she'd listened. A man his age shouldn't have to depend on his mother so much for moral support, but she'd started her own business at one point and understood his need.

"But I can't agree to that without Pa's approval. I work for him, remember? Taking a woman on a Sunday afternoon photographing jaunt isn't exactly my idea of guiding big-game hunters." Or even a first step in progressing to dude ranch status.

His mother sighed. "You have to take the opportunities the Lord sends your way. I can't help but think that was it. You didn't go seeking her out, she came to you."

"I talked to the sheriff, told Bob, people know. So that's not entirely true."

He'd put the word out before talking it through with his father. Mostly he'd talked to people to gauge their reaction. See if they thought it was a good idea. He couldn't help but think his father had been hurt that Sam hadn't come to him with his idea first.

"I need to get supper on," she said. "Let me take care of your father."

Sam would never say it out loud, but he'd always had the feeling he was her favorite. Maybe that was because he was the youngest. But before he could consider it further, a plume of dust rose from the road leading to the ranch, drawing his attention through the front of the cabin. His mother stood next to him and peered through the window.

"Who do you suppose that is?" she asked.

Sam stepped onto the expansive porch held up by pine logs. The sun had already dipped behind the Tetons, though several hours of daylight remained. The white Hupmobile drew near. "The sheriff."

How many times over the years had he looked out this same window to see a horse and buggy coming up the dirt drive to the ranch, or a horse and rider? Seemed strange that within the last few years, most folks drove motorcars—least in the summers. Winter? That was another story here in the valley.

"Looks like he has a passenger, too," his mother said. "A woman. You'd think he'd be too busy trying to get a foothold on the bootleggers, gamblers."

She stepped from the porch in a welcoming stance.

As the motorcar approached, Sam's heart galloped. *Lord, are You giving me another chance?*

Relief swept through him that his father and John were still out working. He'd have to endure teasing otherwise. In fact, he'd be embarrassed if they were here to watch. Guilt slithered through him, longer and wider than the Snake River curved through the valley.

But he jumped to conclusions. He couldn't know if she would ask him again, the way he'd insulted her at the grocery store. In the end, if he didn't want to herd cattle or work the ranch under his father and brother the rest of his life, this could be his chance, as meager as it appeared. In that case, he should apologize and offer to guide her.

Sheriff Daniels steered his Hupmobile around the drive and stopped in front of the house. Before Sam could make it over and assist Miss Kirkland, she stepped out and produced a soft smile to go with her soft hair peeking from her hat. Now that he thought about it, her skin looked. . .uh. . . soft, too, against that pretty lavender dress. He rebuked the unbidden thoughts, but they reminded him of his initial reaction to her request—this wasn't the place for her.

His mother stepped forward and introduced herself. Sam

couldn't help but compare the two women. They were both beautiful flowers, except his mother had proven that she could be a tough weed that could hold her own in this land, and Miss Kirkland looked like a dainty orchid, delicate and unable to survive in a harsh environment. At least she wasn't decked out in the outrageously colorful western clothing of the dudes and dudines populating certain ranches. He wasn't sure why, but that made him smile. Nor was he sure why he wished she would remove her hat so he could see more of her shiny hair.

The sheriff stood next to Miss Kirkland and cleared his throat. Sam realized he'd been staring.

He nodded. "Sheriff, Miss Kirkland."

"Mr. Covington," she said. "I wonder if I might have a word with you."

"You folks come inside," his mother said. "I'll make a pot of coffee, while I get supper on. You're welcome to stay."

The sheriff shook his head. "Thanks, Belle, but I've taken enough time assisting Miss Kirkland and need to get back as soon as possible. No time for supper. But a cup of coffee sounds good."

Inside the cabin, the sheriff hovered in the kitchen with Sam's mother, talking about days gone by. Shame flooded Sam that Miss Kirkland had spent the whole day looking for someone to take Frankston's place, all because Sam had refused her.

He needed to remedy that and fast. He'd hoped they could finish with their business before his father got home, but the telltale sounds of his return resounded out back.

Ann sat on the Davenport sofa, a small lamp on the side table. Light spilled through the large front window that framed Grand Teton. *To live in this house in the shadow of those mountains*—Ann's breath hitched. How very blessed this family was, the people living in this valley were.

She could stare at the view all day but tore her gaze from the window and took in the rustic decor and the walls covered in family photographs on one side, and both elk and moose heads on the other. Barbaric, if they asked her. But they didn't. Regardless, the home was opulent, but in a completely different way from her father's home in New York. Realizing she might look rude in her ogling of the eclectic style, she focused on her hands, pressing them into her lap to keep from wringing them.

The waiting was almost too much.

Coming all this way when the man had clearly rejected her hadn't been her idea, but the sheriff insisted. He'd been kind to assist her in contacting various outfitters and guides throughout the day, as though he had no other matters to attend to. But all were occupied and there was no vacancy in the inn, as it were, though she'd never planned to stay where her father had forbidden.

And here she was reduced to begging. She couldn't go back to her father empty-handed after this deed she'd done. No. She'd have to bring treasure with her to appease the man, and for that, she'd need to convince this cowboy of the importance of her purpose. The value in it, and how it could help him. The sheriff knew the family well and had coached her along the ride out.

She hoped he was right.

Frankston had, in fact, left her a refund she'd discovered at the very hotel where she was staying, for all the good that did her since she'd come all this way.

Oh, Lord, what am I doing here? Already the ambiance and nostalgia of the Old West drew her in, but she was an outsider. Sam Covington's reaction to her plea would go a long way in giving her direction about whether or not she would be forced to return empty-handed.

Mrs. Covington appeared and leaned over Ann, setting a steaming cup on the coffee table. "Here you go, Miss Kirkland. Let me know if I can get you anything else."

Her son, Sam, soon followed, looking as if he'd cleaned up, wearing a clean white cotton shirt and jeans. She might even say he looked spiffy. His jaw was strong and angular, and he'd combed his dark hair back, though she liked how it had curled every which way when she'd first met him in the grocery store. At the thought, she sucked in a breath and hoped he hadn't noticed.

His bright blue eyes warmed, making him appear much friendlier than she'd witnessed this morning. "Sorry for the wait, Miss Kirkland, but my mother won't allow for polite conversation in her home until we're washed up. We do have some culture in these parts."

That news surprised Ann, considering Mrs. Covington wore ranch-hand clothes, the same as Sam. Interesting. But upon meeting her, Ann had instantly liked her.

"Mr. Covington, might we dispense with the formalities? I'd be pleased for you to call me Ann."

Sam positioned himself across from her on the carved-mahogany sofa, catty-cornered to the Davenport. "Call me Sam then. . .Ann."

The way her name sounded on his lips sent a flicker of warmth through her. Ann shifted on the Davenport.

"I'm sure you're wondering why I came all this way when you've already rejected my proposal earlier in the day—"

He drew in a breath to once again reject her, she was certain, and she lifted her palm to stop him. "Please allow me to finish."

After a quick glance back to see Mrs. Covington and Sheriff Daniels caught up in their own conversation, Ann leaned closer. "The sheriff has informed me that it is your desire to start out-fitting and guiding big-game hunters or those from the East that come to stay on the dude ranches. I'm not here to hunt, but I promise I can make this worth your while. You see, I work for a magazine in New York City and these photographs will likely grace the pages, and of course, I would acknowledge the man who made this possible. Don't you see how this could benefit your business goals?"

Sam's eyes narrowed before he leaned against the sofa back, his hand rubbing his mouth and chin. Was he contemplating her words? Or had she failed to convince him by saying too much? Maybe he didn't want the kind of notoriety her offer could bring—and Ann didn't deny she was making promises she wasn't sure she could keep. It all depended on her father's reaction, and she felt confident he would be delighted, or else she wouldn't have gone to the trouble. Then again, maybe she would have. Once she'd envisioned coming to Wyoming, she hadn't been able to let the idea go.

"I want these photographs to be the most spectacular the magazine, and maybe even the world, has ever seen." She was all in now, laying out her heart, and this man could very well tromp all over it, just like Tom had. The only difference, Ann wasn't engaged to Sam Covington.

"Go on," he said, light flickering in his eyes, encouraging her.

She inched to the edge of the sofa. "I've set my goals high, but not unlike other renown women photojournalists of our time. The sheriff, he made it sound like you've done some climbing and adventuring, and know your way around the mountains to places that others haven't been."

Voices resounded from somewhere behind. Sam's eyes flicked over her shoulder then back to her. He leaned forward, placing his elbows on his thighs, giving Ann a sense of urgency that in a few moments she would lose her chance to convince him. Sitting so close, the clean smell of his soap wafted over her.

She drew in a breath to give this one more try in her most persuasive tone, but Sam held up a hand. Ann's hope died.

"My turn, now." He flashed her the hint of a smile, all while monitoring the activities behind her. "Let me extend my apology for turning you down earlier. I'm agreeable to your proposal, and I would have made the offer the minute you stepped from the sheriff's vehicle, had you allowed me. Unfortunately, there is the matter of convincing my father of my new venture. I work for him, too."

Ann contained the squeal inside. She could hardly believe her good fortune. "You mean you'll do it? If you can, that is?"

Sam tensed and rose to face whom she presumed must be his father.

"And who have we here?"

Ann turned to see the face belonging to the deep voice and immediately saw Sam's resemblance to his handsome, much older, silver-haired father.

"This is Miss Kirkland," Sam said. "Sheriff Daniels brought her out to talk to me."

"Pleased to meet you. I'm Sam's father, Zeb Covington." Broad-shouldered and smelling of horses, cows, and hay, the man's smile deepened. "And this is Sam's brother, John."

Another cowboy stepped forward and nodded. He looked more like Sam's mother. "Howdy."

"John, I need to have a word with Sam and Miss Kirkland."

John nodded. "I'll head on home, then, and check on Lucy and the girls."

When John was gone, Mr. Covington's smile dimmed, if

only a little. "What business do you have with my son?"

Mrs. Covington sauntered up to her husband and squeezed his arm. "Now, Zeb, you should get cleaned up, too, before you bother this young woman. See to it now."

He bristled, unwilling to back down. Ann almost felt like she was facing off with her own father. It was clear Sam wouldn't fare well in this conversation.

"Allow me to dispel your concerns. I'm proposing to hire your son as a guide. I work for *View Magazine* in New York." She added that tidbit to garner his respect.

Ann held her breath. She understood Sam's dilemma in working for his father, his need to branch out on his own all too well.

Sam's father stared him down, sending Ann's hopes plummeting.

Chapter 3

S am steeled himself for his father's words, hating that Miss Kirkland...Ann...would hear them, too. And he'd been so close.

Why, Lord? Why did You give me another chance? Why did she come all this way just to have my father shoot me down in front of her?

Sam fisted his hands at his side, reining in his disrespectful attitude. If only his father would respect him as well.

"Go," his mother said, her tone brooking no argument. She gripped the man's arms and made to usher him away. "I'll not have you carrying on with our guest until you're cleaned up."

His mother had come to his rescue again. Sam considered that maybe he should stand on his own, but now wasn't the time or place to face-off with his father about his future, and possibly, the future of the Covington Ranch. Then again, his brother would have his say on top of that.

His father out of the room, his mother returned and smiled. "I'm so glad I put that rule in place when I set up my household."

She turned her attention to Sam. "Now, Son, I hope you've already told Miss Kirkland that you agree to her offer."

"Please, call me Ann."

"All right, Ann it is." His mother smiled. "And please call me Belle."

His mother looked at him, waiting for an answer. "Sam?"

He nodded, opening his mouth to get in a word but failing.

"Good, then that's settled." His mother took Ann's hands between hers. "I'm sorry you had to trouble yourself looking for someone to take on this task. And to make up for any more inconvenience, I insist on having you stay with us for the duration of your business here."

Ann's uncertainty was evident on her face. "Oh no, I couldn't. That would be too much trouble."

Sam's heart jumped to his throat. What was his mother doing?

"It's no trouble at all. I have extra rooms upstairs for guests. This way, you'll save time in your endeavors. Sam won't have to go all the way into town."

But his mother was right in her thinking. The trip to town and back wouldn't leave much time for guiding if she planned on daily outings.

Ann sagged, clearly torn in her decision. "I. . .I thank you for the offer. My father was very specific in that he didn't want me to stay on a. . .dude ranch."

His mother's laughter was musical, bringing harmony.

"Then it's settled. Covington Ranch is nothing more than a cattle ranch."

Ann's forehead creased slightly. "But what about Mr. Covington? I had the distinct impression that he wasn't agreeable to Sam guiding me. Not only that, I'll need a darkroom, so you see, I couldn't possibly stay here."

Sam admired her forthrightness and realized that she was much stronger than he'd given her credit for. He'd made a judgment based solely on her appearance. Looked like his mother had met her match.

"Nonsense," his mother said. "You'll have everything you need here. Won't she, Sam?"

When his mother winked at him, heat rushed up his neck. Good thing the summer had left him suntanned to hide it. He bridled his ridiculous reaction. His mother glanced at the sheriff and ushered Ann to the door, in much the same way that she'd ushered his father out of the room. "Sam will be in town in the morning to pick you up and bring you back to the ranch. I'll get you settled in, and then you can get on with your business. But I must say, I'm looking forward to having another female in this house for a while. How long do you plan to stay in the valley?"

"A month at least, maybe less, depending on the weather. I can't afford to get trapped here if it snows."

His mother chuckled and released her. Ann's gaze flicked to Sam, a question in her eyes. But what question, he couldn't know. "I thank you for your generosity," she said.

Sheriff Daniels followed her across the porch. "I knew I could count on at least one of the Covington's to take this on."

The next morning, Sam arrived in town to pick up Ann, with instructions from his mother to see to the woman's wardrobe for backcountry travel. He'd also make sure Leonard at Jackson Mercantile didn't sell her the gaudier wear of the drugstore cowboys and dudes around town. Sam couldn't abide by that. It was the one thing he agreed with his father on.

He parked the truck in front of the Jackson Hotel, thinking on his father's words to him last night. They'd been so much different from the night before. One day could change everything.

"Your mother's invited a guest into our home, and I'll thank you to accommodate her specific needs." His father had smiled then, and rubbed the back of his neck. *"I can be stubborn at times, Son, I know that. I thank God for the day I married your mother so she can talk sense into me when needed. That said, understand that I'm giving you this chance. Agreed?"*

He and his father seemed to contend like his sister and their mother more than a decade earlier. Back then, his father encouraged Emily in her dreams, like running for the city council. Now his mother took up for Sam.

He hadn't been able to sleep a wink, thinking how his father had given him this opportunity, but escorting a woman photographer around the region hadn't exactly been what he'd hoped for in the way of proving himself. Fear and doubt had eaten away at him all night. He'd understood what his father's words meant all right.

The man had given Sam this *one* chance.

There was nothing for it. He'd give it all he had. He rounded the parked truck to call for Ann just as she stepped from the hotel, the town buzzing with people and businesses—unlike when he was growing up. But Ann stood out from the crowd. Sam wasn't sure if Ann stood out to everyone, or just him. He cleared his mind and made his way toward her, feeling a bounce to his steps today he hadn't felt yesterday.

"Miss Kirkland." Sam tipped his hat.

"I thought we'd dispensed with the formality, Sam. Remember? Please call me Ann."

How could he have forgotten? Something about this woman left him with scrambled eggs for brains. "Ann it is."

Her pretty smile brightened her face even more, and his spirits. "Thank you, Sam. I like that name. It's a good, strong name."

He liked the sound of his name coming from Ann. But he wasn't sure he liked the awkward feeling stirring inside. He wasn't sure what to say to her compliment.

"Before we head back to the ranch, we should get you outfitted for travel in the backcountry. Let's leave your luggage with the hotel for now. We'll come back to retrieve it."

"I was going to suggest the very same thing. Best to take care of that now. There's another chore that I should have taken care of yesterday." She tugged an envelope from her dainty tasseled purse and handed it to Sam. "This was what I paid to Frankston who broke our agreement, so I assume the amount will be acceptable to you."

Sam swallowed. He'd not been much of a businessman to agree to her terms without negotiating the finances first, but then he'd assumed she would be good for the money. He'd been right. He reached for the envelope and their fingers brushed. Sam wished he hadn't noticed. "I thank you for your payment, and I hope I can deliver."

That smile again. "Oh, I'm sure you will. That's only a deposit, by the way. The rest will be paid to you upon completion of our business."

He swallowed to chase away the sudden dryness in his throat. For some reason, thinking of her leaving didn't sit well in his gut. He scraped his hat from his head.

"I'll be honest with you," she said. "I'd love to see this place painted in snow. It would be such a winter wonderland. The photographs would make my heart sing, but I can't stay that long. I need to get out before the first snow."

Sam didn't have the heart to tell her no one could accurately predict when that would be. It could come sooner than expected. Or later than usual. "Because?"

"I need to make it back to New York before my father returns from his honeymoon in Europe. I've heard stories of people getting trapped in the valley because of the Teton Pass."

"Ah yes, the infamous Pass. That doesn't happen too often."

Sam set his Stetson back where it belonged.

"But it does happen." She arched a brow.

"With me as your guide, you'll be done in plenty of time. Don't you worry about the pass."

He hoped he could trust himself on that. Snow would certainly happen on the pass before it blanketed the valley. Then the residents would store their gas-powered trucks and cars away for the winter and bring out the horse-drawn sleighs. The thought of showing Ann her winter wonderland in the Covington sleigh kindled something inside, but he quickly doused that spark.

Ann allowed Sam to escort her around the square and down a couple of blocks, automobiles kicking up dirt and dust from the road. She spotted someone on a horse, just as a motorcar whizzed by and spooked the poor animal.

"Doesn't seem that long ago when there was nothing but horses and buggies," Sam said and ushered her on. "The Jackson Mercantile is just across the way."

"I've seen a lot of changes in the last decade, as well," she said. "Makes my head spin."

"If you stay in the valley until it snows you'll see this place go back a few decades."

"Oh?" She glanced his way. "How's that?"

"The snow's too deep and the roads don't get plowed. Everyone puts away their automobiles in favor of the old reliable horse and sleigh."

Ann gasped. "How beautiful that must be."

Sam's eyes twinkled. "The snow is a lot of trouble, but then again, seeing the horses pulling the sleighs is right pretty."

"Does the Covington family have one?"

He nodded and pressed his hand against the small of her back to direct her. "It's been in the family since my father came to the valley."

Sam regaled her with stories about the valley, the town, and the holidays on the ranch. The way he talked about his home, Ann could tell he loved this place. With the majestic mountains and scenery all around them, she could understand why so many, including herself, flocked here. She predicted that number would increase in the future, but with Sam—his love of his home ran deep. Funny, part of why she'd come here was to *escape* the place she called home.

Though she hadn't met Frankston, and was still perturbed with him for not keeping up his end of their agreement, Ann was glad things turned out the way they had. For some reason, she believed Sam was the right guide for her needs. As Providence would have it, Sam seemed to need her as much as she needed him.

But to make this dream happen, she needed proper clothing and was grateful for his assistance. That he'd offered in the first place surprised her. Now she wasn't sure why. He proved himself more than capable.

He was a completely different sort of fellow than what she

was accustomed to in the city, especially compared to the crowd she spent her time photographing for the magazine. Especially compared to Tom. She chafed at the comparison, wishing she could banish the man from her thoughts.

No. Sam was rugged, tough, and manly in a different kind of way. In fact, he was the sort of ruggedly handsome man that movie stars tried to portray in their movies but in person fell far short, or it seemed to Ann, considering those she'd met.

Ann decided she liked Sam. Though he hadn't seemed too keen on her yesterday, he'd obviously warmed to the idea of assisting her in photographing the region, and the potential for-tuitous benefit of their joint venture.

He cleared his throat, drawing Ann's attention back to the present. They stood in front of Jackson Mercantile and Outfitters.

"You ready?" he asked, gifting her with a smile.

"I am." She nodded, eager to purchase the supplies for their adventure to see the Tetons in all their grandeur, to take the photographs she needed in order to make all this trouble worthwhile.

Her only regret was that she hoped to be gone before the snow that would coat the scenery in white icing, something utterly photographical. With her father due back in late October, no, she had to be home before then. But maybe her pictures would be enough to convince her father to grant her another chance. Possibly spend a few wintry months here. For the sake of the magazine, of course.

"After you, then." Sam gestured for her to enter the premises ahead of him.

Ann stepped through the door he held for her, sucking in a quick breath. She'd fully expected shopping in the "last of the Wild West" to be different than the fashions she'd find in the haute couture shops of Manhattan, of which she was somewhat familiar, considering her father's magazine thrived on featuring the lifestyles of movie stars and the upper class. She'd seen plenty of photographs of western-clad cowboys, especially in the dude-ranch brochures, but standing in the store in person sent a rush through her.

She was really going to do this. Squeezing her hands together, she lifted them to her mouth in glee but then realized Sam eyed her curiously.

"I'm sorry, I must look like a silly schoolgirl to you." She seasoned her words with a smile.

"Not at all," he said, but she wasn't sure she believed him, the way his measuring eyes took her in.

She'd love to know what he was thinking. "Well, Sam, what shall I wear on our excursions into the wilderness?"

Sam's tanned complexion deepened, and he tugged at his collar.

Had she embarrassed the man? She stifled a giggle, or else he would think her a silly city girl, after all.

"I'll have a word with Leonard, who runs the place." Sam leaned in. "I'll instruct him you're not wearing any of that diamond-pointed ornamental western wear you see around town in all the purples and oranges. Just regular work clothes will do."

Sam scratched his jaw. "I'd suggest breeches as opposed to a divided skirt for riding. Are you up for that?"

"I'll wear whatever you think most appropriate."

"We're in autumn now. Don't expect the first snow for another month, if that, but you'll need some winter clothes, too, just in case. You never know in the mountains when the weather will turn, or if it'll snow."

"I never doubted that."

He hesitated.

"Is there something else?" she prodded.

"I'm assuming, since you came all this way wanting someone to take you into the wilds of the Tetons, that you can ride a horse. But I might have assumed wrong." He cocked his brow, looking for some weakness in their plans, it seemed.

She patted his arm. "Rest assured, Sam, I'm an experienced rider, though not in rugged terrain like this." In the English style of riding, but no matter. "I trust you to lead me there and back."

That answer appeared to satisfy Sam. He nodded before calling the proprietor—Leonard, was it?—over for assistance.

Sam clapped the man on the back, obviously familiar with him. "Leonard, I'd like to introduce you to Ann Kirkland from New York City."

"How-do, Miss Kirkland from New York City. Pleased to meet you." Leonard thrust out his hand. "What can I do you fer?"

Funny to think anyone still talked like that, but it was in keeping with the western atmosphere, Ann reminded herself.

She opened her mouth to speak, but Sam rested his hand on her shoulder. She instinctively knew he wanted her silence on the matter. Ann bit back her words, though she'd wanted to speak her mind. This was the twentieth century, after all.

"I'll be guiding Miss Kirkland through the backcountry. I need you to set her up, according to her budget, with the appropriate breeches, shirts, hats, belts, all manner of gear, everything you'd supply to a man going hunting."

Sam's words didn't faze Leonard. "Right this way, miss."

Leonard moved through the store and Ann followed, pursing her lips.

Displeasure rumbled through her chest that Sam had left off the specific purpose of their outdoors adventure. She fought the need to blurt out she would be photographing the region for a magazine, not hunting—why, oh why, did that bother Sam? Or did she have it all wrong, his omission a simple oversight? Nevertheless, she had the distinct impression that he would prefer it if she were actually going on a hunting trip. If she were actually a man, and that way he could prove to his father he should continue outfitting and guiding, rather than playing the part of just another ranch hand on his father's spread. On that count, she wasn't sure she could blame him. She was on a similar mission herself.

But what did Ann care if Sam appreciated her photography or not? She was paying him to do a job. If only her disappointment didn't rankle so.

Chapter 4

Sam sat astride his spunky palomino, Ace, and watched Ann atop Gracie, a gentle brown mare, as she stared across the Snake River, the Tetons looming majestic, distinct peaks pointing to the sky.

"I see snow up there."

"Could have snowed in the summer, but likely it's just old snow from previous winters that never melted, or a glacier. You can get a good close look at the middle peak glacier from one of the mountain trails."

He wasn't sure he'd be able to take her there, but he'd take things slowly. Gauge her abilities before he took her out into the Wyoming wilderness. Today he'd brought her to the Snake River that flowed from Jackson Lake through the valley on its journey west, where it would empty into the Columbia River.

"I might not be here to greet the winter snow, but I certainly came at the right time. The colors are beautiful."

Cottonwoods grew up and down the riverbank, and aspen peppered the hillsides. Leaves were already turning brilliant gold and orange. Add to that the evergreens, making the forest and mountain range look like a canvas that God Himself had painted.

The autumn colors never failed to fill Sam with awe, the same awe he now saw on Ann's face. He smiled to himself. The sun had brought just enough color to her cheeks that his gaze lingered on Ann longer than he had a right. Dressed in the clothes more fitting for their endeavor, thanks to their shopping excursion, Ann's appearance had transformed.

What surprised him was that he couldn't decide which Ann he liked better—he actually missed seeing her in her pretty dress. But maybe he'd get that chance again. Besides, she'd hired him to do a job. He had no business thinking about how he liked the way she looked in her dresses or in her shirt and breeches. No business whatsoever.

Her long sigh drifted to him on the cool breeze. "What's wrong?" he asked.

"I have a collection of photographs of the Tetons back home taken by a local resident, Hank Crandall. Ever hear of him?" she asked.

"A course. Everyone knows him. Takes photographs of the dudes in their drugstore cowboy clown suits, too," he said. "Makes a good living that way."

There'd been plenty of photographers come to capture the beauty; Ann wouldn't be the first. But he'd keep that to himself. Likely, she knew already.

"But those photographs could never do these peaks justice," she said. "I could sit here all day and look at the mountains."

Sam thought he could sit here all day, too, but Ann had drawn his attention from the lofty peaks before them. He forced his thoughts to the business at hand.

"Best get over that because if I guide you to unseen territory, it's going to take time to get there and back." He figured they'd need to prepare for a longer packing trip at some point, as well. Places that would tickle her photographer fancy. Places that even other photographers hadn't seen. But there was no getting in and out in one day.

In fact, the possibilities were endless. She could stay a year and never see everything worth seeing. But she had a month, and that was it. Planned to leave before it started snowing, she'd said.

That was a shame. Nothing more beautiful than Jackson's Hole in the winter. Sam found himself thinking once again about driving her around in the old Covington horse-drawn sleigh. Unbidden thoughts, those.

"Might as well get to work." She climbed down from Gracie, speaking a few soft words to the mare.

True to her word, she was relatively experienced with horses. Sam liked her soft-spoken ways with Gracie, too.

"I know I'm not the first to photograph the mountains from this angle, but this is a good place to start." She began unpacking her camera from the saddlebags. "But I want my own pictures. Maybe I can bring out something not already captured by others."

All photographer-talk to Sam. "Might as well," he said. He slid from the saddle to join her.

She looked at the top of the box camera. "Can you help me with the tripod?"

Sam set to work. "That's some sort of camera you got there."

"Isn't it spiffy? It's a Rolleiflex Twin Lens Reflex. It just came out this year. Daddy got me one as soon as it was available. I can work much faster, and it's not as heavy." Ann talked on about her camera, explaining the new improvements.

She was passionate about her photography. It warmed Sam that she was able to do what she loved. Her camera positioned to photograph the Tetons, Ann stood back.

"Want to see?" Her eyes shimmered with contagious excitement.

"Sure."

"Look down through the viewfinder, like this, see?" She showed him where to look then stood back, but not nearly far enough. He looked through the window of her camera and into her world and saw the mountains he'd seen every day of his life made more special because of Ann.

Far too aware of her proximity, he cleared his throat and pulled away from the camera.

"Well?" Her face was expectant.

"It looks like the mountains."

"Is that all?" Disappointment laced her voice.

"No...well..." Unsure what to say, Sam peered through her camera again.

His mother had charged him with preparing a darkroom for her. He'd set the trunk filled with the equipment and chemicals she'd brought with her in the small closet across the hall from his room. At that moment, he'd known that she was serious about her work.

"I'm sure you're a talented photographer," he said, "and I can't wait to see your photographs."

She beamed. "Sam Covington, you have no idea what you're in for."

He chuckled. Sam had the strong feeling that Ann was entirely correct—he didn't know what he was in for where she was concerned.

Warmth expanded in Ann's chest as she watched Sam gaze through the top of her new camera.

Tom had never shown the slightest interest in Ann's photography outside of the work she did for the magazine, at least, and then it was only to please her father. Of that, there could be no doubt.

Ann frowned. Why did she insist on comparing this man to her ex-fiancé? A breeze sent his hat flying, and he snatched it back. His brown curly hair whipped around his tanned face, accentuating his rugged clean-shaven jaw as his blue eyes pierced

Ann's gaze. She stepped up to the tripod and looked through the camera, hoping he hadn't seen the heat infusing her cheeks.

She'd come here to make a name for herself. Maybe become a female Hank Crandall or some other famous photographer, she didn't know. But she *did* know that she loved the crisp mountain air, the way the sun beat down on her in this valley. She knew, too, that she enjoyed Sam's company.

"Why don't you go and do something while I work."

He angled his head. "What?"

She laughed. "You know, fiddle with your horse, or go down to the river. I can't work with you standing over me like that."

Giving her a funny look, he pressed his cowboy hat back on his head. "You're the boss." Then he took off toward the river.

"Wait, not in my line of sight," she said. "Not in front of the camera. Go that way."

He half smiled, half frowned, and led the horses to the side, mumbling to himself and making Ann smile. The man was definitely photogenic, and she'd get a few of him, too, before it was all over.

But right now, she didn't need the distraction and focused her attention on the Tetons, hoping to compare her work to what she'd seen before, hoping to capture what hadn't been photographed.

The images had been what she expected, but they wouldn't be enough to impress anyone, especially her father. Ann hadn't taken photographs of the Tetons that everyone hadn't already seen. Though she wouldn't trade that moment when she stood across the river looking at the massive peaks for anything, she'd have to do better if she wanted to prove herself.

Except, if she were to believe Sam's reaction to the pictures this morning, she'd already proven herself to at least one person. She hadn't meant for him to see them yet, when she'd grabbed the dry photographs from where they were clipped in the makeshift darkroom. Sam caught her in the hallway on his way to breakfast.

He'd taken them from her and seemed to soak in each image, quirking his brow at her when he'd seen the ones she'd taken of him. "These are wonderful."

And then he'd looked at her long and hard, his approval filling a deep need and expanding in her chest. If only her father ever reacted to anything she'd done like that. If only Tom. . .

But she'd explained she needed to see some place new and fresh, some place not yet photographed. Sam understood, and they now traveled to a place he claimed no one knew about, save him. Ann still hadn't decided what she thought about his willingness to help her in such a way, offering up his secret places.

Gracie trailed Ace into the thick forest, climbing high and aiming for the rocky face of a hill until it finally gave way to a canyon. Sam allowed Ann to stop and take as many photographs as she liked, but he urged her on to their final destination. They'd already been on the trail for a couple of hours when he reined his horse over to a small brook that tumbled over mossy rocks.

He slid from the saddle. "Let's take a break. It won't be too much longer, I promise."

Ann had never spent so much time in the saddle and was already feeling the effects. She climbed from her horse as well, aware that Sam watched her. "If you say so."

"How are you doing?"

She smiled, hoping to hide that she was already weary. "I'm good, thank you. I'm more than good, in fact. I'm enjoying the beauty. Thank you, Sam, for doing this."

"Just doing the job you hired me to do."

Well, that was true. She felt silly. "Are you sure you want to share wherever it is we're going with the world?"

Sam whipped his hat off his head. "I can tell it means a lot to you. You want your photographs to be the best. But I'm curious. Why is that so important to you? That is, if you don't mind my asking."

Ann found a boulder to rest on while Sam drank his water. "The sheriff told me something about you that first day on the drive out. That you were trying to make your own way. Maybe you and I have that in common, Sam Covington."

Sam stared at a point beyond her but didn't reply. When he replaced his hat, beneath the brim, his eyes locked with hers. The quickest of moments, his look made her heart jump.

"Ready?" he asked.

"As I'll ever be," she said.

But Ann wished he'd responded to what she'd said. Maybe he hadn't been prepared for her to turn the conversation to him so avoided the discussion entirely.

A half hour later the trail opened up and Sam rode next to her, the horses climbing over rocky terrain. Somewhere in the distance, water roared.

"I don't want to be just another ranch hand for the rest of my life," he said, "working for my father and my brother, who'll inherit the ranch. And. . ."

"And?"

"I had a girl once. Why would she want to marry me?"

Oh, Sam. . . Ann instinctively knew he wouldn't appreciate pity, but she wasn't sure what to say, so she said nothing. She'd give him the space he needed, now that he finally opened up. Let him talk.

"I shouldn't have said anything." He rode up ahead of her.

"No, wait." She urged Gracie forward and next to Ace. "Look, you don't have to share anything personal, if you don't want to. But we're spending long hours together, and I'd like to know more about you."

He tugged on the reins, bringing Ace to a stop. "Here it is."

Ann didn't need to be told—the waterfall filled her vision and ears. "It's. . .so. . . beautiful."

Her focus drawn to the scenery before her, she wasn't sure when she'd dismounted, but Sam was already helping to unpack her camera. "I can't believe that you've brought me to a place that no one else has seen. How is that even possible?"

He grinned. "Maybe I'm not the only one, but there's not a lot of traffic in and out of here, as you can tell. The game hunters follow the game trails, and the mountain climbers, well, they have their path. This. . .this is all mine, as far as I know. The valley isn't all that populated. Those of us who live here, and grew up here, well, we know places."

"I haven't seen a photograph of this waterfall before." For the first time since she'd arrived in the valley, a real hope infused her that she might actually accomplish what she'd set out to do. All that thanks to this man. "I can't help but be thankful that you're the one to guide me and not Mr. Frankston."

Sam held her gaze for only a second, his mouth pressed in a grim line, and she wasn't sure why. Had he changed his mind about her photographing this place?

Regret burned in her chest. "Are you sure you don't want to keep this place to yourself?" What was she doing? Why was she giving him a chance to back out? She wanted to show the world, even if he didn't.

"Can't see as it hurts to take pictures. Nobody knows how to get here except me. Now you, and I doubt you could find your way back."

"No, but maybe others could."

"No matter." He looked at her long and hard, something dancing behind his eyes. "Besides, I like seeing how happy it makes you."

Ann wasn't sure of what to make of the wrangler's comment, or how it affected her breathing. But she couldn't remember the last time anyone had cared whether or not she was happy.

Chapter 5

Two weeks of trekking through the valley, mountains, and gorges on horseback had gone by much too quickly. He'd even taken the pretty photographer on a four-day packing trip through Garnet Canyon. His mother had come along, too—her old-fashioned ways wanting to protect Ann's reputation.

He'd witness the happiness his parents shared, even when they were mad at each other. But he hadn't thought that would ever be possible for him—and he was crazy because it *wasn't* possible for him. Ann. . .she was heading home at the end of the month—before the first snow, she kept saying, as if anyone could know exactly when that would come. Ann was nothing more than Sam's client, and he'd best remember that.

He took off his hat and scratched his head as he watched Ann climbing over the rocks to get near the stream as it trickled over boulders and finally spilled down the hundred-foot drop. Snow came at any time in the higher elevations, and they were prepared for that. But the way the clouds hung low and dark today told Sam that Ann needed to hurry and take her photographs.

Enthralled with the beauty of nature, she hadn't bothered getting her camera out yet. Though he hated to admit it, Sam was enthralled with Ann. Watching her brought on a smile, and also not a little concern.

"Be careful, will you?" he called, wishing he could pull the words back because Ann jerked up and almost stumbled.

"I'm fine. Why don't you join me?"

Her words held the teasing tone she'd used more often lately. As if they were becoming more than wilderness guide and client. Like they were friends now. Yes, that was it. He and Ann were friends. His heart couldn't help but wish for something more. Would she write him once she was back in Manhattan?

Enough dreaming about a future that could never happen. Sam should have learned that lesson already when he'd fallen in love with Rebecca. But with no future or hope of his own, other than life as a cowpoke on his father's ranch, he had nothing to offer her when a wealthy man from back East came to Jackson and wooed her away from him. That's why he couldn't stand to see the dudes in all their gaudy attire.

The memories lashed at him, reminding him to put all thoughts aside of Ann as more than a client. When she disappeared behind a boulder, he shoved from the tree he'd been leaning against and hiked over. Might need to assist her down and make sure she didn't take an unexpected tumble. Sam climbed over the larger rocks, the roar of the falls filling his ears long before he could get close enough for the mist to leave his face damp.

On her knees, Ann bent down and ran her fingers through the crystal-clear river. In that moment, leaning over to caress the river surging from the falls, Ann appeared more graceful than any creature he'd ever seen.

"I love that you always take me to the waterfalls. I understand why." She glanced back at him and smiled. "Isn't this the most beautiful thing you've ever seen?"

"Yes."

Ann got to her feet and swiped at the knees of her breeches. She blew a stray hair from her face and glanced at the sky then back at Sam. "I'd better get busy."

A slight frown tugged at her smile.

"What's wrong?" he asked, following her back to the horses and her camera equipment.

"Ah, Sam, you know me too well already." Her hand on the saddlebag, she turned to face him. "I'll need to head home sooner than I wanted, if the snow is going to come so soon this year. Getting in and out of the valley won't be fun if I wait too long. Nor can I risk getting snowed in. I. . ."—she averted her gaze—"I don't want to leave."

Sam's chest constricted. *I don't want you to leave.* But she referred to the beauty and grandeur of the Tetons, and all the places he'd shown her. He wanted with all his heart to reach up and cup her cheek. When she glanced back at him, her soft brown eyes searching, Sam did just that.

Her skin felt silky against his rough palm. "And I'll miss you, but at least you have your photographs."

What are you doing?

Ann's gaze took in his face, settled on his lips, and sent Sam's heart into his throat. He leaned closer, and in his head a church bell tower rang its warnings. Not the right time, place, or thing to do.

And to his great pleasure, Ann met him halfway. That was all the invitation Sam needed. He covered her mouth with his, gently, tasting her sweet lips, wanting to wrap her in his arms, but he restrained himself. He cupped her cheeks instead, savoring this moment, wanting to tuck it away and keep it with him forever.

A young elk leapt from the trees, crossing their path and disrupting the moment. Ann stepped back, leaving Sam to drop his empty hands to his side, but only for a moment. He stiffened, wondering what had set the creature running, and hoping they hadn't gotten between the elk and a group of hunters.

"Oh, I'd love to take a photograph!"

Something big crashed through the woods behind them. Sam grabbed the reins of both horses. "Get on your horse."

"Why? What's happening?"

"Just do it." He kept hold of the reins in case the horses got spooked and tried to run, speaking in reassuring tones to the animals. Watching the tree line for movement, he pulled his Winchester from his saddle scabbard and quickly chambered it, glad he'd opted for a bigger caliber weapon than his .22 varmit rifle.

A grizzly crashed through the trees after the elk. Focused on getting his prey, he didn't see them. Sam held tightly to the reins when Ace and Gracie grew antsy. Pulse roaring in his ears, he needed to harness his own emotions. Sam didn't think he'd need to use his rifle, since the bear disappeared.

"Oh my," Ann said. She'd managed to pull her camera out and was attempting to catch what she could. "That's not something you see every day."

"Definitely not. This time of year they feed on whitebark pine nuts, roots, and berries. Rarely see them chasing elk unless it's a young calf in the spring. They'll eat carrion, or winterkill animals, though. Young or old, and injured. That elk looked a little too healthy to me."

"Winterkill?"

"Animals already dead due to a hard winter." Sam climbed into the saddle.

Ace trembled beneath him, and Gracie whinnied. Ann did a good job of soothing her.

"We should leave now," Sam said.

"But I haven't taken photographs yet. I don't think I got a good shot of the bear."

Sam scratched his chin, weighing the situation. She trusted

him to guide her and keep her safe. While it was common to see bears when you trekked through the wilderness, the sight of that six- maybe seven-hundred-pound hungry creature unsettled Sam, and the horses could sense his fear. "I know. We'll come back before you have to leave, I promise."

What are you doing making promises, Sam?

"I trust you to know best." She smiled, though he read disappointment in her eyes. "Something else I'd like to do before I leave is photograph the Covington Ranch. Take pictures of you and your family, the cattle and horses." Ann twisted to stick her square camera back into the saddlebag. "I can't thank you enough for your generosity."

"Don't tell me you thought my mother would have it any other way?" He grinned, urged Ace forward, leading Ann back to the valley, his eyes and ears alert to the danger brought with the grizzly. His heart alert to the danger brought on by his growing feelings for the woman photographer from back East.

For the rest of the day, Ann had not been able to stop thinking about that moment when Sam had kissed her. The way his hands gently cupped her cheeks and the feel of his lips against hers, as though he truly cherished her. How she had wished for him to put his arms around her—but they'd been interrupted by wildlife, no less. The bear crashing through the woods had been exciting enough but hadn't shoved thoughts of the kiss aside.

That evening, Ann headed down the stairs after cleaning up,

her thoughts lingering on the kiss they'd shared. She was grateful they'd returned in time to enjoy dinner with Sam's family. In the higher elevation today, she'd gotten chilled to the bone and couldn't seem to warm up enough, so instead of putting on her usual dinner attire, which consisted of one of the dresses she'd brought, she donned a pair of her denim breeches. She was growing fond of dressing this way.

Loosely holding on to the banister, she descended the steps, taking in the aroma of roasting beef and fresh baked bread, and listening to the laughter and voices of a family who loved one another.

Pausing on the stairs, she savored the moment, soaking it all in.

Over by the stone fireplace, Sam regaled his father and brother with the tale about their near run-in with the grizzly—not so unusual to see bears, but chasing an elk this time of year set the men on edge. They argued over bringing the errant behavior to the national park ranger's attention, expressing concern over their cattle. The discussion launched into whether to drive the cattle or ship them over the pass now. Though the debate had grown serious, she could hear the deep respect and love in the men's voices.

Regret found its way to her bones, just like the chill from this afternoon. Regret of not having a close-knit family, like Sam had. She wasn't sure she'd ever had that, even when her mother was still alive.

"Good evening, Ann." Belle called to her, breaking her from her melancholic thoughts.

Sam's mother smiled at Ann from the long dining table where she set places for seven people. Belle fed the ranch hands, too, until they could replace their cook who'd quit and gone to California.

"Evening." Suddenly aware of the pause in conversation and everyone's eyes upon her, Ann descended the rest of the way. "I had hoped to be down soon enough to help. Let me finish setting the table for you."

She grabbed a dish from the stack.

Sam appeared by her side. "And I'll bring in the stew," he said to his mother but stared at Ann.

"Thank you." Belle squeezed Sam's arm, and he followed her to get the stew.

John joined Ann at the table and started helping set the places. Ann wished it were Sam instead. John's wife, Lucy, had left to visit her family in Idaho until John came to get her.

She glanced across the room to see Zeb Covington cleaning a Winchester rifle—was that the same one Sam had carried today? She didn't miss that he studied her from beneath his thick brows. John reached for another plate, and it clanked, jarring her back to the moment. Sam appeared, carrying a big steaming pot of stew.

During supper, Ann sat between Sam's mother and father, and across from Sam, John, and two of the five ranch hands filling the rest of the places. Sam's father, John, and three of the hands would take the cattle to be shipped over the pass to Victor this week, it was decided. As if to put an end to further discussion on the matter, Mr. Covington asked Ann about her photographs.

His questions told Ann that he now respected what she did, and the approving look he gave Sam said even more. Sam even sat a little taller. She had a feeling this was only the beginning for him. Ann couldn't help but compare this evening to the rare family time she enjoyed with her sister, father, and Marilyn—the woman who'd become her stepmother. And with Tom—that is, before she'd broken off her engagement.

Life in Manhattan couldn't have been further removed. The culture, the people, and lifestyles were worlds apart. Ann had wanted to escape, but she hadn't known then just what she was escaping.

She hadn't known then how this valley would capture her heart. Or how the people would affect her. Or how this family would mean so much to her. Suddenly dishes and teacups rattled and the floor trembled beneath her feet. The table shook and Mr. Covington held it steady.

Ann's heart thundered in her ears. "What's. . .what's happening?"

Sam reached across the table and put his hand over hers, until the shaking finally settled and then stilled. "Just a tremor. A small earthquake."

"Are you all right, dear?" Belle asked.

Sam released her hand.

"How often do you get those?" Ann had never experienced an earthquake, even a small one.

The family chuckled around her.

"There's nothing to worry about," Sam said, watching her intently. "Weeks could go by, months even, between events. I promise there's nothing to be afraid of."

The look in Sam's intense blue eyes told her that he needed her to believe him. But why?

The next morning, Ann rode with Sam into town, the road bumpy and uncomfortable. He suggested they take a rest from trekking through the backcountry today. She could photograph the ranch while he went to Jackson for supplies, but she had a few things she wanted in town as well.

Sam swerved the truck back and forth, eliciting laughter from Ann. She'd never had such fun with Tom. To think Sam seemed to appreciate her as a photographer, too, taking interest in all the photographs she'd developed. He understood her reason for coming here, her need to prove herself.

Once in town, Sam parked and got out and ran around to open the door for Ann. "I'm heading to the grocers first. You mentioned wanting to purchase some more riding clothes, so why don't you go to the mercantile, and I'll join you in a bit."

"You think I'll take longer than you?" She sent him a teasing grin.

With a chuckle, he ushered her toward the sidewalk and tipped his hat to her as they parted ways. She loved it when he did that.

"Wait for me there," he said. "I won't be long."

A warm smile that chased the chill away spread through her as she meandered toward Jackson Mercantile, just across the way. She wanted to purchase a few extra shirts and breeches for her sister. Not that she expected Edith would ever wear them, and if she didn't, Ann found the clothing comfortable. Part of her wished she didn't have to leave, even wished for an early winter. That heavy snow would come and keep her in Jackson a little longer, even if that meant she wasn't home when Daddy returned from his honeymoon.

All she knew was that if she left now, she'd never again see Sam Covington. An unpleasant thought, indeed. When she paid for her purchases, Sam still hadn't come for her, so she exited, deciding to wait outside.

From up ahead, a familiar and unwelcome voice startled her.

The cowboy tumbled out of the Jackson Hotel, wearing big purple chaps and laughing boisterously with a few other dudes of the same ilk. Ann suddenly felt conspicuous in her own western garb, though she rather blended in than stood out.

"Tom?"

The drugstore cowboy froze and turned his attention to her. His eyes lit up. "Ann."

Holding his hands out, he rushed to her. Grabbed her and

swung her around. "Just the woman I was looking for."

Ann twisted from his grip. "What are you doing here?"

"Don't you miss me, baby?"

"We broke up weeks ago."

"Because I didn't appreciate your photography. Your need to come see this place. Well, here I am. I came to see for myself why you're so fascinated. I understand now. So don't be such a killjoy." He lifted her hands, looking her up and down. "Did you get all dolled up for me?"

Boisterous laughter from his friends erupted over his sarcasm. She jerked her hands free. Ann's throat constricted, preventing her from voicing her displeasure with his sudden appearance. How could he do this? How could he follow her out here and ruin this for her? She fought to say something.

Misunderstanding her reaction, as usual, Tom took her hand, lifting it to his lips, glancing over his shoulder to send his gang away. "Come on, Ann. I missed you, baby."

Chapter 6

S am stowed the items he purchased in the truck then headed to the mercantile to find Ann, hoping he hadn't taken too long. He spotted her on the sidewalk in front of the entrance. Just seeing her made him step a little lighter. But he reminded himself nothing could come of his feelings for her, and that was just as well.

Only fifteen yards away, he slowed, taking in the scene before him as an outrageously dressed dude lifted her hand to his lips. Sam drew closer, listening to the exchange. The fake cowboy had called her by her first name. Sam stumbled, and bumped into someone passing him.

"Watch where you're going," the man said.

"Sorry," Sam replied, but his attention was on Ann and the man holding her hand, speaking to her like they were on friendly terms.

His protective instincts kicked in, urging him to rush to her side and interfere. But no, this wasn't a stranger, this was someone she knew.

"I miss you, baby."

The words singed Sam's ears. He backed into the shadows to wait, wishing he hadn't seen anything to begin with. Unwilling to watch anymore, except he'd told her that he'd meet her at the mercantile. He'd give her a few minutes of privacy then come back.

Pulse hammering in his ears, though he had no right, Sam turned about-face and headed in the opposite direction. He couldn't face her until he dealt with his own reaction. He'd wanted to tell that guy to beat it.

Sam was jealous!

He forced his breathing to steady, but it wasn't easy. He had no right to be jealous. Add to that, he'd been through this with Rebecca. Same story, different girl.

He was such a sap.

Ann had hired him as a guide. She had never led him to believe—for even one minute—that she would stay. She had every intention of going back to Manhattan with her all-important photographs. Now Sam understood things better. She had a fella waiting for her back home, only now he'd grown tired of waiting and had followed her here.

Sam leaned against the wall, just outside the bank doors, and blew out a breath.

You've been a complete fool. He squeezed his eyes shut, pushing out the image that didn't want to leave. Just yesterday, he'd kissed her.

"You okay, Sam?" Sheriff Daniels asked.

Sam hadn't noticed when the man had come to lean against the wall right next to him as though commiserating with Sam. Had Sheriff Daniels seen what happened? Sam's reaction?

"Fine, just fine."

"She's a pretty one, Miss Kirkland," the sheriff added. "How long is she staying?"

"Another week, if that." She was as good as gone, as far as Sam was concerned.

He shoved from the wall, hoping to get out of more conversation with the man who'd offered sage advice on more than one occasion, the man who'd been persistent in getting Sam to guide Ann.

"Interested in another job?"

Sam considered the question. "What have you got?"

The sheriff chuckled. "I should get commissions for bringing you business."

Sam smiled at that. "Maybe you should."

"There's a big group come to town. Ran into them this morning. They're looking for a guide."

Sam wondered if Ann's friend was in that group. "I think I've shown Ann everything she needs. I'm guessing she'll likely leave sooner than expected, especially since. . ."

The sheriff quirked a brow. "Since?"

"I can't afford to let this opportunity slip away. I thank you for bringing Ann to me, but I wouldn't want to stake my reputation on that. Tell them to meet me at the Jackson Hotel day after tomorrow. We'll iron out the details, settle our business then."

"I'd say you could tell them yourself, but. . ." The sheriff tipped his hat. "Miss Kirkland."

"Sheriff, how are you?"

Ann's sweet voice wrapped around Sam. He regretted everything he'd just said. She had to have heard.

He turned to face her, forcing a smile he didn't feel. "Did you find what you were looking for?"

She held up her packaged items. "I did, thank you. Thought you were going to meet me there."

"I. . .uh. . .got sidetracked. The sheriff caught me," Sam said.

The way Sheriff Daniels eyed him, Sam wasn't sure the man would be much help on what started to feel like a runaway wagon. He shook Sam's hand and bid Ann good-bye then headed down the boardwalk.

Then Ann pinned Sam with her soft brown gaze, hurt flickering behind her dark irises. Was her lip quivering?

"I heard what you said, Mr. Covington." Her voice shook through her scathing tone. "I'll thank you to keep to our agreement."

Sam hated himself. "I didn't mean anything by what I said. Of course I'll honor my agreement, but you'll be leaving at week's end, or maybe even sooner. I don't want to lose this next opportunity." He wasn't showing much business prowess, but seeing her with that man had scrambled his head. Meeting with those men wouldn't take long. If Ann stayed until the end of the week, he'd have to stall the men.

"Why would I leave sooner unless it starts snowing?" She glanced at the sidewalk then back to Sam. "I know I said I wanted to be gone before the snow, but I kind of hoped it would snow before I left, so I could take a few photographs. It would be a risk, but"—her voice cracked—"but forget it. The end of this week will be fine with me."

She lifted her chin, all businesslike and impersonal, but he experienced the pain in her eyes as if it were his own. Why would she be hurt? He hadn't meant to hurt her. He reminded himself she had a fella and was leaving. Still, he shouldn't have reacted the way he had.

He opened his mouth to say he was sorry, but different words came out. "I'm meeting with my new prospective clients the day after tomorrow. It won't take long. But I'm sure you can understand that I don't want to lose the opportunity, considering you have your own prospects right here in town."

Sam Covington—where is your brother to kick you to the end of the road when you need him?

Her own prospects? *Tom.*

He'd seen her with Tom, but why should that matter?

"I'll consider your obligation to me fulfilled after you take me back to that last waterfall." Ann fought to control the quiver in her voice.

So Sam wouldn't want to stake his reputation, what little there was, on Ann's photography. He didn't respect her or see what she offered him, after all. She hadn't required him to sign a contract like Mr. Frankston, trusting him instead. She'd been a fool in her handling of this arrangement, to be sure. But Sam had become so much more than a guide to her. She was more hurt than she'd ever been, even with Tom.

The ride home was long, with an awkward silence hanging between them.

When they arrived at the ranch, Ann wanted to flee to her room like a scolded schoolgirl, though she should be the one to do the scolding. Mostly she needed free of Sam's presence so she could gain clarity over her runaway thoughts.

Sam caught her arm before she could rush away. "I have a few things to take care of this afternoon here at the ranch, so if you want to get those ranch photographs, today is the day. Tomorrow, we'll see to the waterfall, finish our business."

"Agreed," Ann said in her most professional voice. She hoped.

That night after dinner, the family retired to their rooms; Ann crept down the stairs to the fireplace and stoked the fire, throwing on another log. She hadn't had a moment alone to think on all that had happened today.

Sure, she'd seen plenty of smiles from Sam and his family as she photographed them working on chores around the ranch, gearing up to deliver the cattle to market. Sam had seen to her every need when it came to their business agreement. But with Tom's sudden appearance, everything between them had changed.

On the sofa, she curled her legs beneath her and hoped watching the flames would lull her mind into a peaceful state as she prayed. She'd come here on a mission and needed to return so she could greet her father with smiles and present the proof of her adventure to him at the right time. Now, all she could think was how she wanted to stay here longer. At least she'd wanted that until Sam had said those horrible words.

What had happened today? One moment, she'd savored Sam's company and his friendship, the next moment she overheard his excitement over the possibility of taking on a big-game hunting trip. He'd even commented that he couldn't stake his reputation on the work he'd done for Ann.

His words had pierced her heart. The man had fooled her into believing he actually appreciated her talents. Her photography. Into believing he understood her.

Unlike her father.

Unlike Tom.

She'd gotten it all wrong. He was no better than either of them. Ann was on her own, as always. She needed to toughen up, erect an even taller wall around her heart. This would always be a man's world. She'd have to work even harder than she imagined. But she was grateful that she had the photographs she'd come for—that thanks to Sam's willingness to share his secluded places. Why had he done such a thing?

She'd thought. . .she'd thought that something more had grown between them. None of that mattered. Nor had she come this far to be trampled upon like some withering flower. She would see this thing through with him tomorrow and hope she would be able to take the photographs she'd envisioned since she'd seen the place.

If only the thought of leaving at the end of the week didn't swipe a claw across her heart. Everything had gone downhill with Tom's appearance, but whether or not Tom had found her today, she would be leaving at the end of this week.

She would depart this amazing valley, the Covington Ranch, and Sam's family. She would leave Sam.

"Ann?"

Sam's voice pulled her from her thoughts, sending her heart galloping. She stiffened, hating the interruption.

But glad to see him at the same time.

"What are you doing here?" she asked.

He smiled. How she'd grown to love that smile. "I live here, remember?"

"Yes, of course, you do," she said. "I meant, why you aren't asleep?"

He settled on the opposite end of the sofa and leaned forward. "Same reason as you, I suppose."

Something in his voice made Ann's breath hitch. "And what reason would that be?"

He blew out a breath, stood, and walked over to the fire,

stoked it with a poker. The crackling flames blazed now, reflecting in Sam's eyes. He moved back to the sofa, this time sitting a few inches closer to Ann. She couldn't move away because she was in the corner. But despite the danger this man was to her heart, she didn't try to move away.

"I couldn't sleep," he said. "Haven't stopped thinking about today. I wanted to say I'm sorry if I hurt you."

"One of the reasons it was so important to me to come here on my own was to prove myself to my father, a man who should already know my talents since he employs me to photograph for the magazine. But he gives me no credit. He's not the only one, so you can understand why your words hurt me. I thought you were different." Had she really just said that out loud?

"I am," he said. "If there's anyone who understands being underestimated or devalued, it's me. I know I did that to you today, Ann. I guess I figured that my father was finally giving credence to my ideas. I didn't want to lose the opportunity with those hunters. But my mind started scrambling after. . .after I saw you with that diamond-pointed drugstore cowboy."

"Tom." Ann whispered, almost hating the name.

"It looks to me like you have a boyfriend. Someone to go back to."

Why would that matter? But Ann's heart knew why, and her pulse quickened.

"I mostly reacted to that," Sam continued, "but the truth is you're leaving at the end of this week, regardless. You can't blame me for wanting to line up another opportunity. All the same, I wanted to say I'm sorry, Ann. I can honestly say that I'm impressed with you. All you've done in your life. Your photographs are wonderful. Meeting you, guiding you through this country, has been the best thing to happen to me."

Her heart jumped. Oh, if that were only true.

He shifted a little closer. "Will you forgive me?"

"There's nothing to forgive. You're right, I'm leaving." *I don't want to.*

Could he see in her eyes what was in her heart? She longed for Sam to truly understand her, even if she couldn't figure herself out.

Chapter 7

"Tell me about Tom."

Sam wasn't sure what he was doing now, but he had to know. The thought of her leaving had tormented him all day. When he'd seen her with Tom, he realized just how much she meant to him.

"Why do you care?" she asked. "If I didn't know better, I'd almost say that you were jealous. But you have no reason to be."

He stared at the fire, saying nothing.

"Please. I need to know why," she added. Her eyes had softened, turning her into the Ann he'd grown to care about these last few weeks.

"I have no right to be jealous." How did he explain? He just knew he couldn't let Ann slip away from him without saying everything that needed to be said. He'd made that mistake before.

"When I said you had no reason to be jealous, I meant that Tom and I were engaged, but that's been over for weeks now."

Sam's gut churned. The two had been far more serious

than he'd thought. At the same time, he could hope it was over between them. Hope he had a chance with her. The idea had been growing for a long time, even though he'd buried it time and again. It had bloomed when they'd shared the kiss, but today, that fragile bloom had been destroyed. He couldn't know if Ann had any inkling of how strong his feelings were for her, considering he was only figuring that out himself. He couldn't know if she returned them.

"What happened?"

"Tom didn't care about my photography or about me. Not really. He cared about my father's magazine and money. That's all."

"How can that be true?" Sam's words grated against his own ears. He hadn't meant to give Tom any credit, but he had to know it was over. "You're the most beautiful, most amazing woman I've ever met. I can't help but think Tom sees the same in you."

Even in the dim firelight, he could see Ann's deep blush. It did crazy things to his insides.

"I overheard him saying as much, the same as I overheard you today, Sam. So you'll forgive me if I'm not so trusting as to believe anything you say. As soon as you thought I wouldn't hear, you—"

She didn't finish but rose from the sofa. "If you'll excuse me." She fled the room.

So this was it, then. Sam had ruined the best thing that had ever happened to him. He didn't know how to stop it, but he had to try.

He bolted from the sofa and followed her, catching her wrist just as she made the stairs, and turned her to face him. She teetered from the first step, putting her entirely too close, her face mere inches from his.

Sam didn't take time to think. Thinking hadn't gotten him anywhere. He leaned in, pressing his lips against hers, not worrying that Ann would tear away from him, or slap him, at the very least. Words hadn't worked for him. This was all he had.

When she didn't pull away, he once again cupped her cheeks, like the kiss they shared before, then slowly slid his hands around her head, tugging her closer, weaving his fingers through her soft, brown hair.

The taste of her salty tears brought him back to himself. He ran his thumbs over her cheeks, ending the kiss. "Ann," his husky whisper sounded like someone else. "I. . .I wanted you to know how I feel. I couldn't explain it with words."

She closed her eyes but said nothing.

"Did Tom ever kiss you like this?" The wrong question to ask, but Sam needed to know Ann's thoughts.

Her eyes flew open. "It can't work between us."

He held her wrist, wanting to ask her why she would say that, but then, what was he really asking of her? How could he ask her to stay when he could promise her nothing? He'd professed his love once before. His throat constricted at the thought of saying those words again. He was in no better place than he'd been before. He had nothing to call his own, nothing to offer a wife.

A wife. His heart hammered.

"Do you still love Tom?"

She frowned, looking more confused. "What? No. But that hardly matters. I have a job. My family to return to in Manhattan. You have your business to build here. And we have an early morning and long day tomorrow."

With a sad smile and a tender peck on his cheek, Ann pulled herself from the slight hold he had on her. He watched her make her way up the stairs and then heard the door to her room open and shut. It felt like she'd ripped his heart from him.

If only there was a way for him to come with her to Manhattan. But no, he wasn't from her world. Could never fit in. As much as he loved—and yes, what else could make him feel this way but love?—as much as he loved her, he could not follow her to New York and hope to provide for a wife and family.

The irony wasn't lost on him—the person who'd broadened his horizons and paved the way for him to become a guide and outfitter was the woman he'd fallen in love with. But their worlds were too different. He'd give it all up for her, if he thought it would change anything.

Ann ran her hand along Gracie's neck, talking to the animal she'd grown to care about, too. Sam finished saddling his horse in the early morning chill, only a hint of gray breaking across the sky.

Gracie whinnied, and Ann pressed her hand over the horse's

soft muzzle. "I'm going to miss you, girl," she said softly.

She'd gone against Daddy's will, though she reminded herself she was a grown woman. Daddy was also her boss at the magazine. She'd wanted to prove herself in coming all the way to Jackson. She'd wanted to escape the chaotic culture and see for herself the wonder of the Grand Teton photographs. Her breakup with Tom had merely been a small piece that urged her toward this one goal.

Here in Jackson's Hole, Wyoming, she'd found a freedom she'd never before experienced. She'd found Sam.

She watched his sturdy form climb onto his horse. Remembering the way he'd kissed her, she realized she'd been hard on him, but after everything she'd been through, trusting someone to care for her, for who she was, wasn't easy. Besides, how could their two worlds fit together?

Moisture crept into her eyes and she quickly swiped it away.

"Ready?" He barely looked at her beneath his hat. Once again, he'd shut himself off.

Why shouldn't he? He'd laid his heart out to her last night as best as any man could, better than Tom ever had, even though Tom had proposed, and she had rejected him. She climbed onto Gracie and held the reins.

"As I'll ever be," she said.

Sam urged his horse forward and Gracie followed. Ann and Sam had grown close over the last few weeks, close enough that he'd been compelled to kiss her. And she'd kissed him back. She didn't regret that, except both of them knew she had to return to her world. He did, too. So they both rode in silence—a great rift between them, as big as the Continental Divide that cut across the nation.

Ann tried to reignite her excitement about seeing the waterfall again, but Sam's question wouldn't leave her.

Do you still love Tom?

No. In truth, she'd always held back a part of herself because she knew that Tom didn't see her for who she really was. Hearing Tom's words, learning the truth, had almost given her a measure of relief.

He hadn't looked at her or her photographs the way Sam had. But what could she do? She had to get back to New York before Daddy. Be ready to present her photographs. She couldn't stay here on a whim, or because Sam had kissed her, or because he liked her. Or even because she loved him.

Her heart lurched at the admission, but that was a secret she'd keep to herself. No sense in causing either of them more pain. His expression drawn, it was clear that Sam was in pain.

Two hours into their ride, Sam stopped to rest the horses again.

"You realize that you're taking me to the same place for the second time now. Don't you worry I'll remember how to find my way back?" she asked, missing the light banter and teasing they'd shared so often before. She took a sip of water, hoping her statement would bring some peace, ease the tension between them.

He chuckled. "That would surprise me, but if anyone could do it, you could. His smile tore down the rest of the wall, at least enough for her to cross over.

"I appreciate your vote of confidence."

The horses grew antsy. Ann glanced at Sam, who drew his rifle from the saddle scabbard. He nodded. Ann understood he wanted her to get back on her horse. He did the same.

A grizzly bear lumbered from the trees, and Ann couldn't control Gracie. Despite her best efforts, the horse took off, leaving Sam behind. Unfortunately, the bear gave chase.

Ann turned in the saddle to see Sam direct Ace into the path of the bear. The horse reared and challenged the bear, which stood on its hind legs. Ann finally slowed Gracie and urged her around to watch.

Something went horribly wrong. Ace stepped in a hole, or on a rock. Ann wasn't sure, but the horse went down on top of Sam. Soon enough, Ace scrambled to his feet and limped away.

But Sam had angered the grizzly with his interference. Ann needed to help, but Gracie refused her urges to go back to Sam, who remained on the ground, injured.

He held his rifle steady, aimed at the beast charging toward him. Sam had to have nerves of steel.

Oh, Lord, please help my Sam! If only the bear would lose interest and leave them be.

"Shoot him, Sam, shoot him!" Ann screamed. But she knew he'd wait until he could make the one shot he had count.

He fired the weapon, the shot resounding through the forest. Injured, the grizzly limped away into the forest, away from Sam. Ann urged her nervous horse as close as she could then tied Gracie to a tree. Ace had disappeared. Ann ran to Sam and dropped to her knees.

"Oh, Sam!"

He laid there with his eyes shut. She cupped his head. "Sam Covington, answer me."

His eyes opened. "My leg. I think it's broken."

"You're lucky the horse didn't crush you, or that bear kill you."

Suddenly, Sam smiled. "It's snowing."

Ann looked up, and a few flakes licked her cheeks. She glanced down at Sam. "I don't think that's a good thing, considering we have to get you down the mountain."

"You wanted to see it snow. You're getting your chance."

He had to be in pain, maybe he was going into shock. "I'll get Gracie. We'll get you home."

No matter how hard they tried, Sam couldn't climb onto the horse. Ann wasn't strong enough to lift him.

His face drained of color; he grabbed her arm. "It's no use. You have to go get help."

"But how can I find my way out and back?"

"You have to. You have a real eye for detail, Ann. I know you remember the way," he said, trying to hide the pain. "I trust you to do this."

Tears freely streamed down her cheeks, though she wanted

to reassure Sam. She removed her saddlebag and blanket and made him comfortable.

On her knees, Ann leaned in and kissed Sam, lingering. "I'll be back with help, I promise."

When she pulled away, Sam gripped her tighter. "I need you to know. . . I waited too long to tell someone before. I won't let that happen again. But I need you to know in case things don't work out."

"*Shh.* Don't talk like that. I have to hurry," she said. Though she hated leaving him, she pulled away and climbed onto Gracie.

"I love you, Ann," Sam said. He studied her as though waiting for a response then closed his eyes.

Chapter 8

What was that look in her eyes when he'd told her? The pain in his heart almost equaled the pain in his leg. He'd never wanted to feel this way again—he was no good at love—but he'd risked his heart with Ann.

She'd wrapped him in a blanket, but the snow was getting thicker. It would be hours before she could get back with help, if she could even find her way.

God, please help her. Please, keep her safe.

Maybe he shouldn't have told her he loved her, but he might not get another chance.

He shivered and struggled to stay awake, wishing he could just go to sleep and escape the pain. At some point, a warm, wet tongue stroked his cheek. Sam woke up to realize Ace had returned.

"Good boy." He rubbed the horse's muzzle. Ignoring the pain shooting through his body each time he moved, he worked to get Ace settled in the soft snow next to him. Heat from the horse's body would go a long way to keep Sam warm.

Beyond that, there was nothing more he could do besides wait.

It seemed like a lifetime, and yet no time at all, when Ann brushed the snow from his face and whispered his name. The heat from his horse had likely kept him alive to see her sweet face.

His mother's concerned face appeared in his line of vision. "You're fortunate Ann could remember how to find her way back. Do you know. . ."—she frowned, apparently deciding to hold her scolding for later—"here, I brought something warm for you to drink."

She helped him drink from a Thermos insulated bottle. Sam thought nothing ever tasted so good. It warmed him to the core, which was exactly what he needed.

"Can you get on your horse?" she asked.

Sam was stiff and sore like he'd never been before, even when he'd been thrown, trying to break horses. The two ranch hands tried to assist him to his feet, but blackness edged his vision. They decided it would be best to fashion a travois for him.

Oh boy. It was going to be a long ride down the mountain.

Sam woke the next morning, exhaustion from his battle with the bear and his own horse clinging to him. His mouth dry, he was glad when his door creaked and his mother stepped in, bringing a tray of breakfast food.

When he tried to sit up, the splint on his broken leg reminded him of the doctor's work and his restless sleep. How was he supposed to guide the hunters now? His future seemed completely out of reach. Over. His life would have been, too, if not for Ann.

"You need to eat, Son. Eat and rest. Doctor's orders."

"Ann," he whispered, not recognizing his voice. "She saved my life. I want to thank her."

Something shifted behind his mother's eyes, striking fear in his heart.

"What is it? Did something hap—"

She shook her head and moved to the window, opening the curtains. "Her father arrived yesterday. Sheriff Daniels brought him out."

"She's. . .gone?"

His mother turned to face him. "She didn't want to leave. Not without saying good-bye. But her father had already arranged for travel. He insisted. She wanted him to see her photographs, but he wouldn't even look."

Sam sat up despite the pain. "What are you saying? She left them?"

"Most of them, yes. I snuck a few into her luggage when I helped her pack. Oh, Sam, I was sorry to see that girl go."

Not nearly as sorry as Sam.

More than two months had passed. Ann had no idea how Sam would react to seeing her, especially since it was Christmas Eve. His family already had their own plans, she was sure, but she was fortunate to have persuaded Daddy to her way of thinking. Fortunate to have made it back to Jackson, at all. Before Sam forgot about her. She hoped she wasn't already too late.

Daddy still owned the magazine but had turned management over to someone else, so he could spend more time with his new bride. Plus Ann knew he wanted to escape the depressing atmosphere in New York, especially after the stock market crashed in October, which had spurred his early return from his honeymoon.

She'd convinced Daddy and Marilyn to visit Jackson to see the last of the Wild West for themselves in the winter. She'd shown him a few of the photographs she'd been able to bring back, that is, after his anger abated. Finally, Daddy's eyes had lit up.

For her.

For her photographs of Grand Teton National Park. He agreed she should take photographs of what had to be a winter wonderland. They'd traveled over the pass just fine.

Even if he hadn't agreed, Ann knew she would have found her way back here. Back to Sam. Her photographs had created memories of her with Sam. She longed to see him again.

Packed snow crunched beneath her boots as she strolled around the Covington home, taking in trees and mountains painted in white, while she waited on Sam and his brother to return from delivering gifts to a neighbor. Sheriff Daniels had been kind enough to bring Ann to the ranch before he headed home himself to spend Christmas Eve with his own family, so she'd need a ride back to town where Daddy and Marilyn stayed at the Jackson Hotel. Ann's sister stayed behind in New York to spend Christmas with friends.

At first, Sam's mother had been stunned to see Ann. But her surprise quickly turned to genuine delight. Ann had always liked the woman and took a measure of relief at hearing Belle say that Sam would be pleased to see Ann.

Anticipation danced in her stomach. She was glad the roads over the pass had been clear enough to travel, or else—

"Ann?"

She whirled to see Sam hiking toward her, and favoring his left leg. Ann smiled and rushed to him. He gripped her shoulders and looked her over.

"Is it really you?" He ran his hands over her hair and face.

"Yes, Sam. I've come back to see Jackson in the winter. If you're available, maybe you can be my guide."

His brows flinched. "Is that the only reason you came back?"

I love you, Ann. She hadn't forgotten those words. But had he meant them? He hadn't written to her since she'd left. She'd written only to crumple the letters and throw them out. She hadn't known what to say, where to start. If there was any hope of her return. Once she knew she would return to Jackson, she decided on surprising Sam.

"No," she said, wishing he would inch closer and kiss her. Hoping she hadn't lost him already. "That's not the only reason."

Sam's vivid blue eyes searched hers, a smile edging back into his lips. "Come on. There's something I want to show you."

Holding her hand, he led her through the snow toward the barn. "Wait here," he said. "I won't be long."

He opened up the barn doors and disappeared. Ann saw Belle watching from the window. She waved.

A ruckus drew Ann's attention back to the barn where Sam finally exited, riding in a sleigh pulled along by two beautiful horses with bells on their tack, jingling. Bearing a huge smile, Sam maneuvered carefully from the sleigh.

"Want to go for a ride?" He assisted Ann into the sleigh and covered her with a blanket.

Sam climbed onto the sleigh and sat next to her. "My father made this. When he first came to the valley. Proposed in it, too."

Her heart leapt at the words.

Wrapped in a blanket, all cozy next to Sam, Ann couldn't remember ever feeling more content. Just over a rise, he slowed the horses, the Covington Ranch spread before them.

Ann sighed. "It is, indeed, a winter wonderland."

He shifted toward her. "I never got to thank you properly for what you did for me that day. I wanted to save you, but you saved me instead."

"You don't have to thank me."

"Are you sure?" Sam tilted her chin up and kissed her softly then whispered, "Thank you, Ann."

When she responded, he turned to face her completely and wrapped her in his arms, kissing her thoroughly.

Ann felt a little dizzy when he ended the kiss. Dizzy and happy.

"I didn't mean to startle you with that, but I had to make sure."

"Make sure of what?" *I love you, Ann.*

"Don't you know?" A sparkle flickered in his gaze.

Ann could no longer stand it. "That you love me?"

Sam gave a subtle nod. Ann knew he wanted to hear it from her. "Your words stayed with me all the way to New York. They never left me. Sam, your words brought me back. I. . .love you, too."

Sam cupped her cheeks, taking in her face as if he were afraid he might forget what she looked like. "You once told me it could never work between us. I won't lie to you and pretend to think that I could live in the city."

"You wouldn't be the man I fell in love with if you could." Snow swirled like a vortex around them, landing on Ann's face and eyelashes. But she'd never felt warmer.

"Ann?" Love mingled with terror in his eyes. "Do you think you could tolerate this cold, harsh environment, beautiful as it is, to become my bride? I promise you can take all the pictures you want. I'm not sure what, if anything, I have to offer you, at least yet. And—"

Ann grabbed Sam and kissed him, shutting off his excuses. Tears burned behind her eyes. "Yes, oh yes, Sam. You're all I want—together we'll make beautiful memories."

RIBBON OF LIGHT

by Elizabeth Goddard

Chapter 1

Jackson Hole, Wyoming, Present Day

Hayley Covington drove her Ford Explorer past the antler arches that marked off the town square, where a couple posed for pictures in front of Jackson, Wyoming's, iconic symbols. Downtown Jackson resembled a town from the Old West, and folks liked that, but Hayley had grown up in the valley and the western-styled architecture seemed ordinary enough to her.

On occasion she and her two sisters, Kate and Sarah, would drive to Salt Lake to do major shopping, even after her sisters had married and moved away from Jackson, but the town had everything else Hayley needed, if not everything she wanted. Jackson was home to numerous art galleries, movie stars, the rich and famous, and plenty of folks whose family had been in the valley from the beginning—like hers.

Hayley slowed for a horse-drawn stagecoach carting tourists down a dirty snow-slushed street. Waiting for the coach to move on, she caught site of the Veronica James Art Gallery, and envy rose, burning her throat. Veronica had become so popular that people even commissioned her to create for them. Hayley should have grown accustomed to various artists breaking out with their very own studios by now. The closer she came to her dream, the more she wanted it, and yet, the further away it seemed.

Crazy. It was all crazy thinking. Daddy let her dabble with her pottery, but she was the last of three daughters he'd wished were sons. He had her life mapped out already. For generations, Covington heirs ran the Covington cattle ranch—pure and unadulterated—just like Hayley's grandfather, John, and great-grandfather, Zeb, would have wanted. No dude ranching for Hart Covington, or kowtowing to cowboy wannabes. Hayley's great-uncle Sam had started a dude ranch decades ago over in Cody, where that branch of the family also ran Covington Outfitters.

As for the ranch in Jackson Hole, Hayley's sisters had both gotten married and escaped that life, leaving Hayley alone with Daddy. Of course, Daddy employed a full-time manager and ranch hands to do the day-to-day work, but a Covington must always hold the reins.

Daddy never treated Hayley like he wished she were a son, though she knew he did, and Hayley was all he had left. At twenty-four, she was the only one to stay behind to run the ranch, making her the last heir, as it were, which put tremendous pressure on her. She couldn't be the weak link in the ranch's legacy, and yet she wanted so much more. But even though she had dreams, she wouldn't let her father down.

When the stagecoach finally maneuvered out of her way, Hayley turned between the western-styled buildings of the local cowboy bar and the Blue Mountain Art Gallery. Her palms grew moist as she got out and walked to the back of the vehicle to open the hatch.

Jim Taylor, who owned and managed the art gallery, had offered to display her work three years ago, but Hayley had been terrified. She'd actually been afraid that she'd fail. Since then she'd worked to perfect her art even more, but she was never satisfied. Then Jim stopped by the ranch a couple of months ago and surprised her, coming to her private art studio. She was in the middle of throwing, had clay all over her hands and clothes.

He'd practically dared her to let him feature her pieces. So he'd taken three, and they'd sold within the week. Hayley continued to produce new pieces using her signature sgraffito—a technique where she applied two different layers of slip then scratched designs, mostly scenery, into the clay. Jim was plenty pleased with himself for discovering what he termed a "new" local artist.

She'd yet to tell Daddy she'd found a little success, but he'd hear about it sooner rather than later. She dreaded that moment. Hayley lifted a carefully packed box containing her newly fired vase with the Tetons carved into it.

Her designs were a hit, Jim had said, with the tourists coming through who purchased fine art for a memento or an investment, depending on the artist. She tugged the box from the back of the Explorer and tried the side door of the gallery. Locked, of course. Hayley positioned the box against her hip and rapped on the door.

Finally, a guy peeked out. "Can I help you?"

"I'm here to deliver some more pottery," she said. "Is Jim around?"

He opened the door and shrugged, his Nordic turtleneck sweater accenting his strong clean-shaven jaw, especially when he smiled. His hair was wavy and brown like his eyes, and grew past his ears, scratching the edge of the turtleneck.

"Oh well," she said. "I'll set these in the back and he can figure out where to display them." Hayley walked through the door and peered behind her at the guy. "There's more in the back of my Explorer, if you want to help."

"Sure thing." He winked, his eyes were warm and friendly.

Where had Jim been keeping this one?

Hayley carried the box to the back of the gallery, eyeing several people who browsed through the studio, someone with small children even, which could be hazardous around the more delicate pieces like sculptures, glass, and pottery. Just before she entered through the employees-only door at the back, she glimpsed a salesperson assisting a potential customer with questions about a large nature painting on the wall.

She set the box on an empty shelf and began unpacking. She didn't want Jim to miss this one. He was sure to spot it as soon as he returned. Hayley exited in time to see her helper meandering across the studio floor, searching for her.

"I'm over here," she called.

He grinned and strode toward her, carrying the last two boxes. Didn't he understand what was in them? If he dropped them, all that time and effort would be lost. But Hayley kept her grin in place as she led him to the back.

"Set the boxes on the table, and I'll unpack them. Put these pieces next to this one on the shelf."

His eyes grew wide. "Whoa, you did that?"

Hayley cocked her head. Hadn't Jim informed all his employees of her work? "Yes, I'm Hayley Covington." She let her hands fall from the box she was unpacking. "Jim gave me an opportunity to display my work at his studio."

He reached for the vase.

Hayley reached, too, placing her hand against his. "Please, be careful." Oh, no. She sounded like a prima donna, and there wasn't any call for that kind of attitude.

He didn't appear offended at her overprotective reaction. "May I?"

Hayley liked that he asked her. "Yes, of course."

He lifted the vase and ran his finger over her etchings in the clay. "I've never seen anything like this. Why haven't I heard of you before?"

His praise warmed her insides. Had others who'd seen and purchased her work reacted this way? "I'm just starting out. I've only had a few pieces in the studio, but they've sold quickly."

He gently placed the vase on the shelf.

Ty Walker wasn't sure he could afford this, lovely as it was. He'd come into the gallery to get ideas, just browsing mostly, though he doubted he'd end up purchasing anything so pricey. But prices were all steep in Jackson.

"I can see why, this one is amazing. You might be new on the scene, but I predict you're going to be popular in no time." With her crystal blue eyes and shiny blond mane, she was as amazing as her pottery. Looking into her eyes, he imagined that he saw a depth there, intricately carved into her being, like she'd carved into her pottery.

"Thanks. That's just what Jim said. He's been telling me this for a few years. I finally agreed. I don't know. . . I guess I was afraid of success." The uncertainty behind her eyes confirmed her words and stirred compassion in him.

"Success can be brutal." Not that Ty would know anything about that.

She laughed. "You didn't ask to hear all this."

"I'm good with it. And I know what you mean about being afraid of success." Maybe that had been his problem all along, and this girl, this lovely girl who he'd only just met, had nailed it. She didn't even know him. Ty. . .a ski bum with nothing to offer a pretty lady like her, an up- and-coming artist—found himself wanting to see her again. To know more about her.

"I'm looking for a special present for my grandmother's

seventy-fifth birthday. I know we only just met, but I'm having a hard time finding something that's just right. Something unique. This piece is unique but"—Ty frowned—"I'm not sure it's her. No offense."

"None taken. I completely understand." Hayley stared at nothing in particular, like she was in thought.

Ty figured he'd overstayed his welcome. "Well, it was nice to meet you Hayley Covington. I need to go."

"No, wait, please. I didn't get your name."

"Ty Walker."

"Well, Ty, I have an idea. I'd really like to help you with your grandmother's present. Maybe I could create something special just for her."

"Oh no, that's too much. Thanks for the offer, but—"

"It's no trouble at all, and I insist. You helped me today, and I'd like to return the favor."

By creating one of her special pieces for his grandmother? "I... Hayley, I'll be up front with you. I don't think I could afford your pottery."

Hayley's cell phone chirped. She frowned when she glanced at it, but smiled up at him. "Not to worry. We'll work something out. When can you come over so we can talk about your grandmother and I can give you a few ideas?"

"I'm free for a few hours Thursday afternoon."

"Good. I'll see you at the Covington Ranch. It's easy to find. My studio is in a small cabin off the back of the house. And Ty, please, if you decide you don't want any of my pottery for her, you won't hurt my feelings."

"Why would you want to do this?"

She gave him a half grin. "Have trouble trusting people, do you? I'm kind of impulsive like that, just ask my father. But I started thinking it would be nice to do some commissioned pieces, and I'd like to start with you. So think of yourself as a test."

Ty laughed. "Now that I can agree to."

He left Miss Hayley Covington to unpack the rest of her boxes, revealing her extraordinary pottery, and return her phone call, with a bounce in his step he hadn't felt in far too long. He strolled through the vibrantly decorated studio, eyeing the expensive oil paintings and sculptures and wood carvings, feeling for the first time like he belonged. Feeling like he wasn't out of place in the ritzier places Jackson had to offer. And all because of Hayley's offer. Her warm, unpretentious ways. She was a Covington, for crying out loud—part of that big spread outside Jackson. Had to be worth millions.

When he'd woken up this morning, he'd prayed for direction for his life, and God sure answered in funny ways. Of course, meeting Hayley wasn't exactly a path for his life, but he hadn't expected any of that to happen.

All he'd wanted was to find something special for Nanna to make up for her disappointment in him. He'd fallen in love with skiing as a teenager and moved in with her, convincing his parents in Texas that he could train and become something great.

Yeah right.

All he'd managed to accomplish was working as a part-time ski instructor at Jackson Hole Mountain Resort, and he worked part-time at the National Elk Refuge to bring in extra cash, too. His grandmother thought he was a ski bum. She was right, because he didn't have any other aspirations. He lived to ski. What more did he need? He'd prayed for God to show him.

And meeting Hayley today. . .

I guess I was afraid of success. Her words came back to him.

A gnawing started in his gut and worked its way up into his chest. He just might need something more in life besides cutting through the icing on the most vertical slope in the country.

Chapter 2

*P*erfect.

She'd gotten on top of her ranching chores. A rich beef stew, a Covington family recipe handed down through the years, simmered in the Crock-Pot, filling the spacious home—built in the late eighteen hundreds—with a wonderful aroma. Daddy was in a much better mood when she took good care of him. He was an old-fashioned guy. No getting around that. And considering he'd insisted she join him in discussions with Will, the ranch manager, about selling off some of the horses, she needed him in a good mood so she could beg off. Ranching was hard work, but they had plenty of hands to do the grunt labor. The work could go on forever, from dawn to dusk, if she let it.

Since Daddy hadn't quite stopped thinking of her as his little girl yet, even though she was twenty-four, she'd used that to her advantage. She needed time to explore her artistic side, and she'd started putting more time into that lately. The more she put into it, the more ideas for pottery designs she came up with at all hours of the day and night. Designs even took over her dreams.

The problem was that Daddy didn't know she'd put her pieces in a gallery in town. She needed to be the one to tell him before someone else did. She hadn't honestly thought people would buy her pieces so quickly, or that her work would actually be in demand. Getting permission to put her pieces in the studio when Daddy had never had much respect for artists—though she didn't understand why—seemed futile. But maybe it was more that he wanted her focus on running the ranch. Maybe he was afraid of losing her to other endeavors.

She sighed, feeling her dreams tugging her away from the ranch. Who was she kidding? She was afraid her art would pull her away from the ranch, too, but she had to make it work.

Somehow, she needed to convince him that she could create and sell art, and work the ranch, too. With Ty stopping by, she'd have even more to explain.

She thought about Ty and his warm smile. Helping him with this gift for his grandmother had seemed like the right thing to do. It would help them both. She could find out if she could create a "commissioned" piece especially designed for a particular person—Ty's grandmother—though Hayley had done the commissioning.

In her small studio, Hayley stored away the messy slip, glazes, and clays, and wiped off the counters and her Lockerbie kick wheel. She wanted to make an impression on Ty. For some reason she couldn't explain, the man had stayed in her thoughts since she'd met him, and in a way that had nothing at all to do with pottery.

She promised herself if she ever fell for someone, he'd need to be a cowboy or a rancher, too, so he could be part of her life here. She'd come close once, a couple of years ago. But Daddy had come on strong, and Ray hadn't stuck around long after that. She'd never been sure what happened—if Daddy had run him off, or if Ray had lost interest. But regardless his reason for moving on, Hayley had been deeply hurt.

She hadn't met anyone since who she would be willing to risk her heart over. Maybe she'd been too isolated at the ranch, she didn't know.

All she knew was that Ty had stayed in her thoughts. The problem was he wasn't really a cowboy. Had no ranching experience. What was she thinking? She'd met the guy once. Her thoughts were getting away from her. She lassoed them, reining them in.

Someone knocked on the door. Hayley's palms slicked. *Calm down, girl.* The thought of doing this kind of work made her giddy. When she opened the door, Ty filled the space on the other side like his smile filled his face. Then she was giddy for an entirely different reason.

"You made it." She swung the door wide. "Come inside and see my meager little studio. But hey, it's all mine."

Ty stepped inside, the subtle hint of his musky cologne tickled her nose. He shrugged out of his jacket.

"I'll take that." Hayley hung it on the coat tree by the door along with hers.

He thrust his hands into his khaki pants, his sweater pulled tight over his broad shoulders. Hayley suddenly wondered what she'd been thinking. She had no idea how to go about this. Might as well be honest about that.

"Thanks so much for driving all the way out." She used her hands a lot when she talked, so she clasped them in front of her. "I'll be honest, I've never done this before."

Ty angled his head. "What? Had anyone out to your studio?"

She laughed. "No, actually, but that's not what I mean. Ty, I want to create something special for your grandmother based on what you tell me about her, and of course, based on what you'd like me to create."

He frowned and drew in a breath. "I hope I haven't wasted your time. I don't make a lot of money, so I'm not sure I could afford anything you make."

"You're doing me a favor. Like I said, I have never done this before. You already agreed to be my test subject. We'll work something out, remember?"

He nodded. "That's right."

"Well, see anything you like?" She gestured to the pottery on the shelves around the room—vases, pitchers, bowls, tea-kettles, and more. "Why don't you look around and talk to me about which pieces speak to you. Then we'll talk about your grandmother."

He flashed a lopsided smile. Hayley liked that.

"All right," he said. "I have a feeling this is going to be great."

He moved to the shelves.

"That one is just greenware. It hasn't been bisque-fired yet. And that over there"—she pointed across the room—"has been bisque-fired but not yet glazed. Unless you see some shape you like here, I'm more interested in hearing your thoughts on the completed designs."

She created all these pieces?

Ty eyed her while she busied herself with some jars on the counter. She was beautiful and talented and softhearted, considering her offer to help him with his grandmother's gift. He knew her offer benefited her, too, so she'd said, but still, she was kindhearted.

What was he doing here with this amazing girl? As a ski instructor, he met a lot of intriguing and beautiful women, but none of them held his interest. Not like Hayley. Mostly because they were here today gone tomorrow. They came to the ski resorts for a weekend of fun and weren't interested in anything long term. Ty reminded himself that he had nothing to offer in a real relationship, except, well, himself. He needed to do more with his life in order to provide for a family.

A knot grew in Ty's throat. Wow, this girl had him thinking about marriage and family, and he'd only just met her. He refocused his thoughts to the task at hand, once again perusing her beautiful pottery. Smooth colorful glazes in hues of blues and browns adorned pottery in all shapes and sizes, and then there were the sgraffito pieces, which he loved the most.

"You're so prolific," he said. "My grandmother is really going to be amazed."

"I hope so," she said. "Maybe I can meet her some time."

Her suggestion surprised him. He studied her for a moment, with her crystal blues that took everything in. "Maybe so."

He walked between the shelves, overwhelmed by the amount of pottery her small hands had produced. The artwork took his breath away. "I can't even imagine how much time it takes you to create these pieces."

"See anything you like?" she asked.

Her question startled him. Maybe he hadn't been demonstrative enough over her work. "Everything." He locked eyes with her. "I love everything. Boy, it's going to be hard to figure out what you could create for my grandmother. But maybe. . ."—he touched a porcelain teapot overlaid with blue sgraffito—"she'd like a teapot similar to this, only slightly bigger."

Oh boy. Why had he asked for something bigger? He was already going to be in trouble paying for this. Because he did, in fact, want to pay her for her work, if at all possible.

"I can do that. But I want you to think about it for a few days. Oh my goodness. . ." She slapped her hand over her mouth then dropped it. "I didn't think to ask when her birthday is. I might not have enough time to do this. Please tell me her birthday isn't tomorrow."

Ty smiled. "Nanna's birthday isn't until December twelfth. I started looking early because I wanted something special."

Hayley's sweet face lit up with her cute dimples and just a hint of color in her cheeks. Ty undeniably wanted to spend some time with her outside this joint venture. But he had nothing to offer a girl like her.

"What's wrong?" she asked

He'd never been good at hiding his emotions, and she was an artist. Had an eye for seeing things.

"Ty, if you don't want to do this, please tell me. I hope I haven't pressured you into this."

"There's nothing wrong. I definitely want to do this." Just have to figure out how to pay her.

"Okay, so have a seat. I'll make us some hot chocolate because no matter what the heat is on, I always get chilled if my hands aren't working the clay. Tell me about your grandmother."

"Aw, she's great. She loves people and is very active in her church. Loves crafts."

Hayley handed him a warm mug of hot cocoa and eyed him over the brim of her own. "That it?" she asked, arching a brow.

He scraped a hand through his hair, unsure what else to tell her. But he went on about how his grandfather died when Ty was young, and even told Hayley that he'd come to live with his grandmother as a teenager and why. What else did she need to know in order to create pottery that his grandmother would love? "This isn't going to be easy, is it?"

"I think. . .no." She huffed a sigh. "Have you ever thrown a pot on the wheel?"

He grinned. "I can't say that I have."

"Would you like to?"

The way she tilted her pretty blond head, what guy could turn her down? Good thing he'd taken off the rest of the day, though it would mean a smaller paycheck.

"Do you have to go anywhere? Because those clothes are going to get dirty, even though I have a couple of aprons." She held up what looked like a butcher's apron.

"I'm all yours"—he winked.

Hayley's cheek colored a little. She focused on getting her clay out and prepared for the wheel. Ty stood back and watched, hating that he'd embarrassed her. Maybe he was coming on too strong, and he hadn't meant to flirt with her at all.

Straddling the wheel, she plopped the clay on and explained to Ty about how important it was to center the clay. How difficult it could be. Ty thought about how that was kind of like a person's life. It could be tough to find your way, find the center and stay focused. He was twenty-eight and still trying.

Watching her now, he felt like he'd wasted so much of his life. Look at all she'd created, and he had nothing to show for his efforts.

"Okay, Ty, it's your turn." She slid from the seat. "I've centered it for you and started the process. All you have to do is dig your hands in and make something."

He laughed. "You make it sound so easy."

"It is for some, and for others, not so much." Mischief crept into her eyes. "Let's see what you've got."

He didn't miss the challenge in her tone and straddled the wheel. He pressed his thumbs into the center of the clay, and immediately it went all wonky. Off center. "I see what you mean."

He expected her to place her hands over his and show him that way, but no, she centered the clay again and talked him through it. When he was done, he'd created a squatty bowl.

"Not bad for your first time." She slid a wire beneath the pot and gently removed it from the wheel, placing it on the nearby table. "I've never actually taught anyone to do this before. That part was harder than I thought, too."

Ty stood there covered in clay, unsure what she had planned next. Her gaze flicked over him. "You can clean up at the sink."

She stripped off her apron, and so did he. At the sink, he washed his hands. He never thought he'd enjoy this activity so much and knew it had everything to do with the girl who'd pulled him into her life. While he dried his hands, the door swung open.

"Hayley, you coming to supper?" a deep voice asked.

"Daddy! I'm sorry."

"You got caught up in your art, I see."

Ty turned to face her father. The man then noticed Ty.

Surprise registered in his face before he covered it.

"I didn't know you had company. Don't know how I missed seeing another vehicle out there."

"This is Ty Walker," she said.

Her father thrust his hand out to Ty. "Glad to meet you, son. I'm Hart Covington, Hayley's father."

Hayley looked nervous and flustered. She grabbed his arms and tried to usher him to the door. "I made your favorite tonight, Daddy, and I'll be right in to join you."

The man didn't budge. Instead his gaze stayed glued to Ty. "Aren't you going to invite your friend, Hayley? Where are you manners?"

"Oh no, I couldn't, sir," Ty said. But his stomach chose that moment to rumble. Time had gotten away from them both.

"Nonsense," her father said. "Hayley makes a mean stew. You need to eat." The man winked and left Ty alone with Hayley.

"He doesn't take no for an answer, does he?" Ty asked.

"No, he doesn't." She came over to the sink and washed up, too. "Please let me talk about the pottery, okay? Daddy doesn't know I have pieces at Blue Mountain."

A shadow of guilt crossed her face.

"I won't say a word." As long as the man didn't ask too many questions. "But, why would you keep that a secret? What's to hide?" Ty regretted the words. This wasn't his business.

She blew out a breath. "It's a long, complicated story."

Ty wanted to say he wasn't going anywhere, that he had the

time to listen, but he heard in her voice that she didn't want to share it.

Why would Hayley's father want her to keep her talent locked up in this little cabin studio? Why wouldn't he want to share it with the world? But Ty didn't know anything about her relationship with her father or the family dynamics. Maybe it was a stretch, but he hoped to remedy that.

Chapter 3

Ty took his first spoonful of Hayley's stew and almost closed his eyes to savor the tasty dish.

Suddenly aware that both Hayley and her father watched him, waiting for his reaction, Ty grinned. "This is the best thing I've ever tasted." Certainly rivaled his grandmother's.

That seemed to meet with their approval, and both Hayley and her father started on their own bowls of stew, accompanied by fresh homemade rolls. How did she do it all? Ty could see easily enough that she enjoyed cooking and pleasing people.

Her father had given him a quick tour of the ranch house while Hayley set the table and readied their supper. Ty especially enjoyed all the old photographs covering the walls, depicting the Covington family in years gone by—old ones mixed with new ones. He asked lots of questions, grateful he was able to keep her father talking about himself and the history of the ranch, instead of turning the conversation Ty's way.

There was something he'd been weighing since he first met Hayley. That she might have been confused about his identity.

He wanted to clear that up, but the afternoon had gotten away from him, and he found himself sitting at her table, facing her father.

Finished with his stew, Mr. Covington placed his napkin on the table and leaned back, a gauging look in his eyes. Ty felt like he was on trial. He couldn't imagine what it must be like for anyone with a romantic interest in Hayley. But then her father likely figured Ty had an interest in her. And he wouldn't be wrong, though that's not why he was here.

"So, tell me, Ty, how did you and my daughter meet?" Ty fished his napkin from his lap, buying himself some time, and placed it on the table next to his bowl. He leaned back in his seat as well, with a quick glance to Hayley. She'd not wanted to bring up the fact her pottery was at the Blue Mountain studio.

This was her chance to jump in, which she did. "Daddy, I met Ty when I was in town. He was at the Blue Mountain Art Gallery looking for a gift for his grandmother. I offered to help."

"What were you doing at the gallery? Don't tell me Jim's been bothering you about showing your pieces again."

Ty didn't miss the fear mixed with hurt in Hayley's eyes. "He's already put a few of my pots in the gallery, and they sold quickly, Daddy. That's when I met Ty. I took a few more in, and he works at the studio and helped me carry the pots inside."

A knot constricted Ty's throat. She had brought him into the big reveal—why? So she wouldn't be alone when she told her father? And that wasn't all of it. She had Ty all wrong, just as he suspected. He wasn't sure it mattered all that much, but now he saw that it mattered.

"You don't have time to mess with that, Hayley. There's too much work for you on the ranch. And you know I don't think much of artists or ski bums and all that's grown popular in the valley. That stuff is a waste of time."

The man needed to seriously look around him—Jackson Hole was all about art and skiing, and less about cattle ranching. Regardless, Ty was in a predicament. He didn't want to correct Hayley on his employment in front of her father, but if he didn't, her father would think he'd covered up the truth. No. It was best to get that out in the open now.

"I need to clarify something," he said, dread souring in his stomach. "When I helped you with your pottery, Hayley, I was in the studio looking for something for my grandmother. That's it. I don't work there."

Her father laughed. Ty couldn't help but hear it as mocking his daughter. He kept his anger veiled, though. Hayley's big blues grew wide, and she pursed her lips. Clearly, this wasn't the best time to break the news to her, at least in her eyes.

"Then tell us, son, where do you work?"

He wanted to blurt out that he wasted his time as a ski bum. But he hadn't been raised to disrespect others, even when they were impertinent. "I work as a ski instructor, splitting my time with that and working at the National Elk Refuge." Maybe the man would appreciate that, at least. "In the summer I guide white-water rafting groups." Paint houses. Whatever it took to make ends meet.

Ty mouthed an "I'm sorry" to Hayley.

"A ski instructor," she said. "I've never been skiing."

Laughter erupted from her father again—a strange mix of mocking and yet a teasing warmth in his eyes, confusing Ty. The man pushed back his chair and stood.

"A ski bum and an artist. Don't you make a cute couple?" He thrust his hand out to shake Ty's once again.

Weird, after the insult, but Ty didn't refuse him.

"It was nice to meet you, son. I'm sure your grandmother is proud of you."

Ty wished he could retort that she was, as a matter of fact, but that wasn't true at all. Ty wished he would have listened to his grandmother, all these years. Even if he stayed in his field of work, he could have taken things to the next level instead of working part-time. But until this moment, he had lived to ski and nothing more.

Hayley's father excused himself and left the table, ambling into what looked like a study. Hayley was at Ty's side, pulling him to his feet. She ushered him into the kitchen.

"Oh Ty, I'm so, so sorry. Daddy doesn't really mean to come across rude. It's just his way. I hope you'll still let me make something for your grandmother."

"You sure you still want to? Doesn't sound like your dad is going to let you."

She cocked a brow at him. "I'm twenty-four years old. I can make my own decision, and Daddy knows that. It's just. . . I'm all he has left here. I'm the heir to this ranch, this is the Covington legacy. Lots of ranchers have sold out to kazillionnaires over the years, but my family has held on to this ranch. Daddy wants to keep it in the family. So you see. It's complicated."

"No wonder he was assessing me. Thinks I'm after his daughter, and maybe his ranch one day." Ty was out of his element here. These people were worth a lot of money, but that didn't seem to affect Hayley. She was down to earth, warm, and friendly.

"Don't worry, I'll explain," she said. "I'm sorry you ended up in the middle. I didn't mean to wait so long to tell him about my pottery on display at Blue Mountain."

Still trying to process the conversation, Ty wasn't sure what to say.

"But I have an idea," she continued. "You can trade me ski lessons for your grandmother's gift. That is, if you still want to work with me."

Any guy with brains would ski jump off the highest ramp for the chance to teach Hayley Covington how to ski, but the conversation tonight had sent Ty's confidence plummeting. He liked this girl, really liked her, but he would never get by her father if he imagined something could ever happen between them. She respected the man too much. Ty frowned.

"Ty?" Disappointment lingered in her gaze.

"You grew up here and have never been skiing?"

"No. Too busy with ranch chores, and you heard Daddy. Skiing is for the tourists, not the locals."

Sounded more like the man had said a waste of time, but whatever.

Scraping a hand over his face and then down around his neck, Ty blew out a breath. "I have a feeling you're not the kind of person who takes no for an answer either."

"Are you saying your answer was going to be no?"

Hardly. He sent her an easy smile. "If you can find time between your ranch chores and your amazing pottery, I'll carve out some time for you."

"Thanks." Hayley gave him a peck on the cheek, her crystal blues gleaming with joy.

Ty knew he'd never shake that image from his mind.

After Hayley finished up the dishes, she found Daddy in his study perusing his laptop. He didn't notice that she'd entered, even when she stood right behind him.

Hayley placed her hand on his shoulder and squeezed gently. "So what did you decide about the horses?"

He reached over with his right hand to cover hers, his grip strong and sure. "I'm wondering if I should just sell the whole ranch."

His words punched the air from her. "What?" She came around to sit on the ottoman in front of him. "Daddy, no. Why would you even think that?"

"Why keep it? Nobody wants to run it. What happens when I'm gone?"

A weight pressed on her shoulders. "Are you saying this just because I want to sell my art in Jackson?"

Her father shut the laptop. "Not just because of that, no. But it got me thinking."

He grabbed her hand then. "You really want to be an artist, don't you?"

She huffed a laugh. "Daddy, I *am* an artist—it's inside me, just like Mama, no changing that. But whether or not I can sell enough to make a living, or make a name for myself, who can know. I don't want you to sell the ranch. I love it here. Can't I be an artist, too?"

He smiled and squeezed her hand. "Of course you can. I guess I'm still trying to find my way after your mother passed."

A pang hit Hayley behind the eyes. "Daddy, she died fifteen years ago. This has nothing to do with her."

"I never had a mind to take a new wife." His chest rose and fell with a heavy sigh, and his eyes flicked to hers. "You don't have to tell me that I embarrassed you in front of your friend, and I'm sorry about that."

"Oh, Daddy, it's okay. Ty's. . ." Ty was what? Hayley hated to admit she really didn't know the man, which was obvious enough—she thought he'd worked for the studio. "He understands." She hoped.

Edging forward in the seat, he said, "Make something nice for his grandmother."

Her father stood and moved in front of one of Mama's paintings of the mountains, hanging tall in the center of his study, and jammed his hands in his pockets. Hayley always suspected he resented the time Mama had put into her art, and that's why he struggled with Hayley's creative side. Or maybe art made him think of his beloved wife and miss her all the more. Hayley wasn't sure. But she was sure that Mama had never put her paintings on display in the Jackson galleries because of Daddy.

"She would have loved your work," he said. "Would have told you to put it in those galleries in town a long time ago. I'm sorry if I held you back. She would have liked your guy."

Hayley stood next to him, looking at the painting. "He's not my guy, Daddy. I don't even know him, not really."

"But you like him, don't you?"

Hayley wasn't sure she should say the words, but it terrified her to think otherwise. "You don't have to worry about me getting married and leaving you to run the ranch by yourself, not that I do much around here."

He father drew her into a hug. "The ranch isn't worth your happiness, Daughter."

She loved it when he spoke in what she called pioneer speak. She squeezed him back, thinking it was worth Daddy's happiness to stay. "And I'm happy, right where I am."

Even as the words left her lips, her thoughts went to Ty and how she could make this evening up to him.

Chapter 4

T here you are." Making his way to his grandmother who dug in the white stuff, Ty kicked at the soft snow.

"Got it." She wrapped her gloved hands around a pinecone then stood to face Ty. Crinkles appeared around her eyes as she smiled at him. "Needed some more of these for a craft I plan for my Sunday school class. What are you up to today? Can you stay for supper?"

"Yep. Just finished with my last sleigh ride at the Elk Refuge, and my ski lessons are done for the day."

"Good. I've got chicken dumplings on. Was hoping you'd stop by."

Ty visited his grandmother several times a week between his jobs, and he usually stopped by at suppertime. Sometimes he'd take her out to the local buffet, but he hadn't been by since he'd seen her at church on Sunday. He'd been noticeably distracted then, and she'd picked up on it, asking a few too many questions. Ty had wrestled with his failures after the fiasco meal with Hayley and her proud father last week.

Hayley loved the man too much to truly see how harsh he was, but Ty understood that. Love covered a multitude of sins, the Bible said. But the conversation had forced Ty to face what he'd tried to avoid for too long.

"It's going to be dark soon, do you need more pinecones?" he asked.

"Just a few."

She grabbed a couple near the surface of the snow, and Ty joined her, placing them in the bucket she'd set out for her collection. They filled the bucket then moved inside, where the aroma of her chicken and dumplings made his mouth water and stomach rumble. Warm feelings and memories of living here with her wrapped around him and brought him a measure of comfort. He'd loved how secure she'd made him feel.

He shrugged out of his coat, and took hers, too, hanging them on the coatrack, then followed her into the kitchen. She uncovered the stockpot and ladled dumplings into two bowls, handing one over to him. They settled at the kitchen bar counter.

"Milk or water?" she asked.

"Water's fine. What are you going to make out of all those pinecones?" he asked. "Seems like a lot."

She chuckled. "Some are for the class. But I gathered enough to make a Christmas wreath. I know it's not Christmas yet, but I figured you could use a wreath to hang on your door when the time comes."

He let the dumplings he'd been eating warm his stomach

before he spoke. "I'm not the best at decorating for Christmas. I don't spend a lot of time at my apartment anyway." In truth, he preferred to visit his grandmother, or hang out at the lodge with a few friends. He'd like to add seeing Hayley at her art studio to his free-time endeavors, but he wouldn't make a conscious effort to go back there without an actual invitation. Not after meeting her father.

Coward.

"I understand. You're busy and you're a bachelor. You need a good woman to do that sort of thing for you."

Ty snorted. Nanna was so old-fashioned. "I could buy a wreath. You don't need to make me one."

"Nonsense. I enjoy making something out of nothing, though a pinecone isn't nothing, it's part of God's wondrous creation, put here for me to do something with."

Ty had endured enough of these conversations to know she was likely thinking about him and how he should do something important with his life. But he'd moved out to his own apartment, and she hadn't wanted to push him further away, so she stopped talking about it.

But Ty wanted to discuss that very thing this time. He'd felt duly humbled at Hayley's table, realizing that he wanted to do something more with his life than simply earn enough money to scrape by. Enough money to ski. He'd met a girl he liked, but why would she give him a second look when he hadn't done anything with his life except learn how to ski and instruct others?

"What's bothering you, Ty? This is the first time you've been by this week. I figured you for busy, but I see you have something on your mind."

"Yes"—he nodded—"actually, I do."

"Want to talk about it?"

"You've been right all along. I should have gone to college. Done something with my life. But now look at me. I work part-time at two different places. Sure, I get to ski until I'm sick of it, but that's about it."

She wrapped her mouth around a dumpling and studied him while she chewed. Took a swallow of her milk then settled against her chair back. "What brought this on?"

Ty wasn't sure he wanted to tell her. The more he thought about it, the more painful it was. To share that with his grand-mother would sink the knife deeper into the wound.

"Nothing. Just been thinking."

She got up from the chair and searched in the cabinet, returning with the salt and pepper. She shook a little of the con-tents into her bowl. "Not salty enough for me. You?"

She handed the shaker to Ty, who took it from her but set it on the counter.

"So what happened? You finally meet a girl?" She winked at him.

"Maybe." Ty shrugged.

"Those pinecones were just sitting out there, waiting for me to pick them up and do something with them. It's not too late for you to do something with your life, Ty. Have you got anything in mind? If you could do anything at all, what would you want to do? And don't tell me ski."

Now it was Ty's turn to chuckle.

He thought of Hayley and her art, and how her father appeared to stifle that, or else why would she have hidden that she'd been featured in a local gallery? "That's who I am. I wish I would have worked to at least manage a ski resort. Something."

He got up and rinsed off his dishes then stuck them in the dishwasher.

She sighed. "I've been waiting for you to step up. To see that you have so much more to offer, so now's probably as good a time as any to tell you that you should think bigger. I have a plot of land I've held on to, to give to you one day. You could look into building a resort there."

Ty laughed. "Do you know how much that would cost? We don't have that kind of money. Not to mention permits and zoning. No. That's way out of my league." Only people like the Covington's had the ability to do those kind of things. Who did he think he was, spending even ten seconds with Hayley?

His grandmother frowned. "It's something to start with, Ty. You create a business plan and get venture capitalists. Look into it. But I'll give you one even better than that. There's a man been trying to buy that from me for years to build another ski resort. The mountain is perfect, he says. I kept that for you, Ty."

"Why? Why would you keep it for me like that when you

think I haven't done anything worthwhile? And why didn't you tell me?"

"Because I believed you had it in you. You just needed to realize that for yourself. Or at least want it."

"I don't even have a business degree."

She eyed him, while tugging out a map. "You're full of excuses."

Ty watched as she fingered her land. It was near enough the Covington Ranch, he wondered if it didn't back right up to the property. Hayley's father would just love to have a ski resort next to his ranch, since he thought so highly of the activity.

Hayley exited the Blue Mountain Art Gallery and climbed into her vehicle parked at the curb. She'd gone in to browse and watch when and if anyone stopped to look at her pottery.

There'd been only a few people inside, and her pottery hadn't caught their attention. Oh well, she'd try not to let that discourage her. But one thing that had discouraged her was that Ty hadn't returned her call.

She started the ignition and turned up the heat, rubbing her hands together. Granted, she'd left a message last night, inviting him back out to look at what she was doing for his grandmother's teapot. But since he hadn't called her back, she started to worry. And it wasn't just that.

She hadn't stopped thinking about how she had unintentionally embarrassed him by thinking he was one of the art gallery employees, when it turned out he was something much different. Daddy had played on that, of course. Though she'd tried to apologize to Ty, clearly that hadn't been enough. She'd run the guy off.

Hayley glanced in the rearview mirror. When the traffic was clear she pulled from the curb. She hoped Ty didn't think she was a stalker or anything, but she really wanted to make up for last week. She'd already looked up his grandmother's address and now debated whether or not to follow through with her plan. Meeting the woman would go a long way in helping Hayley create this piece. Though it really wasn't the best way to conduct her little test of commissioned work, she wanted this to be perfect.

For Ty.

He seemed like a thoughtful and kind guy. After all, who would put so much thought into a gift for their grandmother, thinking about it weeks ahead of time? She hadn't been able to get the image of him at the potter's wheel out of her head. Boy was he awful, but she hadn't had the heart to tell him. Besides, it took a lot of training. She hoped he would come back to practice. At the very least, he was supposed to teach her to ski. She would probably be awful at *that*.

She smiled to herself.

Steering through Jackson, she passed by the Aspen Hill Cemetery, onto Pine Drive that curved around the base of Snow King Mountain. She drove slowly up the steep road, reading the addresses until she found the cozy cabin, tucked back in the woods. Pulse hammering, Hayley pulled into the abrupt driveway that spiraled down to the cabin. Fortunately, she didn't see Ty's vehicle. She hadn't thought about what she'd say if she ran into him at his grandmother's.

Coming here had been impulsive and lacked any sort of good judgment. At least she could admit that about herself. She could admit she'd made a mistake.

Hayley shifted into reverse to back from the drive. A knock on her window startled her. Looking at the older woman standing on the other side of the glass, she shifted into Park and lowered the window.

"Can I help you?" the woman asked.

Hayley's throat constricted.

"Are you lost?" The woman's eyes crinkled with concern.

"No, actually. Um...I was hoping to meet Ty Walker's grandmother. I'm Hayley, by the way." She left off the Covington name, just in case the name set the woman off. Some folks didn't necessarily like the cattle ranches, namely Covington Ranch.

"I'm Clara Walker, Ty's grandmother. It's nice to meet you, Hayley. Would you like to come in for some coffee or hot cocoa and get warmed up?"

Hayley spotted the bucket of pinecones in the woman's hand and smiled. "I'd love to."

Maybe this hadn't been a bad idea, after all.

Half an hour later, Hayley finished her third cup of hot

chocolate, her mind reeling with all that Clara had told her about Ty. She'd been right about him—he was definitely a good guy. And she already had in mind what she would create for his kind and friendly grandmother.

"Clara, please promise me you'll keep our meeting between the two of us. I don't want to mess up my surprise. I hope I haven't been too presumptuous in coming here."

"Nonsense. I'm glad to know my Ty has met a sweet girl like you. Of course, this will be our secret, but you won't mind if I invite you to join us for an evening meal now and then, will you?"

Definitely, Clara's statement was presumptuous. Hayley and Ty weren't there quite yet, if they ever would be. Hayley hoped she hadn't overstepped by coming here, but Ty would understand—he had a soft spot for his grandmother. Surely he couldn't fault Hayley for wanting more information to make her present the best it could be.

"Of course not. But has Ty even mentioned me?"

"He's let on that there might be someone special, dear. He is never one to give me too much ammunition, you see." She chuckled.

Hayley found the sound endearing. She was a family girl, and could see that family was important to Ty, as well.

"Hayley, I don't think I got your last name."

Here goes. "Covington."

Clara's eyes widened slightly. "As in. . ."

Heat warmed her cheeks. "Covington Ranch."

Clara pressed her fingers over her mouth just as Hayley's cell phone rang.

Hayley glanced at the caller ID.

It was Ty.

Hayley answered, his grandmother watching. Awkward.

"Hey. I can stop by this evening to see your work, if that's good for you," he said.

Chapter 5

Y ou're getting the hang of that pretty quickly, considering this is only your third lesson."

Hunching over the lump of clay spinning on the wheel, Ty pressed down to center it, Hayley's compliment pleasing him more than it should. Funny. He never thought that helping the girl with her pottery that day in the gallery would have led to him creating his own. But Hayley did so much more to the pieces than throw and shape them on a wheel. She etched images into each piece then glazed the images different colors. It still blew his mind.

The lump of clay now spun asymmetrically, pulling his attention back. He knew she'd been generous with her compliment.

"Here, let me help." She got in close to help him center the clay.

He smiled. Maybe he'd left it a smidge off center on purpose. Her blond hair tickled his nose, so he backed away to give her space. How many times would he get it wrong before she was on to him? She dropped more water on the clay to keep it moist and worked it back into position.

Hayley released the mound and moved away for him. "It can take awhile, but I think you're doing better than most."

Ty went back to work, but he'd much prefer watching her etch those drawings onto the teapot she was creating for his grandmother. The piece was much more whimsical than he'd seen in any of her other work. Somehow, she'd known exactly what to do. How had she gotten it right? Ty couldn't have done better if he'd been a master potter.

He went back to work on the potter's wheel. He'd mostly agreed to learn as a way to make Hayley happy, but he found that he enjoyed being creative, something he didn't realize was inside. Of course, he enjoyed spending time with her, though he'd hesitated after that first meeting. Ty liked her and, deep inside, figured she was the kind of girl he'd want to have a future with. Unfortunately, he couldn't see that happening with Hayley, well, because he was a nobody ski bum. Her father would never allow it. Ty was surprised that Hayley had persisted in inviting him back, persisted in her idea to make a gift for his grandmother.

Hayley cleared her throat, and Ty slowed the wheel, glancing up to meet her gaze. His insides jumped around. Not good.

"What do you think?" She lifted up the teapot.

"My grandmother will love it." Ty slid from the perch at the potter's wheel, wiping his hands on a towel, and moved closer.

"Really? You think so?" Delight danced in her crystal blues.

Ty loved the darker flecks in her irises, but he pulled his

gaze from her eyes and looked at the teapot. Didn't she see how talented she was? Surely she understood that, especially with people buying her work at the gallery.

He peered at the intricate carvings, wanting to run his finger over them, but that would ruin them at this stage. Wanting to run his thumb over Hayley's soft cheek, and without thinking, he did just that. "Yes, really. This is a special gift for her."

His voice sounded husky, and he shook it off, putting distance between them. Inappropriate. Hayley didn't want that from him. Somehow, the two had become fast friends, and he wasn't sure what to make of it, considering they were an unlikely pair with such different backgrounds.

"I'm glad you like it. I hope she will, too." Hayley's whisper told him she'd been caught up in whatever passed between them, too.

"Then you should be there when I give it to her on her birthday." Ty grabbed a clean towel on the table behind Hayley and wiped at her cheek. "Sorry, I left a smudge."

She laughed. "You mean to add to hundreds of other smudges."

Hayley stood close to him now, her sweet, smiling lips so near. Ty cleared his throat and stepped back. "I should get going."

"But what about your pot? You haven't finished." Hayley's disappointment rallied him.

"Okay, I'll finish this piece before I go, but you have to do something for me." As if she hadn't done so much already.

"What's that?"

"You wanted me to teach you to ski. That was our deal. Now, you're teaching me pottery and you've created that amazing teapot for my grandmother, and still I can't get you on the slopes. We're expecting some big snow this weekend, before Thanksgiving. Will you be around? Or do you and your father go somewhere for Thanksgiving?"

"Family comes in from all over. My sisters and their families. Aunts, uncles, and cousins. I'm not the boss in the kitchen then, but I'm around to help. They won't start arriving until a day or two before Thanksgiving. What about you?"

"I'll be in town, waiting to ski with you." He winked, noting her cheeks colored again. *Easy, Ty.* That's not what this was about. Was it?

Hayley is out of your league. He struggled to care about that hurdle.

"I still can't believe you've never been skiing and you live in a skiing mecca."

"Yeah well, I live in an art mecca, too." She laughed. "As long as my schedule isn't filled up with ranching chores, maybe I can make it up there, but I'll need ski clothes and gear."

"I can help you with that."

"Thank you. I just. . . I'll admit I'm a little scared."

"Scared? Of what?"

Hayley released the clip keeping her hair out of the way and shoved the long tresses behind her shoulders. Ty fought to focus on her words.

"Of making a fool of myself out there."

"Don't worry. I'll teach you everything you need to know. Besides, with so many people on the slopes, and plenty making fools of themselves, you'll have anonymity."

She angled her head.

"Nobody will know or care who you are."

And then it hit him, was that what she was worried about? Being seen with Ty Walker on the slopes?

Hayley dumped what was left of her coffee in the sink and finished cleaning up the breakfast dishes she'd left earlier in the morning. She'd finished breaking the ice so the animals could drink and made sure the hands were putting out fresh hay for the horses they hadn't sold off. Daddy had seen to the cattle.

Boots stomping in the mudroom told her he'd returned, and she'd hoped to be out the door before he set her to work on something else. She was beginning to feel like she'd been playing too much with Ty, instead of working the ranch. But he made her laugh and smile. Made her happy. He appreciated her pottery. She'd been thrilled when she'd seen his admiration over his grandmother's teapot. Delighted with the question she'd seen in his eyes—how had she gotten the teapot right?

The piece was much different from all her others. She'd etched in cutesy pinecones. But she'd gone to meet his grandmother and seen that she enjoyed crafts. Had seen the pinecone crafts the woman created. Hayley had fashioned a teakettle just for Clara. She'd keep the fact that she'd already met his grand-mother a secret for now, but how could Ty not be suspicious?

Daddy had already removed his coat and dusted off the snow when he came into the kitchen and grabbed a mug of coffee. "It's frigid out there. Best stay close to the ranch today."

Anxiety kicked up her pulse. She thrust her hair behind her ears and cleaned out the sink. "As a matter of fact, I thought I'd head into Jackson."

"I'll drive you."

Hayley gasped. She turned to face her father. "I'm okay. I know how to drive in this, remember?" Ty had called earlier and offered to pick her up, but she hadn't thought Daddy would be back.

"I don't want to worry about my girl."

Hayley considered how much to tell him and decided to give him the whole story. "Look, Daddy. There's going to be some fresh powder on the slopes."

He stared at her, long and hard. "What did you say?"

Leaving the kitchen to head back to her room and get ready, she just shook her head, and he followed. Now that she thought about it, it did seem a little ridiculous she hadn't tried the sport. "I know you think skiing is a waste of time," she said, "but I'd like to try it just once."

Her disrespectful tone mortified her. When had she ever spoken to Daddy this way?

When Daddy didn't follow her up the stairs, guilt squeezed

her heart. She turned to stare down at him standing at the base of the steps. Hayley couldn't take it anymore, she ran down the steps to her father and hugged him. "I'm sorry."

"It's that Ty, isn't it? He's the one who's influencing you."

Hayley released Daddy and took a step back onto the stairs. "I'm not a child. I work hard for you, here at the ranch. There's no harm in me having some fun once in a while. I like Ty. He makes me laugh. And. . ."

"And he makes your smile a little brighter. How could a father not notice? But darlin', he isn't ranching material. You get your heart set on this boy, and he'll hurt you."

"Why do you say that?"

He stared at her. "I've been around a long time. Men like him—they use people. All he cares about is getting his hands on this ranch so he can sell it off for the money."

Her eyes filled with tears. "Don't. Don't even say that he only cares about the ranch. That he doesn't care about me."

She ran up the steps and into her room. How could Daddy be so cruel? She swiped at the tears, more angry at her father now that she'd gained control over the hurt. He didn't understand that things weren't like that between her and Ty. They were just friends.

As Hayley stared at her reflection in the mirror, she ran a finger over where he'd touched her cheek a few nights ago. His touch had made her skin tingle all over. There was something more between them. At least she'd felt it, but she wasn't sure if

Ty had felt it. Considering Daddy took a long time to warm up to new things, Hayley was happy to take her time with Ty, if their relationship even grew to something more.

Daddy had a point about Ty. He didn't have a lot going for him in the way of aspirations. She wasn't sure if he was even husband material, if things went that far. Should she let herself get closer to him, if in the long run they wouldn't be good together? Her sisters had married good, solid men, one an engineer and one an architect, who provided stability for the families they wanted. But that's why they'd ended up moving to the city and away from the ranch, so their husbands could keep their jobs. Her sisters contributed, too—one a schoolteacher, and the other worked at the post office. What in the world would Hayley do if she couldn't run the ranch? It wasn't like her art made her a living.

She sighed. She wasn't looking for a husband, and she hadn't known she was missing anything until she'd met Ty. But Daddy was right, Ty wasn't a rancher. She shoved those ridiculous thoughts away, all of them, including Daddy's hurtful words. She wanted to enjoy the day learning to ski.

When Hayley was at the back door with her keys in hand, Daddy appeared in his coat. "I'm driving you, Daughter."

She pursed her lips "No, thank you."

"Hayley, I'm sorry about what I said, but I don't want to see you get hurt."

"Then why do you say cruel things?" *Why do you keep me*

shackled here? But that wasn't true either. Daddy needed her. That was all.

He reached for her arm and gently squeezed. "You know I love you. I'm just an overprotective father. You know fathers never like potential future sons-in-law."

"Good thing you're getting way ahead of yourself," she said.

"Uh-huh. And things can heat up pretty fast. I knew your mother five whole weeks before I proposed."

Hayley pushed through the door, her father following, insisting on driving her.

He climbed into the driver's seat, started the ignition, and turned up the heat on his dually truck.

"Ty and I are just friends working on a project together."

"All it takes is a little kindling to start a fire blazing."

Chapter 6

Wishing he had picked her up at the ranch, Ty waited for Hayley outside the entrance to Teton Village Sports, at the base of Jackson Hole Mountain Resort.

He glanced at his watch. She was only fifteen minutes late, so he shouldn't worry. The snow had stopped falling in the lower elevations and the roads had turned to slush. Besides, Hayley was a big girl and had grown up in this town. Lived here longer than Ty had.

A few cars, trucks, and utility vehicles steered into the parking lot, but none Ty recognized. A steel-gray dually pulled around the front, and the girl in the passenger seat waved.

"Hayley?" Ty opened the door for her.

Ty stiffened when her father climbed from the driver's side and hiked around the grill of his truck.

The man adjusted his baseball cap and glanced around. Then he turned his attention on Ty. "Didn't want Hayley driving in this. Figured I'd run a few errands in town then come back to pick her up. How long will you be?"

Technically, Ty should have been working today, and technically he was—giving a private lesson. But he'd had every intention of making today special.

Having her father inserting himself into the mix put a damper on things. But maybe Ty was trying too hard. Pushing too fast. Likely he'd ruin the friendship he had with Hayley, if he wasn't careful.

"A few hours, actually. We have to get her ski gear and rent boots and skis, and then"—Ty cleared his throat, uncertain if he should add the last part—"then I thought I'd take Hayley to dinner. So I'm happy to bring her home. But. . .you're welcome to join us for something to eat later." Ty hoped the man would turn that offer down.

"Oh, that sounds fun, Ty." Hayley's eyes sparkled.

Which part—where they ate alone? Or where her father joined them? Ty waited for her father's answer, though, because it seemed like he was commander-in-chief.

The man studied Ty without a hint of a smile. What was he thinking? Ty had a feeling that her father suspected Ty had a romantic interest in her. Maybe he wasn't worthy of Hayley Covington, but maybe. . .maybe he could get there. Meeting her had definitely changed his perspective on life. He could see that God had in fact answered his prayer that morning—giving him direction. Or more like sense that he needed direction.

He didn't know where he was going, but he knew he was

heading somewhere, and he'd let God be in the driver's seat.

"Daddy?" Hayley spoke up, when her father didn't answer. "Ty will bring me home. I don't want you to have to wait around. And I don't want to have to rush, either, okay?"

The man grumbled something unintelligible and moved around his big manly truck. "You." He pointed at Ty. "Be careful with my daughter. Call me when you're headed out to the ranch, Hayley."

"I will," she said. "I love you." She smiled at her father and waved as he drove away and then her lips flattened.

She blew out a breath and looked at Ty. "Sorry about the third degree. It's like I'm sixteen or something, going on a first date, only this wasn't a. . ." Hayley's blue eyes, accented by the white stuff behind her, searched his gaze. "Was it? I mean, dinner and. . . Oh, Ty, I'm sorry. I didn't mean to put pressure on you."

He hadn't known whether or not she thought about him like that. A person can only suspect that someone else feels the chemistry, but they can't know until words are said or kisses are shared. "I'll never tell."

She laughed. "Oh, you. Now I feel—"

"Don't." He grabbed her gloved hand and squeezed. Even though he couldn't feel her soft skin against his, holding her hand lit a million candles inside his chest. "Let's have fun today."

The next hour they spent in the sports shop buying ski clothes and renting the boots, skis, and poles. No point in buying those until she knew she wanted to do this again. After they geared up, Ty led her outside to a level area to give her the basic skiing instructions, then he showed her the moves in a place where she could practice before they tried the green slope for beginners.

Hayley fell down a few times, and Ty helped her up, but that was to be expected.

She tugged her goggles over her head. "I don't know if I'm ever going to get this. You're not disappointed, are you?"

"Disappointed? Are you kidding me? You're doing great, and in fact, I think it's time to take the lift."

Her eyes grew wide. "Oh wow, I've always wanted to do that. But I. . .just never did."

Yeah. Ty had his own tale of *just never did.* "Then let's go."

They rode the ski lift to where the beginner's slope began then slid off at the right moment. At the top of the ski run, Ty positioned himself next to Hayley. "You can do this, just take it slow and easy, and stop if you need to. I'll be right behind you."

"Thanks." Hayley held his gaze for a few seconds longer than necessary.

Was Ty reading too much into that? She pulled her goggles down over her eyes and pushed off with her poles. She took off a little too fast, and since Jackson was considered one of the most vertical slopes in the continental United States, maybe even the green was too hard.

Hayley screamed as she skied.

Ty yelled at her to throw her skies into a wedge, which would stop her.

But she just kept skiing faster.

Ty yelled for her to drop on her backside. If nothing else, that would bring her to a stop.

Finally, she fell, and Ty skied up to her. He tugged off his sunglasses. "Are you okay?"

Breathless, she looked up at him and grinned. "That was awesome!"

"You scared me to death." Ty gasped, trying to calm his racing heart. "You're some kind of crazy, Hayley Covington."

Hayley finished the ski run and went back for more.

She and Ty laughed and talked as they rode the ski lift, and he showed her all the other green runs. She hoped to advance enough before the season ended to try the intermediate, but he cautioned her. She wouldn't worry, she had Ty Walker as a ski instructor, didn't she?

At the bottom of the slope, on their last run, Hayley could feel the endorphins kick in, just like if she'd gone jogging, or after an exhilarating ride on her horse. She followed Ty to take off her boots and return her skis.

"No wonder Daddy never let me ski," she said. "He knew I'd get addicted and wouldn't have time for the ranch."

Ty helped her get out of the jacket she'd gotten tangled in. "Well then, I sure hope he doesn't hold that against me," he said.

"Of course, he'll know your new evil vice is because I'm a bad influence."

When Hayley turned, he was oh, so close. Hayley could have kissed him at that moment, and the thought took her breath away. It seemed a natural next step, but they were in a public place. Ty hadn't exactly said they were on any kind of date. But he just stood there and stared down at her. Was he thinking the same thing?

"Are you ready?" he asked. His voice cracked a little.

For you to kiss me? "For what?" she asked.

"To eat. I know the perfect place."

"Yes, I'm famished."

Ty took her to a wonderful restaurant featuring international cuisine instead of Bubba's Barbeque—which she loved—but she and Daddy went there far too often. This was a seriously high-end place. A fire blazing in the fireplace—and suddenly Daddy's words came back to her:

"All it takes is a little kindling to start a fire blazing."

She had a feeling she knew what he meant. She'd met Ty in the art gallery only a few weeks ago, and from the moment she'd met him, they'd connected. Felt comfortable together. Enjoyed each other's company. Hayley found herself thinking about him a lot, thinking about something more than friendship. But did he feel the same way?

Ty sat across from her, his gaze penetrating. "What are you thinking about?"

"You said you wanted to teach me to ski, and I wasn't expecting all"—she gestured to the ambience—"this."

Hayley couldn't hold his gaze any longer and wished she'd kept that to herself. If they were to be more than friends, how did they go there? Was it even a good idea?

"I hope I haven't made you uncomfortable choosing this place," he said.

"No, not at all."

"Earlier, you mentioned that this wasn't a date, and then you asked if it was."

"Right. You said you'd never tell."

He grinned, one cheek lifting into multiple dimples. "If I had asked you on a real date, what would you have said?"

He kept the tone light and fun—that was who Ty was—but she understood the serious nature of his question.

"Yes." She swallowed. "I would have said yes."

"Well then"—he swirled the water in his glass—"what do you say we make this a real date?"

She smiled, feeling that tingling over her skin again. "I think you know the answer to that."

He leaned forward. "I want to hear you say it."

His question and demeanor seemed out of character. But Hayley decided that she liked it. She liked it a lot. But then Daddy's other words came back to her—the words that warned her of guys who only wanted her to get to the ranch and her money.

"Yes, I want this to be a real date."

Leaning back, he smiled. "Can I ask you something?"

"Of course." She looked at the waiter, who finally appeared with the dishes they'd ordered.

Once he'd left, Hayley cut into her steak and savored the tenderness. "What did you want to ask me?"

"You're a beautiful girl, Hayley. And you have a rich history here...and I'm just... Why aren't you with someone? Why aren't you already married? I guess what I'm really asking is what are you doing here with me? Why would you want to be on a date with me? The local ski bum?"

Hayley heard both the accusation and the insecurities in his question. She liked his honesty—that he was transparent. She sensed he didn't want to play games. Neither did she.

An ache burned behind her eyes. "I don't know, Ty. There was someone once. But things didn't work out. I think maybe, I think...Daddy ran him off. Daddy was scared Ray was only after me to get at the ranch. And in turn, Ray didn't want to deal with my intimidating father. But you... I don't know. When I met you, you didn't treat me like you were on the hunt and I was the treasure."

Ty didn't say anything, just studied her as if considering her words. Measuring his own. Then finally—"I hope with dinner tonight, I haven't been too forward. That I haven't ruined our friendship."

"You haven't." Ray sure hadn't taken an interest in Hayley's pottery like Ty had. Maybe he hadn't cared about her, after all. Maybe Daddy had been right and Ray had only been after the ranch and money, though without liquidating the ranch, there was no real money.

An awkward silence grew between them. Hayley wondered if she'd scared Ty off all by herself. "So tell me about yourself," she said.

"What would you like to know?"

"I know about your grandmother, but what about the rest of your family. What brought your family to Jackson?"

Fair enough question, without probing too deeply, she hoped. But the evening was suddenly turning serious, and Hayley wished they could rush back to the slopes. Back to the laughter and smiles.

"My parents are in Texas. We'd come to Jackson to see Nanna—my grandmother—for the holidays or vacations, and I fell in love with skiing early on. Moved in with Nanna when I was a teenager so I could train and make something of myself." He half laughed, half scoffed. "And the rest is history."

Hayley searched his gaze, hating how he talked about himself. "You sell yourself short, Ty. You're a very good instructor. And you pointed out a few of your students to me today. They looked like they were having a ball."

"You know that's not what I meant. I wanted to make racing history, but I took a few falls and just never got up. And here I am. I never did anything more with my life."

She laughed, hoping to inject a lighter tone to their conversation. "Well, it's like Daddy said, we make an interesting couple. Me an artist, and you a ski—"

"Bum. I'm a ski bum."

"I was going to say instructor. You're a ski instructor, and there's nothing wrong with that profession. It's honest work, and it's what you love. I saw that today."

That seemed to ease his tension, his shoulders visibly relaxing. "I love to ski. And I love teaching others. I loved seeing your face shine when you finally got it."

They finished dinner, reminiscing about their afternoon on the slopes. Ty paid the bill for their meal, which had to cost him, considering the restaurant. He insisted this was a date the old-fashioned way, so he would pay.

"Thank you." Hayley hoped he knew how happy she was that she was officially dating him.

He offered his hand. "You ready?"

"Are you taking me home now?" She didn't want to go. Not yet.

"I don't want to lose the battle with your father."

Hayley liked his answer. That meant he was willing to fight, even after everything he'd just revealed. But she dreaded the trouble her father might cause over another man in her life.

In Ty's vehicle, they held hands as he drove the dark highway, a comfortable silence between them. When it started sleeting, making the roads more hazardous, Ty released her and kept both hands on the steering wheel. On the curve around the base of the mountain going to the Covington property, he pulled over before the ranch house lights came into view.

"What are you doing?" she asked.

He shifted closer to her. "There's something I've wanted to do all day, and I know I won't get the chance once I turn into your driveway. Not with your father watching over us."

Hayley's breath hitched.

He pulled her closer and gently brushed her hair from her face. He searched her gaze, as if trying to read whether or not she wanted him to kiss her. She hoped he read in her eyes an emphatic yes.

But just in case he didn't, she inched closer and pressed her lips gently against his. He put his palms against her cheeks and kissed her back. Soft. Gentle. And sweet.

Ty was a gentleman. She'd always believed that and had wondered if they would ever move their relationship to the next level. If he would be too shy or gentle, or intimidated by her father after that first supper. But even Daddy hadn't stood in his way.

Headlights shined brightly into the cab, interrupting the moment. Ty and Hayley shielded their eyes.

Daddy. She groaned.

The vehicle pulled next to them and stopped. Ty lowered his window.

"Hayley, you were supposed to call when you headed home.

The roads are bad. I got worried when I couldn't reach you on your phone. A good thing I'm here. Looks like you broke down."

She'd turned her phone off to enjoy her dinner without interruption and forgotten to turn it back on. Hayley squeezed Ty's arm, whispering, "I'm so sorry, Ty." Then to Daddy, "We stopped to talk for a minute before going all the way home."

Daddy looked off in the distance, the sleet shifting to snow. "Looks like I interrupted something. For that, I'm sorry." He glanced at Hayley then backed up the truck, turning around. She watched the red lights of his vehicle disappear in the night.

Chapter 7

On the drive back to Jackson, snow and sleet pounded the windshield and danced in the beam of his headlights.

What had he been thinking to move so fast in his friendship with Hayley? Obviously she returned his interest, but where could this really go except giving them both a broken heart and putting a wedge between Hayley and her father?

Ty was surprised the man had been so congenial, because no way was Hayley's father going to let her be with a guy like Ty—someone who hadn't made something of himself. Ty couldn't blame the man. If he were Hayley's father, he'd want her to have the best sort of person for a husband.

Right now, Hayley didn't seem to care about Ty's simple occupation, and there was nothing wrong with it as long as you did something solid with it. Something besides working part-time. That wouldn't take care of a family.

But her father cared about it, and eventually Hayley would care, too. Ty couldn't stand to think of a day when she might be disappointed in him. Or come to resent him.

Given half a chance, he would change his future for himself. For her.

Thanksgiving proved to be ridiculously busy, with Ty's parents coming to town. They stayed with his grandmother, thank goodness, but he still cleaned his bachelor pad just in case. Plus, he worked double shifts at the ski resort and the National Elk Refuge, driving the sleighs for the tourists wanting to see the herd that wintered near Jackson.

He'd only had a short visit at the Covington Ranch, meeting Hayley's sisters, their families, and other relatives. Wow, she had a big clan. She'd held his hand and acted proud enough to introduce him. Of course everyone asked what he did for a living, and after his reply, he couldn't help but notice the questions in their eyes, her father notwithstanding. But maybe his own doubts and insecurities made him see questions that weren't there.

On Friday, he'd managed to tear away from his work schedule and bring Hayley to his grandmother's to meet his family. They were all duly impressed, and unfortunately, he could read his parents well enough. They didn't think it would work.

Instead of letting anything get him down, Ty focused on making something of himself. Just like he'd always dreamed of doing, only different. He couldn't be a champion ski racer, but he could do something productive, and that would last even longer. At the end of the day, when he had the evenings to himself, he worked on creating a business plan for a ski lodge on Nanna's plot of land. Researched possible venture capitalists, and he found he enjoyed the business side of things.

He hoped he'd get the chance to share his plans with Hayley before it was too late.

Saturday morning, Ty worked at the refuge as usual, driving the horse-drawn wagon-sleigh. The sleigh took the tourists right to the elk herd of about seven thousand head. Today's group had him a little nervous, with a few members of Hayley's family, including her father, in the twenty-plus group. They'd said hello, and were warm and friendly enough, but mostly left him to do his job.

He couldn't help but wonder if they were there to enjoy the herd—people who, for the most part, lived in this region—or if they'd come to watch Ty work. Maybe even put him in his place, as it were. He wasn't good enough for Hayley. For a Covington. As he directed the sleigh back he left those kind of thoughts behind. They wouldn't do him any good.

When the group exited the wagon, Hayley's father hung back.

"Did you enjoy the ride? Seeing the herd?" Ty asked, trying to ignore how much her father intimidated him.

Hayley adored her father, and Ty wouldn't give the man a reason to hate him, if he could help it.

The man thrust his hand out and shook Ty's. "You do a good job, Son."

"Thanks." Ty suspected that wasn't all he would say.

"Hayley's a special girl," her father said.

"I know."

"And I know you care about my daughter."

Pulse ratcheting up, Ty nodded. "Yes, I do." Where was he going with this?

"And that's why I want to ask you to do what's best for her."

"Sir?"

"Since you care about her, then surely you can see that you can't offer her the best future."

Heart thrumming, Ty didn't know what to say. He couldn't believe the man would actually say those words to him. How did Ty respond?

"Let me rephrase that for you, Son. If you care about Hayley, like you say you do, then you will let her go. You want the best for her. We both do."

And you're not the best man for her. That's what he was saying.

Hayley's father walked off, leaving Ty standing there to reflect on his statement.

Today was Ty's grandmother's birthday.

There was a party to attend. Somewhere. Sometime. Staring at the teakettle she'd created for Ty's grandmother, Hayley chewed on her nails. She'd never done that before. But she'd never been in this position before.

He'd been busy the weeks since Thanksgiving, or so he'd

claimed, so he hadn't had time to see Hayley. Still, he should have contacted her about the gift and the party.

Something was wrong. Very wrong.

Hayley knew she'd been dumped, and the hurt was palpable, even as she tried to comprehend the truth of it. What else could it be? But she couldn't figure out why, unless. . .unless Daddy had interfered. But she couldn't fathom him doing that. Not this time. Couldn't he see that Ty was a good man? A hardworking man. A man who wasn't interested in the ranch because it was worth millions. What did it matter if the guy didn't have money of his own?

Hayley had decided she didn't care what he did for a living— he wasn't the bum he had termed himself at all. She had hoped that over time she could convince Ty to spend time with her on her ranching chores. Maybe she could transform him into a cowboy or a rancher, and they could all be happy. But if not, it wouldn't change how she felt about him.

They'd had such a good friendship, and Hayley hurt that their friendship had been ruined because they'd taken things a step further, but it was the only natural course. No point in dancing around the obvious.

No point in sitting around feeling sorry for herself either. Ty had been straight with her from the beginning. She wouldn't let him change that on them now.

She grabbed a box and gently packed the teakettle inside. Then pasted a few Christmas stickers on and decorated with some ribbon and bows she kept handy for this time of year. She would deliver this present to his grandmother, whether he liked it or not.

And after she'd have her say with Ty, then she'd face Daddy, if he was involved in Ty's backing away.

An hour later, Hayley drove the curvy mountain road to Clara Walker's home. Unsure if she would be early or late to the party, though she wasn't even sure she was still invited. Hayley had called and left a voice mail with Ty that she would stop by to deliver the gift, and she'd texted him to give him an out if he didn't want to call her back.

Whatever.

Her relationship with Ty aside, she'd put time and effort into this project, and the more she thought about it, the more aggravated she grew. This wasn't like him at all. She hoped it was all a misunderstanding. That he was really busy and she'd become some dependent, clingy girl. Wow. The option didn't sound any better.

Hayley steered down Clara's steep driveway and saw Ty's vehicle. Her heart jumped to her throat.

He hadn't called her back.

He didn't want her here.

What am I doing? *Deliver the gift.*

She had to at least give Clara the gift she'd created per Ty's request. But that was just it—Ty hadn't requested the teakettle at all. Hayley had been the one to insist.

As she parked the car, she debated over following through and shifted into REVERSE. But just like the first time she'd come here, she was caught before she could leave. Ty opened the door and stood on the porch, hesitant.

Oh. Not good.

Panic inserted itself in her chest. She couldn't breathe.

He closed the door behind him and walked out to her. Hayley let the window down. "Hey," she said.

"Hi." He tucked his hands in his jeans.

With no jacket on, he would probably get cold. Maybe he wanted that as an excuse to make this quick.

"I brought your grandmother's gift."

He nodded and glanced at the house then back to Hayley.

"Look, I'm sorry for coming out here. I was invited to her party, remember? But you didn't get back to me."

Regret flickered in his gaze. Mingled with longing. So. . .he wasn't over her?

"What are you kids doing out here?" Clara's aged voice called from the door. She pulled her wrap closer and stepped off the porch, making her way toward Hayley. "Hayley, dear, come on in."

Ty opened the door before she could protest.

Hayley got out and went to the back of her Explorer, popped the hatch and lifted the gift, handing it over to Ty, her vision blurring. "Here. I hope she enjoys it."

"You might as well come in and see her open it," he said.

That was it?

Hayley wasn't sure she could stay with the hurt pinging through her. Daddy was right. He'd been right all along about Ty hurting her.

Clara's loving arms wrapped around her. "Hayley, Ty has missed you something awful. I'm so glad you could be here today. Please come inside. Have some cake. Ty is cooking me dinner."

Ty had missed her? Hayley looked at him, hoping he saw the accusations—and the questions—in her eyes. She had a few questions for him all right. And she strongly suspected her father had everything to do with this. The thought eased her pain, if only a little. She'd give Ty a chance to explain.

"Hayley made something special for you, Nanna." Ty escorted the two women back to the house, holding the box close.

"Oh?" Nanna said. "I can't wait to see it."

Hayley laughed, feeling better by the moment. "I guess you could call it a joint project. Ty wanted something special for you."

"And I commissioned Hayley to make it."

Hayley glanced at Ty, and he winked. She smiled back, glad she made the decision to come here, but she couldn't wait to get Ty alone so they could talk.

Chapter 8

Nanna fingered the teakettle with the sgraffito-carved quirky, crafty pinecones and teared up.

Ty wasn't sure what that meant but figured it was one of those women things. Then when she hugged Hayley and her eyes pooled, Ty had to look away.

Nanna hugged Hayley for a long time. He knew she liked Hayley and thought she was the one for Ty, though she never said anything. Ty could just tell.

He couldn't thank Hayley enough for her creation, for coming into his life, and now he'd hurt her. His own pain was palpable.

But he wasn't the man for her.

Not yet.

He hadn't known what to say to her. Didn't want to bring her father into it, so Ty had kept busy with his part-time jobs and working on the business plan, talking to potential investors. He hoped and prayed things would work out and that he could be the man she needed him to be.

But Lord, how can I do this without hurting her more? Without losing her in the process?

It was clear when she looked at him that she was disappointed in the way he'd treated her. Ty didn't have a clue what he was doing, or how to handle this odd situation.

Nanna released Hayley and wiped her eyes. "You didn't know but Hayley came out to see me, long before you two. . ."

Nanna trailed off, knowing that things weren't good between them. Knowing she'd said the wrong thing.

Hayley smiled, but Ty guessed she hid her true feelings. "I wanted to get to know your grandmother, and that's how I came up with my idea for this teakettle. Thanks, Ty, for letting me see if I was capable of creating something special for someone. Something that would match their style in keeping with my own."

"You're going to be a famous artist one day, dear." Nanna patted her arm. "Now sit down and let Ty finish the dinner he was preparing for us."

"The sausage and penne is baking, Nanna. Not much for me to do at the moment." Only there had been no *us*, not since Ty hadn't called Hayley back to invite her, give her the details.

"Oh, no, I can't stay." Hayley studied him, her question apparent—did he want her to stay?

Yes and no.

"We'd love to have you, if you can stay," he said. *If your father isn't going to come looking for you and find you with me. I need him to like me.*

She nodded. "Okay, but I need to get my purse."

Hayley exited through the front door. Nanna swatted him. "You go with her. Tell that girl how much you like her. I don't care what her father said. He's a fool if he can't see his daughter loves you."

Loves? Did Hayley love him? Had she fallen for him as well? Ty went after Hayley, following her out the front door. She was digging around in her purse when he caught up with her.

"I can leave if you don't want me to stay." She looked at him. "I just didn't want to hurt your grandmother."

Ty pulled her to him and kissed her full on the mouth. Felt how much he missed her, the longing and. . .yes, his love for her stirring. They were both breathless when he released her.

She stared at him. "What was that, Ty? What is going on? Why have you been avoiding me? Is it my father? Did he say something to you?"

"I'm not the guy for you, Hayley."

"I hear my father in that statement."

"Your father is right."

"So. What? You kissed me just now. What am I supposed to think?"

"You're supposed to see how much I care about you because I'm backing off. Your father—and I didn't want to tell you—said if I cared, that I'd let you go."

"So, just like that. You're letting go. You can't fight for me? Regardless, I'm a big girl and I can make my own decisions.

I don't have to answer to my father."

"No, you don't. But you will because you love him and respect him too much. You're all he has left. That's what you said."

"This is it then?"

He grinned, seeing the plan unfold clearly. "I hope not."

Now if he could just make it work.

In her studio, Hayley packed up her recent creations—etched, glazed, and fired—to take to Blue Mountain Art Gallery.

Her hands trembled, making her concerned she might drop one of the pots. Too many hours went into her art—and she had a feeling that Daddy had noticed that she'd spent more and more time in her studio, and less attending to the endless chores that went with ranching, meaning more work for the cowhands. But her heart just wasn't in it.

She'd told Daddy she'd be here for him, be the one to take up the Covington Ranch legacy, but she wanted nothing to do with that right now. She hadn't anticipated Daddy or his need to protect her and the ranch would interfere in her life in such a drastic, crazy way.

She hadn't expected when she asked Ty—a man she thought was a gallery employee—to help her, that she could feel this way about anyone. Her future, her happiness, was on the line. But it tore her up inside to think of hurting Daddy.

He'd been working at the north end of the property this week—some problem with the fence. He'd always been one to get his hands dirty and expected the same from her. Enjoyed the physical labor, though he had the means to pay someone else to do things. Hayley had left his meals out for him on most nights, heading to the studio or up to bed before he'd gotten home.

She just couldn't face him right now.

The door creaked open behind her. Probably Daddy. She missed him, but she was still trying to sort her feelings out. Didn't want to face him until she had.

"Hayley," he said, his voice more gentle than she could remember.

Getting a box ready to pack another pot, she stopped what she was doing but didn't look up. "Hi, Daddy."

"Never thought I'd see the day when I'd have to come out here if I wanted to talk to you."

Hayley forced her hands to stop trembling. She straightened and turned to face him, holding the pot. "I'm sorry. I've been focusing my energy on creating more pieces for the gallery. They're selling well."

He eyed the one she held.

"I know. Stopped by there this afternoon to speak with Jim."

"You didn't. Daddy, please tell me you didn't interfere there, too?"

Hurt flashed across his gaze. "Interfere? No, Hayley. I wanted to see Jim to ask him how your work was selling because I care about you. He sold a couple of the pieces this morning, as a matter of fact. I'm proud of you."

Daddy came close. "I didn't understand what this meant to you. Thought it was a waste of time. That it would interfere with our life here at the ranch. Thought it would…take you from me."

"Is that why you went to see Ty? Why you told him to stay away from me?"

He frowned. "I knew he wasn't man enough to keep that to himself."

Fury exploded inside Hayley, and she hated it. She'd never been so angry with her father. "Man enough. Man enough!" She threw the pot she held to the floor. "Ty has avoided me like the plague. I went to see him and dragged it out of him. He thinks he has to let me go because he cares about me. He's not the man for me. He believes that because of you."

Her legs shook now as she looked down at the pot. At what she'd done. "Oh, Daddy, I'm sorry. I didn't. . ." Hayley crouched to pick up the pieces, tears making it hard to see.

Big sturdy hands appeared in her view, helping her pick up the pieces. Then they took hold of her hands and lifted her to stand.

"Daughter, I didn't know you felt that way about him. I let things go too far."

"That's not what I want to hear from you," she said. "I need you to realize you shouldn't have interfered in the first place. I know you think you have to protect your assets. But I'm not one of those. I'm simply your daughter, who has a heart and mind of her own. I don't want to leave the ranch, Daddy, and I wouldn't hurt you for the world, but. . ."

"I'm the one who hurt you," he said. "I'm sorry, Hayley."

He hugged her to him and held her for a while. Then he let go and left her to herself, to pick up the shattered pieces.

Ty loaded his gear into the back of his vehicle, glad he was done with the ski lessons for the day. Glad he didn't have a shift at the refuge after this. He was exhausted from staying up late, working on putting his ideas together to present them to a potential investor for his ski lodge.

Part of him wanted to give up. What were the chances this guy would be interested in investing in Ty's business proposition? Hayley's father had done a good job of knocking him down a few notches, but at the same time, the man had given him something to work for.

Himself.

His daughter.

The only problem was he might be too late where Hayley was concerned. He'd wanted to make something of himself and prove himself to her and her father, but he'd only ended up hurting her.

Dusting the snow from his shoulders, he stomped around the vehicle, opened the door and climbed inside. A familiar steel-gray dually pulled in right next to him, a little too close for comfort. A vise squeezed his chest.

The truck door slammed, and Hayley's father walked around to greet Ty.

Funny, seeing the guy here.

"Hey," the man said. "Glad I caught you."

"What's up?"

Hayley's father tugged off his cap.

"I don't like to be one to interfere." He gave an odd, nervous laugh. "Well, not too much anyway, but I made a big mistake, so I need to remedy that."

"I'm listening."

"I think you know what I'm about to say, Son."

"I'd like to hear you say it, just the same."

The man grinned at Ty, really grinned at him. "I knew I liked you."

Huh?

"I don't want to say too much," he said, "but I was wrong to try to come between you and Hayley. She'd kill me if she knew I was here, but I hope I'm not too late."

Ty offered his own grin. "You mean you don't care that I'm just a ski bum with no future?"

The man kicked at the snow then looked at Ty. "You can't blame me for wanting the best for Hayley. But you're a good man, Ty. I see that now. And you're mighty important to my daughter."

"Well then, sir, it's not too late at all. In fact, I'm on my way to a meeting I think you might be interested in."

Her father arched a brow. "Is that so?"

Though somewhat humbled, the man was still intimidating.

Ty wasn't sure what he was doing. Not sure at all. But he had a feeling that letting Hayley's father in on his plan had been what he'd hoped to do all along. To prove himself to the man. He hadn't intended to share things until he was well on his way, but then again, he hadn't expected her father to apologize and to give his blessing, of a sort, on their relationship.

Here goes nothing.

Or everything.

Chapter 9

On Christmas Eve, Hayley finished preparing the last casserole—cheesy broccoli and rice—ahead of time so she could simply pop it into the oven with all the dishes for their Christmas dinner tomorrow.

While her two sisters, Kate and Sarah, and her cousin Cindy and Aunt Cheryl, Daddy's sister, chattered away and baked more pies, Hayley tried to sneak out of the kitchen. She needed to catch her breath. Grab a moment alone. She'd received a call from Ty and let it go to voice mail. She couldn't talk when he'd called, and now she couldn't wait to hear the message.

For the first time, Hayley knew that no matter what Daddy said, she had made her own decision about Ty. If he felt the same way about her, then she needed to somehow get him back. She listened to his voice mail. "I'm skiing in the Ribbon of Lights tonight. I know you have family obligations, but I wanted to wish you a Merry Christmas Eve."

That was it. He didn't ask for a call back. She whirled to look at the big clock on the wall. Three o'clock.

Barely enough time to get there and find a place to watch the skiers make their way down the mountain with the lights.

"I'm going to watch the Ribbon of Lights at Teton Village. Who is with me?" Hayley asked.

Cindy was in, but her sisters, aunt, and uncle declined, and of course, Daddy and her sisters' husbands declined. Hayley smiled. This would be just like old times, her hanging out with Cindy, though her sisters had been around then, too. Giggling about boys and life and just having fun. But Kate and Sarah had husbands now. Families and children. Hayley thought the kids would like to see the lights, but everyone grumbled it was too cold. And it was Christmas Eve, after all.

Christmas Eve or not, if there was any way she could see Ty tonight, she had to find him.

At Teton Village, just twelve miles north of Jackson, Hayley and Cindy almost didn't find a place to park. She stole a spot half on the road, half on the snowplowed curb, right up against a berm.

"You sure this is okay?" Cindy asked.

"It has to be." Hayley got out.

In her thermal ski jacket, she hugged herself and searched the area, large snowflakes caressing her face. Anticipation hung in the air with the crowd of people who gathered to see the Ribbon of Lights, along with the children's parade. A current of excitement charged through her.

"Let's go." She motioned for Cindy to follow. They tromped

between the buildings that made up the Jackson Hole Mountain Resort and made their way up the slope and found a place to wait.

And watch.

Cindy ran off to buy hot chocolate and returned just as dusk began to fall. "Thought I'd never find you out here, I just kept looking at that one tree so I wouldn't get lost. I'm glad you didn't move."

"Thanks for the hot chocolate." Anxious to see the skiers, Hayley took a sip, letting the creamy warmth slide down her throat as she watched the mountain. She wasn't sure if she'd be able to pick out Ty among the skiers or even connect with him tonight. But she had to try.

Finally, she spotted the lights at the top of the ski run, carried by a line of skiers who crisscrossed down the mountain. A brilliant, awe-inspiring sight, Hayley watched with wonder— her heart filling with the joy that was Christmas. Although she wanted to watch the flow of torches streaming down the mountain, she looked closely at each skier that skied passed.

Which one was Ty?

She wanted to surprise him.

But it was dark, and the skiers wore facemasks, completely understandable given the temperatures. When all the skiers had come down the mountain and the Ribbon of Lights display had concluded, Hayley was disappointed she hadn't seen Ty. The crowd began dispersing, many making their way toward the café and restaurants in the resorts before heading to the streets for the children's parade.

"Hey, let's go inside. Grab something to eat," Cindy said. "You rushed us out of there so fast we didn't get supper."

"Hayley," a voice called. She looked around, skimming the area. Someone snatched her from behind a tree.

Ty's laughter caressed her ears, and he hugged her to him, kissing her neck.

"Okay, I'm outta here," Cindy said. "I'll catch you later. I'm assuming you have a ride home. But how about me?"

Hayley tossed her the keys. "Thanks, Cindy."

On the drive to Jackson, Hayley had shared everything with Cindy, so her cousin understood what was at stake.

Aware her cousin was leaving her alone with Ty, she playfully pushed him away. "What are you doing?"

Smiling, his gazed roamed over her face and landed on her lips. "What am I doing? Kissing you."

Hayley never wanted anything more. Ty leaned in and kissed her thoroughly. Passionately. When he released her, he let his ungloved thumb trace down her cheek. "You came to see me."

"I. . ."—a knot grew in her throat—"I had to see you on Christmas Eve."

She almost didn't care, but on the other hand, she had to know. "Where are we, Ty? You and me, I mean? Our relationship."

"Well, I'm not sure where you are, Hayley Covington, but as for me, I'm in love with you."

And Ty kissed her again.

Christmas morning, Hayley woke up with a smile on her face, feeling like she hadn't slept that well in far too long. She stretched, dreamy with the memory of kisses. Of Ty's profession of love.

She didn't care what he did for a living. And best of all, neither did Daddy. As for Ty, he was an honorable man who tried to abide by Daddy's wishes, loving her from a distance. Ty explained that her father had given him permission to see her, so he'd called her. Hayley still wasn't sure how she felt about that. She'd wanted him to fight for her, stand up to her father, and yet she wasn't anyone's property. Neither of them had any right to talk about her, make decisions for her, like that. On the other hand, she found it endearing that Ty would adhere to her father's old-fashioned ways. That Ty had wanted to please her father, and somehow he'd done just that.

She got up and dressed then glanced out the window at the snow-blanketed earth. Would that sight ever get old?

Hayley bounded down the stairs, the aroma of bacon and eggs wafting around her. Soon everyone would gather around the tree to exchange gifts. Her two nieces and nephew were already playing with the toys that Santa Claus had left under the tree, though they understood perfectly the true meaning of Christmas, celebrating the birth of Christ the Lord and their Savior. Daddy would read the scriptures from Luke, chapter 2, after breakfast.

Hayley loved that the whole family gathered for Christmas here at the ranch. She never wanted to leave this place, with its legacy of Covington family memories.

Yes, she'd made the right decision to stay here, close to Daddy and his beloved Covington Ranch. Her ranch.

When a knock came at the door, Hayley left the table and opened it to see Ty standing there, a grin on his face. He could have made The Sexiest Man Alive on the cover of *People Magazine* with that look.

Hayley just wanted to stare at him.

"What?" he asked. "Aren't you going to invite me in?"

She giggled and opened the door wide.

"I come bearing gifts," he said.

"Oh, you didn't have to." She grabbed the bags, loving this moment—yet another Covington memory.

Loving this man.

She tucked his gifts under the tree, and Ty joined them for breakfast. He'd promised his grandmother he'd be back for lunch, but Hayley hoped he would just bring her out to the ranch. They had plans to fly to Texas the day after Christmas to see his folks in Dallas. Hayley would miss him.

After breakfast everyone opened presents. They'd chosen names well in advance, and each person got two gifts for the name they'd drawn. But of course, Hayley got a few extras for Daddy, the only man in her life until. . .well, until Ty. She opened a gift from Aunt Cheryl, a wonderful crocheted Afghan, and a new ski suit from Ty. She loved her gifts.

Hayley pulled out a big box she'd wrapped and handed it over to Ty. "I didn't know if I'd see you again, but I've been working on this for a while. I wrapped it and put it under the tree, hoping things would work out between us."

When Ty opened it to reveal a large platter, skiers on a mountain etched in with sgraffito, admiration infused his expression. He ran his fingers over the image that she'd scratched into the clay, then he looked at her, seeming to absorb her very essence.

Love flowed from his eyes. "Thank you, Hayley. I'll treasure this, always."

He set the platter on a table, safe and out of the way, then tugged her aside. "Can I talk to you alone?"

"Sure."

"Um, I need you outside, actually. So go get dressed in something warm."

She looked at him for a couple of seconds then ran upstairs to gear up in her winter wear.

Back downstairs, Ty opened the door for her and they went outside. "What's going on?" she asked.

Bells jingled, warming her heart even more, if possible, as the Covington horse-drawn sleigh—pulled by one of Daddy's favorite horses—made its way to the front of the house. Daddy lifted his Stetson, greeting them, and climbed down.

"I've seen Ty drive one of these at the Elk Refuge, so I'm confident he'll be fine," Daddy said, his smile genuine.

"Or I could do it," Hayley offered.

"You could, sure, but that would ruin my show." Ty assisted her up, and she let him, though she didn't need any help.

"Your show?"

"The ambience. Magic. You know, the romance." He winked.

After he placed a blanket over their knees, he urged the horse to pull the sleigh down and around the trail the Covingtons had used in years gone by, as though he'd done this a thousand times before. Hayley wanted to ask how he knew where to go.

But then she knew. Daddy. Had to be.

She leaned her head on Ty's shoulder, her arms wrapped through his, and imagined what it might have been like to ride in this sleigh fifty years ago, or even when Zeb, her great-grandfather, first came to the valley, built this sleigh, and proposed to his bride in it.

Ty slowed the horse, reining to a stop.

Hayley sighed her contentment and took in the Tetons in the distance behind the Covington spread, the small cabin Zeb built, now a beautiful home filled with the memories of generations of Covingtons. The image on this Christmas morning would make a perfect postcard.

Ty turned to face Hayley. "You warm enough?"

"I couldn't be warmer."

He cleared his throat, unusually nervous. "Hayley, I know we've had a rocky relationship lately."

Ty removed his gloves. "I can't stand these things." Then he took her hands in his. "I want you to know that I backed off from you because your father said I wasn't good enough for you. From the moment he said that, I have been working to change it. And, I have a surprise for you."

"*Shh*," she said, pressing her finger against his lips. She'd removed her gloves, too, so she could feel his hands. "I don't need you to be anything but who you are, Ty. I don't care about any of that."

"I believe you. But I care about it. You made me remember I had big dreams. You inspired me to not let them die. I'm working on building a ski lodge and resort on Walker Mountain, my grandmother's land."

Hayley gasped. "Ty, that's. . .huge." But it scared her. What if all this changed the Ty she'd fallen in love with?

"If you're willing, I'd like to include a Hayley Covington Art Gallery in the resort, dedicated to your work. But you'll still hold the reins to the Covington Ranch."

She cupped her hands over her mouth. "All this for me? But. . ."

It seemed like too much, and she realized that despite all the effort he'd put into proving himself to her father and to her, she had been expecting something much different from him just now. She'd obviously gotten ahead of herself, the Covington sleigh proposal stories getting the best of her. Still, he'd mentioned something about her holding the reins to the Covington Ranch.

"And"—Ty tugged something from his back pocket—"this is

why I really brought you out here."

He held out a small velvet box.

"What, Ty?" Hayley was far more excited about what the box might hold than she was to learn she would finally have her own art gallery. "I want to hear you say it."

He popped it open. "I should get down on one knee."

"No," she said. "Stay right there and say it."

Ty grinned the way she loved. "Hayley Covington, I love you more than life itself. I'd do anything for you. Will you marry me?"

"I think you know the answer to that."

"But you're going to say it, right?"

"Yes, Ty Walker, I'll marry you." Hayley let Ty slip the engagement ring on her finger, and then she put her chilled fingers on his red cheeks and kiss him long and hard, remembering Daddy's words:

"All it takes is a little kindling to start a fire blazing."

About the Authors

Elizabeth Goddard is an award-winning author with over twenty novels and novellas, including the romantic mystery, *The Camera Never Lies*—winner of the prestigious Carol Award in 2011. After acquiring her computer science degree, she worked at a software firm before eventually retiring to raise her four children and become a professional writer. A member of several writing organizations, she judges numerous contests and mentors new writers. In addition to writing, she homeschools her children and serves with her husband in ministry.

Lynette Sowell is an award-winning author with New England roots, but she makes her home in Central Texas with her husband and a herd of five cats. When she's not writing, she edits medical reports and chases down stories for the local newspaper.